THE ONE WHO
WAITS FOR ME

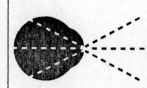

This Large Print Book carries the
Seal of Approval of N.A.V.H.

THE ONE WHO WAITS FOR ME

LORI COPELAND

THORNDIKE PRESS

A part of Gale, Cengage Learning

GALE
CENGAGE Learning·

Detroit • New York • San Francisco • New Haven, Conn • Waterville, Maine • London

GALE
CENGAGE Learning

Thorndike Press® Large Print Christian Historical Fiction.
The text of this Large Print edition is unabridged.
Other aspects of the book may vary from the original edition.
Set in 16 pt. Plantin.

LIBRARY OF CONGRESS CATALOGING-IN-PUBLICATION DATA

Copeland, Lori.
  The one who waits for me / by Lori Copeland.
    p. cm. — (Thorndike Press large print Christian historical fiction)
  ISBN-13: 978-1-4104-4166-9 (hardcover)
  ISBN-10: 1-4104-4166-0 (hardcover)
  1. North Carolina—History—1865—Fiction. 2. Large type books.
  I. Title.
  PS3553.O6336O55 2011b
  813'.54—dc22
                                2011030204

Published in 2011 by arrangement with Harvest House Publishers.

Printed in Mexico
1 2 3 4 5 6 7 15 14 13 12 11

In Memoriam

My brother, Joseph Patrick Smart
1936–2011

My aunt, Madge Pottenger Martin
1914–2011

Willow and Ditto,
two very special cats who gave
amazing love to their owner
1988–2010
1994–2010

I am God, and there is none like me.

ISAIAH 46:9

PROLOGUE

Roanoke, Virginia, summer, 1865

"You can't be serious," Pierce said. "If we take the west road, it'll take days longer to get there."

"Serious as a rusty nail," replied Preach. He stood back and traced the narrow line on the map running from Richmond to North Carolina with a lean, tanned finger. The men stood in the dirt road with a hot sun baking their backs. "I agree it's the longer route, but the roads are better kept and we'll make faster time."

More discussion broke out among the men: Second Lieutenant Samuel "Preach" Madison, twenty-six, and First Lieutenant Gray Eagle, reportedly the finest scout in the 212th Company. Gray Eagle was twenty-five and Cherokee. Both men had fought for the Confederacy. Captain Pierce Montgomery, twenty-four, had fought for the Union, though neither Preach nor Gray

Eagle held it against him.

The war was declared over last spring when General Robert E. Lee surrendered on April 9, but it wasn't until General Stand Watie rode into Doaksville on June 23 that the last Confederate officer surrendered his command. The shaky cease-fire held, but the stench of war still permeated the soft Southern air.

The soldiers had met some two hundred miles back at a crossroads. Pierce and Gray Eagle had ridden the first hundred miles together, and when the pair bumped into Preach at a trading post, he accepted the invitation to join them on the long trek home.

Everywhere the men looked they saw a country struggling with upheaval and plagued with instability as newly freed slaves sought to find work and shelter for their families. The old adage "safety in numbers" rang true, and the men heeded common sense.

Straightening, Pierce flashed a white grin sheathed in sun-bronzed features. "So what say ye, gentleman? Do we choose the shorter route with admittedly bad roads and more rivers and streams to cross, or do we take the west trail that's longer but with supposedly fewer headaches?"

Preach removed his hat and studied the map again. "Trust me. We'll make faster time if we ride west."

Pierce shook his head. "And I say we take the shortest route available. Let's just get home."

Gray Eagle stepped up, his black eyes solemn. Tall and heavily muscled from long hours in the saddle, he was a striking man. "Shall we flip a coin?" The Native American's precise English was in stark contrast to his looks. Taught by his white mother, the Confederate scout had the highest education among the group.

"Well, I suppose that's fair," Pierce conceded. "But I still say the shorter way is better."

Removing a coin from his leather pouch, Gray Eagle rested it in his hand. "Who calls?"

"The captain," Preach said.

Pierce shook his head. "I thought we'd agreed that the war is over. I was 'captain' on the field. Here I'm just Pierce."

"Sorry." Preach's white teeth gleamed in his glistening mahogany features. "A man gets used to takin' orders, and it sorta feels like mutiny not to let a superior officer lead."

Shaking his head again, Pierce said, "Flip

11

the coin. I call heads."

Gray Eagle looked at the other two. "Heads, we take the shorter route with bad roads and more rivers to cross. Tails, we take the longer route but make better time."

The black man grinned. "Either way, I shore do want to get home as fast as possible. I can taste those hot biscuits baking in the oven now. Flaky and dripping with butter and blackstrap molasses. Umm, umm."

None of them had seen butter in years. Or hot anything.

Their eyes were focused on Gray Eagle's nut brown hand as the Cherokee tossed the coin. It twirled in the air, over and over, and then landed in his palm. Closing his fingers over it, his normally serious features broke and he smiled. "What will it be? Heads or tails?"

"Just look at it," Pierce said, snappishly. He removed a bandana from around his neck and mopped at the sweat now rolling down his temples.

Gray Eagle's eyes twinkled. "Oh? Is the captain anxious to get home? Got a lady waiting for him?"

"No lady. Just a fine piece of land." Despite the heat, he couldn't help grinning. "Bought me a small tract not far from my pa's plantation." Pierce patted the vest pocket where he kept the deed close. He had spent every last cent he had in the world on that land. He was going to eventually build a home, raise a few cattle, a little cotton, and maybe consider taking a wife — some fine filly with a longing to serve her man. Grow fat and lazy. He'd had a bellyful of fighting. He was never going to lift a hand in violence for the rest of his life. A man could shoot him in the back, and he wouldn't return fire. He'd lie down and die with a sigh of peace, that was how sick he was of turmoil. Once he got to his land, he was going to sit back and drink pitcher after pitcher of sweet tea, something he hadn't enjoyed in years.

Preach couldn't help smiling as well. "I'm with you, sir. I can't wait to smell the magnolia blossoms in the front yard and eat Ma's sweet potato pies. How come you bought that passel of land, Captain? Didn't you say your pa has thousands of acres?"

"That's Pa's land. I want my own." Pierce patted his pocket one more time for reassurance. In a few days he'd see his land. Pa would most likely be upset that his son had bought property nearby without consulting him first, but when Pierce had seen the advertisement for the acreage in the

13

Savannah Daily News and Herald, he'd wired the money and became a landowner faster than a loose woman could wink her eye.

"Same goes for me," Peach said. "A roof to call my own. I can't wait to sleep in a decent bed."

"And take a bath," Pierce added. "Hot water and clean towels."

"Sissies," Gray Eagle said. "Clean beds, hot food. Didn't the war make men out of you?"

"Look at the coin!" the other two shouted.

Grinning, Gray Eagle began, "Now, gentlemen. You're —"

Pierce reached for the scout's hand and pried open his palm. Three pairs of eyes focused on the coin.

Tails.

Pierce groaned. "Flip again."

"Sorry. We ride west." Gray Eagle slid the coin back into his pouch. "Don't worry. We probably won't be delayed more than a couple of days at most."

Saddling up, Preach said, "You could take the shorter route, Captain. A coin flip doesn't mean we have to stick together."

"You certainly could go your own way . . . if you were a fool." Grinning, Gray Eagle reined in beside his friends. "Which you aren't. Right, brother?"

Sometimes Pierce wondered, but he knew the wisdom of the scout's words. He'd counted the hours till he'd be back home since he'd ridden away five years ago, and it irked him to waste even a day. Delay was pure aggravation. Tightening his hold on the reins, he said quietly, "Okay, but we pick up the pace. If the roads are better and we have fewer rivers to ford, we should be able to make it in the same amount of time."

Preach frowned. "You're sure anxious to be home."

"I thought you were too."

"I am, but a couple of days isn't going to sour the milk."

Pierce nudged his mare's flanks. "No, but there's no point in delaying."

Nodding, Preach shifted in his saddle leather. "Okay. Let's go home."

Pierce fell in behind the two men and the group started off again.

Home.

Peace and quiet. *Thank You, God.*

He was sure he'd seen the last of misery.

ONE

"Joanie?"

Beth's sister stirred, coughing.

Beth gently shook Joanie's shoulder again, and the young woman opened her eyes, confusion shining in their depths.

"Pa?"

"He passed a few minutes ago. Trella will be waiting for us."

Joanie lifted her wrist to her mouth and smothered sudden sobbing. "I'm scared, Beth."

"So am I. Dress quickly."

The young woman slid out of bed, her bare feet touching the dirt-packed floor. Outside, the familiar sound of pond frogs nearly drowned out soft movements, though there was no need to be silent any more. Ma had preceded Pa in death two days ago. Beth and Joanie had been waiting, praying for the hour of Pa's death to come swiftly. Together, they lifted their father's silent form and gently carried him out the front door. He was a slight man, easy to carry. Beth's heart broke as they took him to the shallow grave they had dug the day before. Ma's fever had taken her swiftly. Pa had held on for as long as he could. Beth could still hear his voice in her ear: "Take care of your sister, little Beth." He didn't have to remind her that there was no protection at all now to save either of them from Uncle Walt and his son, Bear. Beth had known all of her life that one day she and Joanie would have to escape this place — a place of misery.

It was her father's stubborn act that started the situation Beth and Joanie were immersed in. Pa had hid the plantation deed from his brother and refused to tell him where it was. Their land had belonged to a Jornigan for two hundred years, but Walt claimed that because he was the older brother and allowed Pa to live on his land the deed belonged to him. Pa was a proud man and had no respect for his brother, though his family depended on Walt for a roof over their heads and food on their table. For meager wages they worked Walt's fields, picked his cotton, and suffered his tyranny along with the other workers. Pa took the location of the hidden deed to his grave — almost. Walt probably figured Beth knew where it was because Pa always favored her. And she did, but she would die before she shared the location with her vile uncle.

By the light of the waning moon the women made short work of placing the corpse in the grave and then filling the hole with dirt. Finished, they stood back and Joanie bowed her head in prayer. "Dear Father, thank You for taking Ma and Pa away from this world. I know they're with You now, and I promise we won't cry." Hot tears streaming down both women's cheeks belied her words.

Returning to the shanty, Joanie removed her nightshirt and put on boy's clothes. Dressed in similar denim trousers and a dark shirt, Beth turned and picked up the oil lamp and poured the liquid carefully around the one-room shanty. Yesterday she had packed Ma's best dishes and quilts and dragged them to the root cellar. It was useless effort. She would never be back here, but she couldn't bear the thought of fire consuming Ma's few pretty things. She glanced over her shoulder when the stench of fuel heightened Joanie's cough. The struggle to breathe had been a constant companion since her younger sister's birth.

Many nights Beth lay tense and fearful, certain that come light Joanie would be gone. Now that Ma and Pa were dead, Joanie was the one thing left on this earth that held meaning for Beth. She put down the lamp on the table. Walking over to Joanie, she buttoned the last button on her sister's shirt and tugged her hat brim lower.

"Do you have everything?"

"Yes."

"Then go outside and wait."

Nodding, Joanie paused briefly beside the bed where Pa's tall frame had been earlier. She hesitantly reached out and touched the empty spot. "May you rest in peace, Pa."

Moonlight shone through the one glass pane facing the south. Beth shook her head. "He was a good man. It's hard to believe Uncle Walt had the same mother and father."

Joanie's breath caught. "Pa was so good and Walt is so . . . evil."

"If it were up to me, he would be lying in that grave outside the window, not Pa."

Beth tried to recall one single time in her life when Walt Jornigan had ever shown an ounce of mercy to anyone. Certainly not to his wife when she was alive. Certainly not to Beth or Joanie. If Joanie was right and there was a God, what would Walt say when

20

he faced Him? She shook the thought aside. She had no compassion for the man or reverence for the God her sister believed in and worshipped.

"We have to go now, Joanie."

"Yes." She picked up her Bible from the little table beside the rocking chair and then followed Beth outside the shanty, her breath coming in ragged gasps. Pausing, Joanie bent and succumbed to a coughing spasm. Beth helplessly waited, hoping her sister could make the anticipated trip through the cotton fields. The women had planned for days now to escape if Ma and Pa both passed.

Beth asked gently, "Can you do this?"

Joanie held up a restraining hand. "Just need . . . a minute."

Beth wasn't certain that they could wait long; time was short. Dawn would be breaking soon, and then Walt would discover that Pa had died and the sisters were missing. But they had to leave. Joanie's asthma was getting worse. Each gasping breath left her drained and hopeless, and Walt refused to let her see a doctor.

When Joanie had mentioned the notice in a discarded Savannah newspaper advertising a piece of land, Beth knew she had to buy the property and provide a home for

21

Joanie. Pa had allowed her and Joanie to keep the wage Uncle Walt paid monthly. Over the years they had saved enough to survive, and the owner was practically giving the small acreage away. They wouldn't be able to build a permanent structure on their land until she found work, but she and Joanie would own their own place where no one could control them. Beth planned to eventually buy a cow and a few setting hens. At first they could live in a tent — Beth's eyes roamed the small shanty. It would be better than how they lived now.

Joanie's spasm passed and she glanced up. "Okay. You . . . can do it now."

Beth struck a match.

She glanced at Joanie. The young woman nodded and clutched her Bible to her chest. Beth had found it in one of the cotton picker's beds after he had moved on and given it to Joanie. Her sister had kept the Bible hidden from sight for fear that Walt would spot it on one of his weekly visits. Beth had known, as Joanie had, that if their uncle had found it he'd have had extra reason to hand out his daily lashing. Joanie kept the deed to their new land between its pages.

After pitching the lighted match into the cabin, Beth quickly closed the heavy door.

Stepping to the window, she watched the puddles of kerosene ignite one by one. In just minutes flames were licking the walls and gobbling up the dry tinder. A peculiar sense of relief came over her when she saw tendrils of fire racing through the room, latching onto the front curtain and encompassing the bed.

"Don't watch." Joanie slipped her hand into Beth's. "We have to hurry before Uncle Walt spots the flames."

Hand in hand, the sisters stepped off the porch, and Beth turned to the mounds of fresh dirt heaped not far from the shanty. Pausing before the fresh graves, she whispered. "I love you both. Rest in peace."

Joanie had her own goodbyes for their mother. "We don't want to leave you and Pa here alone, but I know you understand —"

As the flames licked higher, Beth said, "We have to go, Joanie. Don't look back."

"I won't." Her small hand quivered inside Beth's. "God has something better for us."

Beth didn't answer. She didn't know whether Ma and Pa were in a good place or not. She didn't know anything about such things. She just knew they had to run.

The two women dressed in men's clothing struck off across the cotton fields carrying everything they owned in a small bag. It wasn't much. A dress for each, clean underclothes, and their nightshirts. Beth had a hairbrush one of the pickers had left behind. She'd kept the treasure well hidden so Walt wouldn't see it. He'd have taken it from her. He didn't hold with primping — said combing tangles from one's hair was a vain act. Finger-picking river-washed hair was all a woman needed.

Fire now raced inside the cabin. By the time Uncle Walt noticed the smoke from the plantation house across the fields, the two sisters would be long gone. No longer would they be under the tyrannical thumb of Walt or Bear Jornigan.

Freedom.

Beth sniffed the night air, thinking she could smell the precious state. Never again would she or Joanie answer to any man. She would run hard and far and find help for Joanie so that she could finally breathe free. In her pocket she fingered the remaining bills she'd taken from the fruit jar in the cabinet. It was all the ready cash Pa and Ma had. They wouldn't be needing money where they were.

Suddenly there was a sound of a large explosion. Heavy black smoke blanketed the night air. Then another blast.

Kerosene! She'd forgotten the small barrel sitting just outside the back porch.

It was the last sound Beth heard.

Two

The sun topped the crest of Spanish oak that hung thick with moss. Long rows of white dotted the landscape. Cotton pickers with their heads swathed in white cloth straightened to shade their eyes and watch the passing spectacle. Two soldiers wearing Confederate gray and one wearing Union blue rode past. Men going home to waiting family. Two baritones sang "Dixie."

The Union solider, singing in a deep bass, led the strange pack with a rousing "Battle Hymn of the Republic." The result was an odd clatter of

"Mine eyes have seen the glory!"
"Oh, I wish I was in the land of cotton!"
"Of the coming of the Lord!"
"Old times there are not forgotten!"

Puzzled gapes followed the strange procession as the men's laughter trailed them down the road. The war ended months ago, and the sight of troops moving along the road was nothing new to the pickers. No doubt it was the returning men's strange way of celebrating that caught their attention.

Preach broke into the second verse of "Dixie," wincing when a wadded-up hat hit him in the back. Grinning, he lifted his chin and sang louder.

The men's infectious laughter filled their surroundings. Pierce drew in a deep breath of the hot, stifling air. Freedom. The word had never sounded so good.

"I can taste those mudbugs now," Preach declared. "And potatoes, onions, and corn."

"Hah!" Throwing back his head, Pierce laughed. "We will celebrate the joy of living, my friends." Closing his eyes, he soaked in the soft breeze playing across his face. *Thank You, God, for bringing me home.* Breathing in another deep draught, he paused, frowning.

Smoke?

They rounded a curve in the road, and ahead of them a bellowing black cloud filled the horizon.

"Grass fire?" Gray Eagle wondered.

Pierce lifted a brow. "Might be." His gaze rested on the heavy blanket of smoke sweep-

27

ing across a nearby cotton field. The light wind was catching the fire and spreading it across dry fields. "Could be a homesteader burning off his land."

"Don't think so. The wind's blowing too strong. Any farmer with a lick of sense wouldn't burn today."

All laughter gone, the men spurred their horses and rode toward the smoke.

Flames licked across parched fields, devouring cotton like a hungry beast. The soldiers drew up as the inferno threatened. Lifting an elbow to shield his eyes as the wind caught burnt embers and scattered fiery darts, Pierce called out, "Is that a homestead?"

The men's gazes focused on a distant dwelling and small outbuilding, now engulfed in flames.

"Think we should check on the livestock?" Preach's gaze focused on the small holding pen that sat to the side of the shanty. Smoke shifted and clogged the men's view. "Can't tell if there's anything in there. Can you?"

Shaking his head, Pierce said, "I can't." Pulling his handkerchief over his mouth, he said, "I'll ride in and see."

"I'll ride with you." Preach pulled up alongside him.

Keeping to the rim of the fire, the men's

eyes fastened on the crudely constructed corral. Moments later the shanty's roof collapsed to the ground.

Heavy smoke roiled upward. Pierce's eyes teared up from the searing inferno. "Easy, Sue." He spoke softly to the mare, nudging her closer. The animal veered from the heat. He lifted his voice to get his friend's attention. "Preach!"

"Sir!"

"I'm going to check the gate!"

"I'll do it, sir!"

"You ride ahead and see if you can spot any sign of life." The owners had to be around — unless they were burnt alive in the inferno. Spurring the mare, Pierce rode toward the flames.

Sue stepped lightly, shying, but he pushed her closer. Heat nearly blinded him when he reached the pen and found it empty. Giving Sue her head then, he galloped on, holding his left arm up to shield his eyes. He didn't breathe until he burst through the fiery perimeter and rejoined the men. Preach was back. His mahogany face was smoke blackened, his eyes sorrowful. Two women were draped across the back of his horse.

Pierce's bleary gaze skimmed the strange sight. "What's that?"

Glancing back at the two inert forms, Preach said, "The way I see it, sir? Trouble." His dark eyes rested on the female forms. "Pure trouble."

Wiping his eyes with his handkerchief, Pierce tried to focus. "Are they the homesteaders?"

"Don't know, sir. I found this one —" he rested his hand on a seared trouser — "trying to pull this one" — his hand moved to the second form — "out of the flames. If I hadn't come along when I did, they'd both be goners."

Able to see now, Pierce rode up, eying the strangers. "They're too young to be homesteaders. Where are their parents?"

"Didn't see anyone but these two crawl out of the field." He motioned to his passengers. "Don't know why they're wearing men's clothing, but they ain't men, sir. They're women. If you and Gray Eagle will look after them, I'll ride back and look for others."

Pierce dismounted and moved to Preach's horse. The Indian scout joined him. Together, they gently moved the limp forms to the ground. Pierce bent close to one, sighing with relief when he detected life. "This one's breathing." He turned to the other. "And so is this one."

Preach rode off as Pierce and Gray Eagle poured water from a canteen on their handkerchiefs and wiped the women's faces. One started to come around, fighting off Pierce's assistance.

"It's okay, lady," he said. "You're safe."

The woman looked at him, and Pierce met a pair of clear hazel eyes. Their gazes locked, and then she struggled to break his hold.

Pierce's nodded to the second woman. "Easy, ma'am," he said to the first. "There's another woman with you. Any idea who she —"

The girl shot upright and leaned over the other female lying beside her. She lightly shook the unconscious form. The young woman stirred, coughing.

"She's going to be fine." Pierce gently lowered the first girl back to the ground. "You've eaten a lot of smoke, but you're going to be fine as well." When Pierce realized she hadn't yet said a word, he frowned. Could she talk? "Where are your folks?"

She broke his hold and reached to cradle the other woman to her chest.

"She's okay." After pouring more water on his handkerchief, he gently wiped the coughing girl's face again. She was young — late teens or early twenties — and jackrabbit scared. "Is she your sister?" The observation seemed a likely connection. The two women favored each other — same blond hair streaked by sun, petite build, and fragile bone structure. The younger girl's hacking breaths went far beyond smoke inhalation. Pierce recognized the struggle taking place in the girl's lungs. "She has asthma."

The older sister nodded and then latched tightly to his hand, looking up at him with pleading eyes. The coughing sister managed, "Please, sir, take us away from here."

Pierce glanced away. "Is anyone else here? Your family?"

She shook her head. "Only Beth and me. Ma and Pa are dead. Died this week." She turned and focused on the flames. "The fire started in the shanty . . . and it took over so quickly. Before we knew it, the flames were burning the field."

Piece swiped off his hat, respectfully observing the women's great losses. The countryside swarmed with rebel bands intent on doing harm. He figured the raids and destruction would continue for a while and that he was likely looking at the evidence of this violence. He turned to glance at the shanty's blazing inferno, his eyes searching the area for signs of brewing trouble. There were bound to be many types of lowlife looking for ill-gotten gain.

Turning, he gently lifted the coughing woman, who introduced herself as Joanie, into his arms even as another spasm wracked her frail frame. Preach, who had come back empty-handed, stepped up. "Sir? If you'll allow me. My family suffered the same affliction."

Joanie's strangled breath sucked in the smoky air when the captain handed her over. Her frantic wheezing filled the silence. With the gentleness of a caring soul, the black solider smoothed hair back from the girl's oval-shaped face.

"Can't breathe —"

"Hold tight to my hand." Preach glanced at Pierce. "We have to get her away from the smoke, sir."

The captain motioned for Preach to take the lead. Lifting the other girl in his arms, Pierce carried her to his horse and asked, "What's your name?"

She spoke for the first time. "Beth"

"Well, Beth." He gently set her on Sue and then mounted up in front of her. "Looks like we came along at the right time."

"I want to be with Joanie."

"Preach has your sister. She's in good hands." He fell in behind the other two men.

"Where are you taking us?" He recognized stark fear in her tone, and he realized she had every right to be afraid. Three strange men on a deserted road. Any woman with good sense would be frightened.

"We're not going to harm you. Right now we're getting your sister out of the smoke."

The young lady shifted to peer around him to Joanie, who was lying in the black man's arms across his saddle. "Is she breathing?"

"She's breathing. And once she's out of the smoke she'll rest easier." Pierce had fought alongside men with the affliction. He even had an aunt who suffered with the ailment.

Beth settled herself behind his back again, her small frame breaking into heaving sobs. "I have to get help for Joanie," she said, her tone muffled.

"Ma'am?"

She cleared her throat. "I have to get help for my sister. She's very sick." She peered around his shoulder again, and as he turned his head back toward her he caught a glimpse of her fear-filled eyes roaming the area.

"Are you looking for someone?"

"No, sir. Can you ride faster?"

"I'm afraid I can't. I can barely follow the

34

road now." Heavy black smoke filled the hills and hollows.

"Then no one can see us — right?"

"You're right. Is someone looking for us?"

"Um . . . no."

Pierce kept his eyes on the path. The girl was hiding something, but what? And why? He'd assured her they meant them no harm.

He shook off his thoughts. He was a stranger. Her troubles didn't concern him.

"You have kinfolk nearby?"

"No. I have to get help for Joanie."

The wind shifted and the smoke temporarily cleared. Ahead, two other riders appeared holding cloths over their mouths. Beth stiffened when she caught sight of them. She reached out and grasped Pierce's arm. "Please . . . please don't let them take us."

Frowning, Pierce studied the men. "Do you know them?"

Her muffled answer came to him softly. "My uncle and cousin."

Pierce pinned his eyes on the impending company and kept a steady hand near his sidearm. "Thought you said you didn't have kin nearby."

"I . . . misled you. I'm sorry for that, but I'm scared of this man and his son."

The horses drew near and stopped. A gust

of wind sent smoke spiraling into their faces. When his vision cleared, Pierce skimmed the men's unkempt appearance, heavy black beards, and flint-hard eyes.

Preach was right. These women were going to be trouble.

THREE

Pierce sat quietly as the older of the two riders silently assessed the soldiers, lightly skimming the Confederate uniforms and then Pierce's Union blue.

"You got my nieces," the man said harshly. "Hand 'em over."

Pierce didn't have a vested interest in this fight, but he did have two helpless females, one claiming that she wanted to avoid this man. The frightened woman seated behind him was shaking like a leaf in a gale. His gaze met the stranger's. "One is having hard time breathing. We're moving her out of the smoke."

"I'll do that," the older man said. "Don't want to put you out."

Joanie's cough filled the stilted silence. Deep, congested attempts to breathe. Smoke shifted and blew back in the riders' faces. Tension in Pierce's neck mounted as Preach and Gray Eagle waited behind him, silent

37

but alert.

"No trouble at all," Pierce said. The way he figured, he was stuck between a rock and a hard place. If the girl's trembling was any indication of her terror, she was bone-scared.

The younger man, whom Pierce assumed to be the older man's son, made an attempt at pleasantries. "We'll just take Beth and Joanie, and you gents can be on your way."

The two men faced off. Pierce wished the cousin wouldn't take this stance. It made it real hard to be polite. "Gentlemen, we're not looking for trouble, but I believe the ladies would prefer that we escort them away from here."

The older man's face hardened into granite. "Don't matter what they want. I'm their uncle, and I say I'm taking them with me."

"No!" The girl's muffled voice softly pleaded. "Please . . . I'll do anything. Just don't let him take us."

Pierce glanced back at her again. Anything? The broad statement both disarmed and amused him. He'd have to warn her about making such proclamations to strange men. Some would take her at her word. He lifted his eyes to the two men in front of him. "Appears the lady doesn't want your company."

The older man lifted the reins and stepped his horse forward, threatening. The sound of rifles rising to shoulders filtered from behind Pierce.

"Easy, gentlemen." Pierce took a deep breath. No use getting shot over the incident. The females meant nothing to him, and Preach and Gray Eagle were antsy enough not knowing what awaited them at home without getting involved in this situation. "We'll take the ladies to safety, and then you four can work it out among yourselves."

"No," his passenger hissed. "Don't *leave* us with them! You have no idea what they'll do to us."

Pierce glanced down. She was being mighty persnickety. Did she fear the man this much or was it sheer stubbornness he heard in her tone?

"Look, mister," the older man spoke. "You're sticking your nose in family matters. Hand the women over and ride on. They're my responsibility."

Pierce didn't like the man's tone. A muscle in his jaw worked. "Afraid I can't do that." He wasn't spoiling for a fight, but he wasn't running either.

The man lifted his shotgun and pointed the barrel. Behind Pierce, hammers cocked.

Horses shied.

No more fighting. Wasn't that my vow? The words raced through Pierce's head. If a man wanted, he could pick a fight any day of the week, and the ladies' uncle had a point. Pierce was sticking his nose in where it didn't concern him. Lifting his right hand, he motioned for his friends to lower their guns.

"No," Beth cried. She clutched Pierce's shirt. "You *can't* let him take us. Please."

"Ma'am, your uncle's right. I have no authority here."

"You have every authority to save us if we ask you. This man is evil, and he'll beat us."

Glancing away, Pierce gathered his thoughts. Fifty miles from home and he had to run into this. The last thing he wanted was trouble. Silence stretched as he considered the matter. Beth's clutch tightened.

"I'd be happy to help, ma'am, but it sounds like a family feud, one we got no call to intrude on." He turned around a bit to really get a good look at her.

"It isn't," she said. Hazel eyes met his. "This man means nothing to us."

He cocked a brow. "I heard you call him 'uncle.' "

"He is our uncle," the sick girl managed between breaths. "But he doesn't care a whit about us. He's mean and hateful, and he only wants us to pick his cotton."

The uncle spit and then added a curse. "You ungrateful . . ." His words trailed off. Pierce glanced at the man. Common sense told him to ride on.

"You can't leave us." Beth's gaze locked with his again. "You have to help us!" Hysteria now tinged her voice.

Pierce silently went over the options. He could risk a shootout and get himself and his friends killed over a family squabble, or he could set down the women, ride on, and avoid the conflict. Though from the look of terror in both the women's eyes he suspected their fate might indeed be perilous. His gaze moved to Gray Eagle, trying to gauge his expression.

Fight.

Then to Preach.

I'm game.

"If this is a family spat, it's none of our business," he quietly reminded his companions.

"On the other hand," Preach argued, "if the women are in real trouble and we're ridin' away, what does that say about us?" His kind dark eyes clouded with concern. "Family or not, what happens to these females if what they say is true?"

41

His leather saddle creaked when Pierce turned to face forward again. "It's your call, gentlemen. I'm just part of the group like the rest of you."

Gray Eagle spoke up, addressing the two strangers. "I say you two had better move on. We're escorting the women out of the smoke."

Pierce sighed. He just wanted to claim his piece of land, build a cabin, and settle down. Drink sweet tea. He shifted in his saddle again.

The battle-fatigued soldiers were hot, tired, and in no mood for a delay — and in even less of a mood, it seemed, to abandon a couple of innocent, fearful females. "Move aside. We're coming through."

Preach whooped, his mahogany skin glistening with sweat in the blistering sun. "Yes, sir! We're comin' through!"

"You and whose army?" the uncle sneered.

This was not going to be pleasant.

With a leap, Bear went after Pierce while his father attacked Gray Eagle. Pierce thrust his reins at Beth as he dropped from the saddle. She quickly moved his horse to the side of the road, dismounted, and hurried over to Preach. He gently lowered Joanie into Beth's arms and then went to join the fight. Grunts, the sound of fists meeting flesh, and curses flew. With a hard left, Pierce dealt a swift blow to the younger man, but Pierce's foe was instantly back on his feet, now lunging for Preach.

Burying Joanie's head in her shoulder, Beth held her there, her eyes fixed on the ruckus. Blows and shouts echoed. She had witnessed many a melee in the cotton field, but she'd never seen men fight with such precision, such commanding, brute force. The captain took his blows, but his large hands were weapons easily subduing her cousin. Almost as soon as it had started, the fracas was over. Bear and Walt lay unconscious on the road.

Wiping a drop of blood from his lip, the captain shot a triumphant grin at his friends. "You were a little slow on the uptake, Preach."

"I had your back all the way, Captain." The black man grinned.

"And here I thought you had mine," Gray Eagle grunted, knocking dirt off his buckskin vest. He flashed a bloody grin. "Actually, I was covering both of you little sissies!" The men whooped, exchanged some hard hand slaps, and then turned to the women.

Beth's mouth gaped as her gaze shifted to

her unconscious kin.

Pierce bent, and with one large hand he gently lifted her to her feet while Preach attended to Joanie. The black man's expression went from joyful to grim. "We got real trouble here, Captain. She ain't breathing."

Stepping to the woman's side, Pierce knelt and the two men feverishly set to work. Pierce listened to her chest. Beth stood back, a hand over her mouth to hold back paralyzing fear. How she wished she'd learned how to pray. Joanie had tried to teach her, but Beth decided long ago that prayer was wasted breath. She'd watched Joanie pray for release from Uncle Walt so often and so long that she'd decided He couldn't exist. At least He didn't care for them. Her gaze centered on the men's grave expressions.

Don't leave me, Joanie. You're all I have. If you die — she couldn't finish the thought. If Joanie died, Beth wouldn't want to live.

I should have told Walt where the deed is hidden. Nothing is worth Joanie's life. This is punishment for burning the shanty and running away. I should have known Walt would never let us escape.

Her sister lay on the ground, silent. So silent. Even as the stifling smoke moved closer. Burying her mouth in her sleeve,

44

Beth sobbed. The black man they called Preach rose and took her gently by the shoulders, easing her a short distance away. "I know you're scared and hurtin', ma'am, but you got to stand aside and give us room to help your sister."

Beth's eyes searched the prone woman. "Is she . . ."

His soft molasses-colored eyes tore at her heartstrings. Joanie was dead.

"Are you a praying woman, ma'am?"

Beth mutely shook her head.

"Ah . . ." He flashed a tender smile. "Then I'll be standing in the gap for you."

"Thank you," she whispered, not really sure what he meant but sensing the kindness in his words. She might have never fully gained faith in God, but Joanie's belief never wavered. If it were Beth lying in the road and Joanie were watching, she'd be on her knees petitioning Him for her sister's life. Slipping to the ground, she clasped her hands and bowed her head, hoping that if there was a God He'd see that she was trying. She hoped He'd hear the black man's prayer.

Finally, Beth heard her sister's breath catch in a whoosh. Fighting now, Joanie tried to stave off Pierce's supporting hands. Beth rose and half crawled, half walked to her sister's side, where she knelt and whispered, "It's okay, Joanie. You're going to be fine." Joanie's questioning gaze searched the captain's eyes. The coughing started again.

Preach whispered, "That was close."

"Too close." Pierce rose, his height towering above Beth's. "Saddle up. We have to get her out of this smoke."

He carried Joanie to her uncle's horse and lifted her onto the saddle. She seemed to be breathing a bit easier, and she smiled at him appreciatively. Once he was sure she wouldn't collapse again he glanced around. Moving to Beth's side, he gently tapped her nose. "You didn't actually think we were going to ride off and leave you to fend for yourselves?"

Beth found her voice. It was a sputter. "Ye . . . Yes!" She had never met a man that would stand up to Walt Jornigan. Her eyes focused on the other two men, who were tying up the troublemakers.

Pierce reached for the saddle horn of Bear's horse and pulled up on the reins. "You don't talk much, do you?"

"Only when I have something to say."

He handed her the reins and motioned for her to mount up. A mischievous split-lip grin met her. "I take it you're not much interested in talking to me."

46

"No, sir." She glanced away as he lifted her effortlessly onto the seat. "No offense intended."

"None taken." He mounted his horse and picked up his own reins. "Come on. We're getting out of here."

"Wait." He'd have to know about the woman she and Joanie were headed to meet. They couldn't ride off and leave her. The fellow cotton picker was waiting beside the road, no doubt gasping for breath in the heavy smoke. She knew Trella wouldn't move until she and Joanie came. "I . . . I have to tell you something."

He nudged his horse forward. "It'll have to wait until we get clear of the smoke." Leather creaked when the other soldiers mounted up.

"It can't wait." She grabbed his hand and forced him to look at her. "Trella is waiting up the road."

"Trella?" Wrinkles between his nose and forehead deepened.

"Our friend."

His jaw dropped. "Another female?"

She nodded.

"More kin?"

"No, a field worker who also desperately wants to escape Uncle Walt." She took a breath. "I set fire to the homestead, but the

47

wind came up and the field caught —"

"I guessed as much. But what's this about Trella? You didn't mention her earlier."

"I was meaning to mention her. She's waiting about a mile up the road." *I'm doing this for Trella. Joanie and I don't need to be a burden on these strangers,* she told herself. The brush with Uncle Walt and Bear had been close, but Beth was sure they were safe now. She'd take Joanie and find their land, but Trella would need help. She was defenseless, especially with the war not long past. She glanced at the captain again, deciding. She'd let him think she was depending on him for her safety — for the time being. Then she and Joanie would break away.

Pierce put his forefingers to his lips and whistled. The sharp sound caught the others' attention and they reined up.

"What is it?" Gray Eagle called. Smoke rolled from the fields.

"Change of plans!" Pierce said.

Grumbles rose as the two men rode back. "What now?" Preach asked. "We have to get the girl out of this smoke. She can barely draw a breath."

"There's one more waiting up ahead."

The men turned incredulous looks to peer through the thick haze. Gray Eagle spoke first. "One more what?"

"Woman."

Heads swerved back. Pierce's eyes switched to Beth. "She says there's another women waiting up ahead. They're all running away together."

Into the brief but tense silence that followed that announcement, Preach voiced the obvious, "This complicates the situation."

Pierce shook his head. "That's an understatement, but obviously we can't leave them here. As soon as the uncle and cousin come around, they'll be after them." He appeared to weigh the situation, one Beth was certain he didn't welcome. How far did one go to be a Good Samaritan? As far as rescuing three women?

Shaking his head, he said, "We don't have a choice. We take them with us."

"To the first settlement we come across," Gray Eagle clarified.

"To the first settlement."

Beth wilted with relief. Pierce glanced down. "To the next town," he confirmed. "Then you and your friends are on your own."

"Yes, sir."

Pierce picked up the reins. "You don't have to call me sir. My name is Pierce." His teasing mood had vanished with the latest delay.

"Mister," she corrected nicely. He might have saved her neck, but she wasn't going to be beholden to "Pierce." Any man worth a grain of salt would have done the same. Other than with Walt and Bear, she had never referred to a man by his given name, and she wasn't about to start now.

"And your last name?"

"Call me Beth." When she left here she never wanted to hear the name Jornigan again.

He tested the name. "Beth. Pretty name, Beth."

Her eyes narrowed. "Miss Beth," she said primly. Nobody had ever called her "Miss" before, but from now on men were going to show some respect.

"Miss Beth? Then you can call me Pierce Daniel Montgomery the Third."

She bristled at the formal title. He was true Arcadian. The soft French tones came through loud and clear. "I thought you said to call you Pierce."

He flashed another grin, and she knew without a doubt that while this man was more efficient with his fists than a canon, he'd also be hard to best in a verbal squabble as well.

50

"If you stay close and don't cause any more trouble, we'll get you where you need to go."

Nudging Sue's flank, he set his horse in motion.

FOUR

Face it, Pierce. Trouble's got you cornered. A mile up the road another woman waited. A young black girl writing on the ground immediately caught Pierce's attention.

Reining up, he slid off his mare and then helped Beth down from her mount. They quickly approached the moaning girl. "Is she having some sort of seizure?" he asked.

"No," Beth said briefly.

"She's ill?" That's all he needed. Three females, two of them ailing.

"No, sir."

Beth knelt by Trella as her own panic rose. She'd feared this. Could nothing go right today? She looked up at Pierce. "She's having a baby." She turned back to the young woman lying on the ground and tried to soothe her. "It's okay, Trella. We're here."

We're here? Pierce mouthed. Baby? The woman was having a child? The situation was fast getting out of hand.

The girl's round dark eyes focused on Beth. "The baby's comin' early, Beth. I'm sorry. I've tried to hold it in —"

"Shush . . . how far apart are the pains?"

"They're right on top of each other!"

"Oh, gracious." She glanced at Pierce and the urgency in her tone lifted a notch. "Hurry. The baby's coming."

He took a step back. "Ma'am?"

"Have you ever delivered a baby?"

"Me?" He took a second step away and glanced at the expectant mother.

"I can assure you that Trella will do all the work." She motioned to the girl as she bent to assist Preach, who by now was kneeling over her. "Preach?" She glanced at him, hoping she had gotten the name right.

He nodded. "Yes, ma'am?"

"Have you ever delivered a baby?"

"Yes, ma'am."

Gray Eagle moved in to help as well, and Pierce found his voice. "I've delivered one," he finally admitted. "I helped Ma once with a neighbor when her time had come."

"That's good enough. Trella, this is Preach, Pierce, and . . . and Gray Eagle." She glanced at the scout for verification.

"Yes, ma'am. I'll get a piece of leather for her to bite down on. It sometimes helps." The scout walked back to his saddle while

53

Beth stared at the writhing young woman. It would take more than a piece of leather to get her through this.

Kneeling, she whispered, "These men are going to help us deliver your baby."

"Thank you, sirs," the black girl gritted out.

Proper greetings made, Preach's eyes switched to Pierce. "I've delivered many a young'un. Ordinarily we'd need a few things, but —" He winced when a shrill, agonizing scream escaped the mother-to-be. "I don't think we have time to worry about anything but cuttin' the cord."

Gray Eagle returned and gently inserted the piece of leather into Trella's mouth. "Bite down hard when the pains come."

With grateful eyes, she bit into the leather, sweat rolling down her temples.

"I hope one of you gentlemen has a clean knife." Beth scooted over to allow Preach room. "I've delivered a few babies, but I always welcome help."

Preach's strong, brown hands took command. "Don't push yet, ma'am. Take a deep breath."

The girl — who looked to be in her late teens — clamped her eyes shut, bit down hard on the leather, and waited. After a bit Preach said, "Now give me a push. A good

54

hard one."

Trella did, biting the leather against the pain. Not a sound escaped her now.

"I know it hurts," Preach encouraged, "but we want your pushes to do some good." He glanced at Beth. "Dampen a cloth or a rag."

Before she could move, Pierce poured water from a canteen onto his handkerchief and then bathed Trella's face as if she were a small infant. "Why don't we sing? Nothing like a good tune to take your mind off your troubles."

It was obvious pain racked the girl's body. Gritting her teeth, she whispered between the leather, "You lead."

A low sonorous bass started. "The Gospel train's a comin'."

Pierce removed his hat as their voices blended in sweet harmony. "I hear it just at hand."

Beth tried to follow along, harmonizing with Joanie. She'd heard the song on occasion but didn't know all of the words.

Trella's tormented alto blended, offering something about children getting on board.

"Push," Preach encouraged.

The about-to-be mother reached out and latched onto his strong hand, pushing for all she was worth.

Men's voices harmonized, getting louder. "Get on board, little children."

"Again," Preach urged. "We're almost there."

Music swelled. Another hard push, and the baby slid out into Beth's waiting hands. She wiped the infant with the damp rag. Trella silently motioned toward a cloth bag next to her on the ground, and in it Beth found soft blankets, diapers, and tiny baby clothes. Taking one of the blankets, Beth quickly swaddled the infant.

"You got a fine girl, Trella." Beth placed the newborn in her mother's arms, whispering. "You did good."

Between tears and laughter, Trella focused on her child as Preach delivered the afterbirth and cut and tied off the cord. "She's so tiny!" She counted the baby's tiny fingers and toes. "She's just perfect!"

"Ladies." Pierce glanced down the smoke-filled road. "I know this isn't the ideal time, but we have to move on." He felt bad for asking Trella to make the effort, but he knew that Indian women often had their young beside a stream or field and then rode on. Because of the danger of fire and smoke, Trella would have to do the same.

Struggling to sit upright, she wiped tears from her eyes. "I can ride, sir. You've done been too kind. I don't want to delay you any longer."

"We'll look for a grove of trees out of the smoke and let you rest a spell just as soon as we can. Pierce glanced back at the fire that jumped the road in places. It should slow the uncle's chase.

Preach took Trella's arm and led her to his own saddle, placing a soft blanket on the worn leather. Then he assisted her up, handing her the baby once she was seated.

Smoke blinded Pierce's eyes. He searched for the trail. Now what? He decided the sisters would be safer riding with him and Gray Eagle. They could lead Walt and Bear's horses. Making that happen, he then turned to call out, "Can anyone see the road?"

Preach answered, "I can! I can barely make it out!"

"Take the lead."

Hooves pounded as the group rode almost blindly through thickening shroud. Beth was silent behind Pierce. He couldn't help wondering who this woman was who could so adeptly help a young woman birth a child and yet burn down her own homestead.

It took longer than they would have liked, but to the relief of the entire party, eventually the smoke began to thin. Eyes watered. Lungs ached.

Turning in his saddle, Pierce glanced at Preach, taking note of Trella. She was secure in his arms, cradling her newborn. "How's the new mother holding up?"

"I'm fine, sir," she answered through gritted teeth.

"Sorry, ma'am. We'll stop as soon as it's safe."

She nodded.

Pierce met Gray Eagle's eyes. Joanie lay limp in his arms across his saddle, gasping for air.

The Indian looked grim. "She's not going to make it."

Preach stated the obvious. "She can't breathe, Captain."

Pierce turned back to Beth. "Does your sister have an herb or anything at all to help her?"

Beth shook her head. "Uncle Walt wouldn't allow it."

"Wouldn't allow it?" He tried to think of the natural remedies the army used for the affliction. Then it came to him.

"Preach!"

"Sir!"

"We need grindelia."

"Don't know that it grows in these parts."

Beth drew back. "What is it?"

"A miracle for your sister, if we can find

some." What manner of man was this woman's uncle to not allow her to use a simple weed that could help his niece draw a deep breath? And where was her pa in the matter?

"Lobelia will do," Gray Eagle said from the back. The smoke had cleared enough to spot a small stream ahead. Pierce glanced down at Beth's small hand around his waist and odd warmth passed through him. He quickly brushed it aside as a result of the fatigue eating at his bones.

The group pulled up, and once Gray Eagle settled Joanie on his blanket, he remounted his horse and went in search of the herb.

The day passed, and night began to fall. Pierce and Preach tethered the horses so they could sleep for a few hours. They made camp in a thick row of cypress. Trees stood like towering sentinels shielding their young.

The stars began to come out as Pierce paced the campsite. Gray Eagle had been gone for hours. Had he failed to find the plant? He was notably one of the best army scouts that ever fought for the South. He'd find the medicinal plant if any grew in the area.

Preach remained with Trella and the

newborn, clucking over their needs. Pierce observed the display and thought, *He's going to make a fine pa one of these days.* Then, glancing down the road, he muttered, "What's taking Gray Eagle so long?"

Joanie's coughs and wheezes filled the air.

"He'll be here. Try to relax," Preach said.

"How can I relax when I have a sick woman on my hands?"

"Then pray, sir. Keep your mind occupied."

Then Pierce heard the call he'd been waiting for. A soft hoot. Twice.

He returned the signal, and within moments Gray Eagle rode into camp. Dismounting, the Indian reached into his saddle and brought out the medicinal weed. "This was hard to come by. I had to go far."

Pierce took the small bag. "I'm glad you found it. And the way back to us. Even with the moon, it's dark in the woods."

"Yes. Let's pray it will help the young woman to breathe easier." He reclaimed the bag and stepped to the fire to prepare the hot tea.

A little while later he and Pierce approached the pallet where Beth sat cradling Joanie's head in her lap.

Beth's hand flew up to shield her sister.

"What is that?"

"Tea made from lobelia. We used it on the battlefield to help —"

"No!"

"There's nothing to be afraid of, Beth, but your sister isn't going to make it without some relief —"

"I said no!"

"Look, lady." Pierce gripped the cup as he felt his anger rising. "Do you *want* your sister to die? She can't last much longer."

Beth eyed him, torn with emotions. She didn't know him. Yes, he had fought to save her and Joanie from Walt and Bear's clutches, but she didn't know his true intent. In her desperate need she had asked him to help, yet now that they were free of Uncle Walt and Bear, she couldn't decide if she could trust him. He was a man. No man she'd ever met had good intentions. Her eyes skimmed his uniform. Not only was he a man, he was the enemy.

"You're going to poison her," she accused.

"Why would I poison her?"

"Because . . . you . . . you . . ." she paused and then said, "because you're a man."

"I'm *not* your enemy. The war's over."

Beth blinked. She'd never met a man yet who didn't lie and cheat and beat and dominate.

61

"I speak the truth, Beth."

Her eyes focused again on his uniform. Lee had surrendered his army to General Grant in April. The North won.

She shook her head, feeling unsure and helpless. She didn't know enough about war to dispute his claim that he was not now her enemy. She'd heard the workers fretting over their future. Where would they go if the plantation owners no longer provided jobs? She'd heard the refrain over and over, and she had envied their pending freedom. If only she were black, she'd thought, and could walk away from her uncle and Bear, what a blessing that would be. But she didn't believe in blessings. One had to take one's own interests in hand.

Stirring, Joanie coughed. Her body was weak with fatigue from the rattling that hadn't left her chest in weeks. "I'll drink it, Beth."

"I can't let you drink something that might harm you." She glanced again at Pierce before looking at her sister. "We don't know these men."

Joanie caught her hand. "I'm going to die, Beth. If I don't get some air I'm going to die. Let me take it. I don't have a choice."

Beth glanced up a second time, meeting the captain's eyes. He was trail worn, but his blue eyes were filled with compassion. Her gaze shifted back to Joanie.

Biting her lower lip, she consented. "Go ahead."

Pierce slowly brought the steaming tea to Joanie's mouth. The young woman fixed on him with trusting eyes.

"Sip slowly. The liquid will open your air passages."

Joanie obediently sipped. "Are you a doctor?"

"No." He smiled, and Beth noted that he was older than her. Dark blond hair hung to his collar. He was sturdily built but not fat like her uncle and cousin. His bulk was rock-solid flesh. She glanced away when he caught her staring at him.

"Here." He stood and handed Beth the cup. "Have her drink this slowly. Once she gets it down, she'll be able to sleep."

Joanie closed her eyes. "Sleep. What a joy that would be."

Beth took the cup and then looked at her sister. "Don't get your hopes up, Joanie. We don't know that this will work."

Settling his hat, Pierce smiled. "I can assure you, ma'am, that it will. I am not in the habit of poisoning women."

Beth fixed him with a cold stare before turning to help Joanie sip her tea. "I can only hope for your sake that you're telling me the truth."

"I'm also not in the habit of lying to women."

"I'll be the judge of that."

FIVE

By early morning Joanie had stabilized. Because her breathing had eased, the small group decided to push on a bit to get beyond the reach of Uncle Walt and Bear. Gray Eagle's early scouting indicated that the men had managed to free themselves of their bonds, but as of yet there was no sign of any pursuit by them. Given that the sisters had their horses, it was unlikely they would make a surprise appearance, but the soldiers still felt it wouldn't hurt to be cautious.

After some twenty or so miles up the road, Pierce and his friends decided they were safe enough to take the day to rest and recover. Trella's and Joanie's weakened conditions made a respite necessary, but it was welcome to all. The men set up camp on the east side of a stream, suggesting that the women take the north end, where it was cooler. Beth approached Pierce once they had a fire was going. "If you'll shoot some game, we'll cook it."

It had been a spell since Pierce enjoyed feminine company, and this one was easy on the eyes. "Thank you, ma'am." He tipped his hat. "We would be much obliged. We get tired of our own cooking."

"We have no supplies —"

He inclined his head to Preach, who was bent over the campfire arranging a large soot-covered coffeepot along with breakfast. "He'll give you anything you need." He glanced toward the women's side of the camp. "How's Joanie?"

"Weak, but alive. After we eat, would you see that the men stay well downstream? We'd like to wash off the road grime. I'm sure both Joanie and Trella would feel better if they could clean up."

"I'll do that." He tipped his hat again. When she walked away his gaze followed her. She was a looker, the exact opposite of Joanie in temperament and features. She had sun-streaked hair that had come loose from a braid and now hung to her waist, and green eyes whose centers turned dark when she was angry. And she was little. Feisty but little. His hands could practically span her waist. She seemed to want to keep her distance from the men, unlike Joanie, who welcomed a man's company with smiles and kind words.

Preach approached. "Heard the ladies are cooking today."

"Beth offered. I didn't ask." His gaze shifted to the female camp. "You got to admit that those are mighty good-looking women."

"Haven't you got someone waiting for you at home?"

He shrugged. "There was one girl, but we had no real commitment when I rode away. I can't even remember her name." He patted his pocket where the deed rested. "Footloose and fancy-free. Isn't that what they say?"

"I believe it is," Preach said.

"What about you? Got anyone waiting for you?"

"Had a neighbor girl sweet on me when I rode out. Don't know if she made it through the war . . ."

Nodding, Pierce watched as the campfire grew stronger. Most of the men he'd served with hadn't heard anything from home in years. When he'd ridden off five years before, he recalled seeing his father standing on the verandah, hands on his suspenders, sadness filling his eyes.

Lex Montgomery owned one of the largest cotton plantations in North Carolina, and he begged both his sons to fight to keep slavery — not because he was an evil dictator, but because he loved his slaves like family and feared that if the North had its way, families would be separated and displaced. The blacks would have nowhere to go and no means of support. Yet Pierce believed that freedom was a God-given right, and no man should be another man's slave. Father and son spent hours arguing the matter as the war drums beat louder.

When the fighting broke out, Pierce rode off to defend freedom, while his father remained to give his slaves a home and food on their table.

He blinked back painful memories. What would his father say when he rode home? Would he turn away in disgust? Already Pierce was starting to notice an influx of displaced servants. Families with hopeless eyes, hungry men and women with no assurance that they would fill their children's belly that day. Some joined hands and sang spirituals while they wandered the back roads.

Guilt tinged Pierce's once rosy perception as the hard truth started to hit home. A man was only as free as the means he had to provide for his family. Most blacks in the area could not afford freedom.

"Well." Preach stretched. "Let's find some game, and Beth can put the meat on the spit."

His remark pulled Pierce's attention back to the spirited young woman. She was pretty all right, but instinct warned that she could be a handful.

And what was it about men that apparently set her teeth on edge?

"Miss Trella?" Preach loomed above the new mother's pallet.

"Yes?" Soft, trusting eyes met his.

"Are you comfortable? Can I fetch you anything? A cup of cool water?"

"No, thank you, Preach. I'm doing well."

Removing his dusty hat, Preach took the liberty of sitting down next to her. "You must be real hungry. Can I bring you something to eat?"

Giving him a grateful smile, Trella nodded. "I would deeply appreciate a bite of something."

The young mother must be exhausted, yet she never spoke a word of complaint. His eyes centered on the tiny bundle she held close to her heart. "How's the little one faring?"

"She's good. Fine as pure silk." Trella

gazed at the infant. "She's so perfect."

"Yes, ma'am. I can't recall ever seeing a prettier child." And that was the honest truth. He'd been around kiddies all his life, and he'd yet to see an infant so instantly beautiful.

Trella glanced up to meet his eyes. "Had you noticed? I thought it was just me, but do you see how well her head and hands and feet are formed? She's —"

"Perfect," he supplied. "Yes, ma'am. I'd noticed. The good Lord shined on you with this baby girl." He wondered about the papa. Shame he had to miss this moment so filled with pride and the incredible awareness of how God had created this sweet child. Life breathed into something so tiny, so innocent. It was a memory a man would carry to his grave.

His eyes refused to leave the miracle. "She's something, all right."

The pair just sat and admired the infant in silence.

Finally, Preach shifted. "I'd best be getting back. I shot some game earlier, and the minute it's cooked I'll bring you a plate."

"Thank you."

As he stood and turned to leave, Trella said softly, "I wanted to thank you . . . Preach? Is that your real name?"

70

"No, ma'am. My name's Samuel. Everyone just calls me Preach."

Her eyes softened. "Thank you for helping me to bring my child into this world."

"Don't be thanking me, ma'am. It was an honor." His eyes focused on the squirming bundle. "Seems the good Lord wanted to give Preach a special blessing."

"Seems the good Lord always knows what we need and when we need it."

"Yes, ma'am." His gaze caught and held hers. "That shore is the truth."

Six

In the last part of the day, after the meal had been prepared, eaten, and cleaned up, Beth and Joanie went downstream, picking their way through a tangled path. Rest and some good food, combined with the herbal tea, had eased Joanie's symptoms. Color had returned to her sister's cheeks, and she'd been breathing a bit easier all day.

The men provided a bar of lye soap and a couple of towels, but after close inspection, the women decided to wade in with their garments on. Trella had stayed behind to nurse her infant, encouraging Beth and Joanie to take their time and enjoy the luxury.

When they arrived at the water's edge, Joanie said, "You search for gators while I look for snakes."

Nodding her agreement, Beth concentrated on the task. She detested reptiles of all sorts. The long slimy coils of snakes that filled the swamps and bayous close to home were a constant source of aggravation. Shuddering, she tasted the fear that rendered her nearly paralyzed as her eyes scanned the banks and shallow reeds. Fortunately, this stream appeared free of creatures.

"All clear?" Joanie called.

"All clear."

Joanie had brought along the bag holding all their things — everything they had in the world except the clothes on their backs — and she set it down on the bank. After joining hands the sisters cautiously entered the water, Beth's gaze still shifting back and forth for possible critters.

"We can't be overly trusting," she said when Joanie's gaze met hers. Then she realized she was talking about more than the possibility of snakes in their bathing hole. "The men seem harmless, and they did come to our rescue, but we don't know if we can fully trust them."

"Because they are men," Joanie clarified when she sank into the cool stream and lay back. "I understand your general distrust for males, Beth, but do you honestly think we can't trust these men? Perhaps if they fully knew our situation . . ."

"No. We don't trust any man, Joanie. Not

even one."

Joanie's flushed features turned puzzled. "They have been perfect gentleman. Kind, attentive to our needs, and they have gone out of their way to serve us. If they hadn't come along when they did, we might not have survived." She sank deeper into the cooling water. "Think, Beth. Because of them I'll soon be able to see a doctor and get help for my asthma."

That was the only consideration that drove Beth, the single reason why she would permit the soldiers' presence in her life. She had to attain that goal. But hers and Joanie's safety now depended on them. But her worry remained. A man like Captain Montgomery surely thrived on power.

She worked up lather on the soap and cleansed her shirt. It felt heavenly. Walt allowed one bath a week, but as often as she could she'd slipped into the cool bayou below the plantation and washed her grimy clothing. "Joanie, I think we should break away and be on our own now that we've escaped."

Joanie's soft intake of breath didn't surprise Beth. Joanie would err on caution's side. "That would be crazy. We're safe with these soldiers for the time being."

"Maybe. Maybe not." Beth scrubbed her

elbows. "I think we'd be safer — and more likely to reach our destination — without the others."

"Are you suggesting that we run away?"

"Yes. As soon as possible. We'll leave the men and Trella in camp and slip away. They won't care."

"But we'd be betraying Trella —"

"We won't be betraying anyone. Trella wouldn't be with us at all if she hadn't overheard our conversation and begged to come along."

"True, but —"

"No buts. We break away as soon as possible. It won't be long before Uncle Walt and Bear give up and return home. Trella and the baby would be safe. The men will drop her off at the next community, and she will find help and shelter there." Beth didn't like the idea of deserting the new mother, but she had to do what was best for all concerned.

"We can't know that —"

"Walt and Bear have a plantation to run. They're not likely to waste a lot of time looking for us."

Lifting a foot, Joanie scrubbed at the grime. "I wouldn't count on it."

Once their grooming was over, the women floated in the stream, absorbing the last mellow rays of the sinking sun. If Captain Montgomery was a man of his word — and Beth had yet to meet that sort of man — the group would reach a community soon. Every hour the road traffic had increased. She'd learned to turn away at the sight of homeless families wandering the byways. Small hungry children turned soulful eyes on her. She suddenly sat up, her eyes searching the thicket that shrouded the stream. There it was again . . . the distinct snap of a boot meeting undergrowth. She glanced at Joanie. "Did you hear that? Someone's coming."

Joanie smiled. "It's probably Trella. Besides, we're dressed."

Yes, they were dressed. Perfectly proper. Beth sank back into the gurgling stream to enjoy the last precious moments of daylight. Overhead a dove cooed. The picturesque setting was perfect, and Beth knew she wouldn't experience such a peaceful haven again for a while.

Guilt nagged her and she tried to shake it aside. But she couldn't get past the thought that when the men dropped Trella off in the next town, she'd have no home. No job. No means to support herself. If the masses they had passed on the road were any indication of the probability that any one of them would find work in the cotton fields — well, they would have little opportunity. But what could she do? She had not promised to look after Trella's welfare, only Joanie's.

She sensed the approach of others from the corner of her eye and sighed. Why couldn't Captain Montgomery at least whistle or shout her name? Why must he personally come to check on their where-abouts? Men were so wearisome.

Joanie's breath came in a soft gasp. Glancing toward the thicket, Beth focused on a male figure coming into view and her heart sank. Her cousin stood in the clearing, dark and threatening.

"Don't make a sound, Beth," Bear said, steadying his shotgun.

Beth's heart nearly stopped. Where was Captain Montgomery when a body needed him? If she screamed, she had no doubt Bear would shoot.

"Beth." Joanie's whimpers floated across the stream.

"Do as he says," Beth said quietly. There was no use fighting him. He always won. There was no escaping her cousin's or uncle's tyranny. Ever.

The two women waded out of the water at a snail's pace and up onto the bank. Their clothes dripped water.

Bear motioned with the gun. He focused on Beth, who defiantly met his eyes. "Make a sound, and I'll blow your sister's head clean off."

Nodding wordlessly, she reached for Joanie's hand.

"We got horses waiting."

"What about the others?" Had he taken them too? Were Trella and her baby waiting ahead in the thicket to return to the plantation? She was tempted to ask about the soldiers, but she bit her tongue. For all she knew, they were all dead at the campsite — though she would have heard the shots.

"Hold on." Joanie reached for her rucksack and slipped her arms through the straps. Both women put their socks and boots back on. "Okay, now we can go."

Beth and Joanie started through the thicket, assisted by the barrel of a 12-gauge shotgun at their backs.

SEVEN

Pierce glanced up when the setting sun receded behind a cloud bank. "Shouldn't Beth and Joanie be back by now?"

"You know women. They like to take their time prettying up," said Preach.

"Yeah." The captain sat back and stared at the fire. "It's been a good long time since I've seen women that pretty."

Preach gave him a good-natured punch. "It's been a good long time since you've seen a woman, period."

The men's easy camaraderie filtered through camp. Smoke from yesterday's field fire still hung in the distance, but the wind had died and the flames would eventually burn out. No sign of the uncle and cousin so far, but Pierce really wasn't expecting trouble. What were three soldiers and three women to a plantation owner and his son? The man probably had hundreds of pickers. He surely wouldn't miss the women, even if two were kin.

The campfire crackled. A metal coffeepot gave off the smell of perking coffee. Pierce wasn't concerned that the grounds were bitter chicory. He'd drunk nothing else for the past few years. Glancing toward the stream where Beth and Joanie had disappeared more than an hour ago, he said, "Think one of us should walk downstream and check on them?"

"And have them accuse us of lechery?" Gray Eagle laughed. "Not me. The one called Beth would be the first to take your head off."

Preach reached for the coffeepot. "They're all right, Captain. Let them enjoy their bath."

Pierce's gaze strayed to the women's pallets. "Seems real quiet without their chatter."

Checking his pocket watch a few minutes later, Pierce stood up and stretched. "I think I'll walk down that way and check on them."

Rolling to his feet, Gray Eagle said, "Okay, Mother Hen. I'll walk with you." The two men started off carrying their rifles.

River ferns and tangled vines grew thick along the shoreline. Pierce filled his lungs with the honeysuckle-scented air. He'd missed this — the smell of rich fertile earth without the stench of war. He'd waited a long time to plant his boots on home soil. Dread filled him again when he thought about facing his father and having to admit he'd been wrong about the fight and his father had been right. Freedom came with a price, and from what he'd seen the price was steep. He wasn't sure if his conscience would ever let him forget his part in the war. The reminder of those he'd hurt rather than helped daily confronted him. His father would forgive him; God would forgive him. Now he had to reconcile his thoughts and forgive himself.

Once I claim my land, I'll find peace.

Parting the thicket, Pierce listened for the women's voices. Other than the music of the water, a night bird calling to its mate was the only sound that met his ears.

"Strange. I would have thought we would be able to hear them this close," Gray Eagle observed.

"Those two don't talk all that much." Unless Pierce missed his guess, some man — or men — had abused the sisters. Their father? The uncle? They had mentioned that they picked cotton for Walt, and even a fool could see that he and his son scared the wits out of the girls.

Pierce and Gray Eagle approached the

end of the stream and still the women weren't in sight. Pausing, Pierce's eyes skimmed the area. "Maybe they took a different path back to camp."

"Maybe — but they would have had to cut their way through." The men's eyes roamed the thick vegetation.

"You wouldn't think they would have wandered this far downstream."

Gray Eagle looked down at the still waters. "There could be gators in there."

"You think those women would take a bath if they saw gators? They would have screamed."

The scout's eyes scanned the murky water. "Looks a little snaky too."

"You afraid of a snake?"

"No, but I'd as soon not share a bath with one."

"I'll take the opposite side, and you walk back the way we came. They have to be here somewhere." Stripping off his boots and socks, Pierce stepped out into the shallows. A water moccasin didn't bother him, but he also didn't cotton to taking a bath with one. Something brushed his leg and he paused. A log floated by.

Gray Eagle called from the opposite bank. "Jumpy, Montgomery?"

"I wasn't checking for snakes." Pierce

smothered a grin. "I stepped on a rock and I'm tender footed."

"Yeah."

Pierce reached underwater, found a good sized rock and pitched it up onto the bank. Gray Eagle jumped as if he'd been shot.

"Something in the bushes, Gray Eagle?" Pierce called.

"I'll break your neck, Montgomery."

Grinning, Pierce waded across the stream and sat down on the opposite bank to put on his socks and boots. Half an hour later, both men stood in the camp, puzzled.

Gray Eagle spoke. "They wouldn't have run away. They were too desperate for help."

"And they wouldn't have left Trella behind if they feared us," Preach added.

Pierce agreed with both men. Neither sister would desert Trella. That left only two options: They had either wandered off the main path and were lost in the thicket or . . .

"The uncle."

Preach tossed out the coffee dregs from his mug. "You think their menfolk caught up with us?"

"Either that or Beth and Joanie have become lost."

"It's possible."

"Spread out. We have about fifteen minutes of light left."

Trella appeared. "What's all the commotion?"

"Beth and Joanie are missing."

"They're taking a bath —"

"How long does it take to bathe? They've been gone the better part of two hours."

Uncertainty entered the woman's eyes. "I drifted off to sleep and didn't realize they'd been gone so long. That isn't like them."

"We're going to look for them. You stay put." Pierce handed her a loaded pistol. "Do you know how to fire this?"

"Yes."

"If they come back to camp, fire once into the air."

"All right." She gripped the pistol handle.

"Don't leave for any reason." Pierce rechecked his rifle.

"Do you think Beth and Joanie got lost?"

Pierce met her stricken eyes. "I don't know what's happened to them, Trella. Stay close to the campsite and fire that pistol the moment they come back."

Wordlessly, she nodded.

When he walked away, Pierce tried to concentrate on his original purpose, which wasn't babysitting three women and a newborn. He just wanted to get home, claim his land, and live in peace.

Suddenly his life was more complicated than a traveling minstrel show.

EIGHT

Full moon.

Beth searched her mind for a reason other than the present circumstance to let its brightness bother her. Fighting back hysteria, she muffled a panicked laugh. What more could worry her? She'd been rescued once from Uncle Walt and Bear, and now they had recaptured her and Joanie. There would be no Captain Pierce Montgomery riding to her rescue this time. Her eyes followed Walt and Bear around the camp. Fool. She'd been a fool to consider leaving the captain's protection. Heaping wood on the fire, Bear created a huge blaze. Apparently his last concern was that Captain Montgomery might spot them.

Joanie snuggled closer. "Now what?" she whispered.

Too weary to think, Beth lifted a shoulder. "I don't know." For the first time since she'd hatched this idiotic plan to leave the plantation and escape Uncle Walt's tyranny, she didn't have a solution. Her gaze roamed the heavy thicket. There was no way out. Uncle Walt sat opposite the fire, shotgun leveled at her. If she tried to make a break, he'd have no difficulty shooting Joanie.

"We're going to let Uncle Walt take us back?"

"Do you have a better plan?"

Shaking her head, Joanie said, "Maybe it would be better to let him shoot us."

Beth didn't disagree, but she didn't agree either. She was helpless and hopeless, but she wasn't ready to concede defeat yet.

Sneering, Walt flashed an ugly grin. "I can see those wheels turning, girlie."

"I don't see how." Beth pulled Joanie's trembling body closer. "I'm not thinking anything."

"I'm not thinkin' anything," he mocked. "I know you, girl. You're thinkin' plenty."

"Am not."

"You are!"

"Okay, I am. I'm thinking that we're hungry and thirsty." They hadn't made much progress when Walt had decided to stop for the night, but that had been hours ago. He didn't like traveling in the dark this far from home. Beth wasn't certain where they were. Because of the circuitous route they had-taken, she was completely turned around.

"Oh, poor babies." Walt glanced toward the fire. "BEAR! You're gonna burn the dad burn camp to cinders! Ease up on the wood!"

Straightening, Bear looked sheepish. "Sorry, Pa."

Logs caught and the fire burned even hotter. Walt sat the shotgun down beside him, and by his expression he was thinking seriously about something. "We're gonna have to kill our supper."

"Okay, Pa."

"You go scare us up a few rabbits. I'll make a pot of coffee."

"What kind?"

"What kind of what?"

"What kind of rabbit?"

"Dad burn it, boy, how many kinds are there?"

"Well, there are brown ones and black ones —"

"Jest get us some grub!" He swore under his breath. "Takes after his ma. That boy ain't got a lick of sense."

Bear left, his shotgun tucked under his arm. Walt rose and walked to his horse, where he fished a coffee tin out of a leather saddlebag.

Joanie snuggled closer to Beth, making herself comfortable despite the knapsack on her back. "I'm so tired. I don't care if I eat or not."

Beth wasn't hungry either. Her head ached, and she could hardly hold her eyes open. What a mess she'd gotten Joanie into — and Trella. Maybe they would have been better off picking cotton all day instead of running like criminals from Walt and Bear. Walt bent over the fire, scooping grounds into the pot. Eyeing his backside, Beth wondered if she was strong enough to kick him into the fire and scorch his worthless hide . . .

Shaking the ugly thought away, she closed her eyes, trying to form a plan. There had to be a way out of this.

Sounds of Bear thrashing through the bushes met the silence. If there was any game, it would be long gone by now.

The thicket snapped. More rustling bushes.

Joanie sat straight up. The fire popped. The faint smell of coffee permeated the air.

Eyes still closed, Beth murmured, "Sit still. You'll start coughing again."

"Bear," she whispered.

"Don't worry about him. It'll take him hours to scare up some food."

"Beth . . . bear."

"Idiot," Beth corrected. "The *idiot* will be gone for a while. With all the noise he's making, it will take him until morning to gather enough food to feed four of us."

"No. *Bear!*"

Beth's eyes flew open when Joanie sprang to her feet. Walt spotted the black bear at the same time Beth saw it. Grounds spilled from the can as he started to slowly back away from the fire. His shotgun sat ten feet out of reach.

The bear lumbered into camp and paused, its beady eyes focused on the prey.

Joanie clutched Beth's arm. "What do we do?"

"Don't bat an eyelash."

Walt froze into place, his eyes fixed on the animal. Beth could see that though she wasn't full grown, she could still do serious harm.

For long moments, the animal and humans assessed each other.

Then the bear lunged for Walt, and Beth grabbed Joanie's hand. "Run!"

Uncle Walt took off and the women ran in the opposite direction. Bushes thrashed and twigs snapped. Glancing over her shoulder, Beth saw that the bear was single-minded after Walt. The animal loped after him even as Beth and Joanie scrambled into the thicket.

Running until her sides hurt, Beth refused to let up. By now she was pulling Joanie's limp frame along beside her. "What happens . . . if we run into . . . bear?" her sister called, gasping for breath.

"Which one!"

"The animal!"

"Run faster." Beth didn't have a plan. She hadn't been expecting this . . . miracle? Well, if it was a miracle, she wasn't going to waste it. "Are you praying?"

Joanie's answer came through a wracking cough. "I . . . always am!"

It figured. Praying while running your lungs out. That was a different twist on prayer. Beth's eyes darted in and out of the tangled bush. She hoped they wouldn't run into Bear. Her cousin was somewhere foraging for supper. If she saw him, she'd run right past and not give him the chance to catch her.

Moonlight spilled across a road when Beth finally slowed the pace and then stopped. They couldn't run another step. Dropping to her knees, she spied cedar trees surrounded by a thicket of bushes. Cedar aggravated Joanie's condition, but their choices were hiding in there or face running into Bear. The man.

"I know this isn't the ideal hiding place. The cedar will only worsen your lungs, but —"

"I can handle it. I have to. I haven't breathed well in so long that I think I'm getting used to it." Joanie collapsed in a heap after Beth shoved her through the bushes, safely out of sight. Beth crawled in behind her.

"We'll only stay long enough to catch our breath," Beth promised.

Joanie's feeble voice came back in a whisper. "I think God has shone on us again."

"Really?" It was hard to imagine their present circumstance as a gift, but she guessed it wouldn't hurt anything to let Joanie think of it that way.

"He's given us yet another place to hide." Yawning, Joanie closed her eyes.

"But listen to your breathing," Beth said as fear rose up in her again. "Maybe we shouldn't be doing this. We could give up. We could return to camp and let Walt and Bear take us back to the plantation."

Settling back to rest, Joanie slipped her arms from the knapsack and used it for a pillow. "That's crazy talk, Beth. God's taking care of us. Besides, we can't go back. If we do, we're doomed for life."

"It seems we're doomed every way we turn."

Beth wondered if maybe they should give up right now and stop fighting the inevitable. Or was Joanie right? Had God intervened on their behalf just now? And before, when the men found them at the edge of the field, inches from death? She scoffed at the idea. If God had been working on their behalf, He sure hadn't done a good job of making certain His protection stuck!

Closing her eyes, she dropped into a fitful sleep next to her sister.

NINE

Daybreak shone through the cedar branches when Beth and Joanie climbed out of the bushes. Dusting off the seats of their pants, the two sisters set off at a slow but steady pace and didn't stop until they came to a long line of once-groomed hedges. Parting the greenery, Beth's eyes scanned the sight before her. A dilapidated yet stately three-story brick dwelling on the other side appeared to be occupied. A certain beauty shown through its neglected exterior. Honeysuckle twined around wide white pillars that led to a belfry, where a bell tolled. Listening to the lovely sound, Beth counted the number of peals. Six. Overhead, chirruping birds flittered in and out of overhead roosts. Her gaze found the small plaque near the door: Saint Elizabeth Ann Seton Abbey.

"What is it?" Beth asked. She had never stepped foot off the plantation, so every new sight was met with wonder and trepidation.

Peering over her shoulder, Joanie whispered, "It's a convent."

"A what?"

"A convent. I've seen pictures of them."

"Who lives here?"

"Sisters."

Beth turned slightly to face her. "How many sisters, and what family do they come from?"

"Not like us," Joanie said, laughing softly. "They're nuns. Religious folk."

Religion. Beth didn't know anything about religion. She'd heard the field hands praying to God and singing, but she'd never understood why they took the time to talk to somebody they couldn't see. Some put a lot of store in God, but if there was such a being, Beth hadn't met Him. She thought their appeals sounded pretty silly, and when Walt caught Joanie praying she had felt the sting of a whip across her back.

"Do you think they will help us?" She knew Walt and Bear wouldn't be far behind. If they didn't find shelter quickly, the men would likely overtake them again.

"Perhaps." Biting her lower lip, Joanie kept close watch over her shoulder. "Maybe if we hide long enough, the soldiers will catch up with us."

"Don't be silly." Beth's eyes searched the tall, elegant mansion. The structure towered over the run-down outbuildings. "The solders aren't coming to our rescue, Joanie. They are probably glad to be free of us."

"But they said they would take us —"

Beth turned to her sister. "They're not coming to save us a second time. We're strangers — women strangers in need — and those men are on their way home. Why would they waste more time rescuing us from a hateful uncle and cousin yet again?"

"I thought . . . they seemed so caring . . ."

"Caring." Beth turned again to peer through the hedge, where the faint scent of frying meat caught her awareness. Her stomach rumbled. How long had it been since she or Joanie had anything to eat? It was yesterday's afternoon meal, and her strength was drained.

Casting another wary glance over her shoulder, Joanie whispered, "We have to do something."

Hoofbeats sounded in the distance. Beth wasn't fool enough to think Walt and Bear wouldn't search the area thoroughly. Grabbing Joanie's hand, she moved forward. Crossing the yard, she led the way to the back of the house, searching for an entrance. Perhaps some kind soul would take pity on them and offer a hot meal. "Let's go."

Crouching, they moved quickly across the expanse and tapped lightly at a large wooden door.

"What do we say?" Joanie's eyes rounded. "They'll want to know who we are and why we're out so early in the morning." The sun was just peeking through the trees, spreading rays of light across the dew-soaked grass.

"Let me do the talking. Make yourself presentable." They licked their fingers to smooth their hair, and then they straightened their masculine attire. At least yesterday's bath made them somewhat presentable.

The heavy door swung open, and Beth met a pair of friendly eyes. Golden, like an old tomcat they once had, but with the most pleasant warmth in their depths. The rotund figure dressed in black offered them a quick smile. "Yes?" A large gold cross hung around her neck. Beth focused on the object, speechless. She'd never seen such a sight.

Joanie found her voice first. "We're terribly sorry to call so early, but we are very hungry and thirsty —"

The door swung open wider. "Welcome!"

Still without her tongue, Beth followed Joanie into a massive kitchen that smelled of frying bacon and warm bread.

Closing the door, the woman locked it and then turned, smiling. "Please have a seat at our table."

Beth realized then that they weren't alone. She lifted her eyes to see a large oblong table with a dozen or more elderly ladies in black staring at them. Her heart thumped. The woman who had opened the door appeared to be the youngest of the bunch. The others looked to be very old.

Joanie reached for her hand and led her around the massive table to a spot with two empty seats. Smiling, she made the introductions. "I'm Joanie, and this is my sister, Beth."

"Joanie. Beth." Words of recognition were softly murmured.

An austere-looking woman seated at the head of the table noted, "We are pleased God has sent you to join us. We were just about to give thanks."

Nodding, Beth still couldn't speak. Her surroundings were almost as frightening as the knowledge that somewhere nearby Bear and Walt searched for them. She pictured their spiteful eyes scanning the nearby woods as though they were hunting prey.

The women bowed their heads. Joanie, and then Beth, followed.

"Bless, O Lord, this food. For Thy name's

sake, grant that all who partake of it may obtain health of body and safety of soul through Christ our Lord. Amen."

Safety of soul? Beth would have to ponder that one. After-making the sign of the cross, the women unfolded their napkins.

The leader, whom the rest called "Reverend Mother," reached for a large bowl of scrambled eggs and passed it to the guests first. "Please. Eat."

Exhausted and hungry, Beth accepted the warm bowl. The women were very kind and gentle with their guests. One poured hot tea while another passed a plate of thick ham slices. When Beth realized she was eating like a ravenous animal, she purposely slowed her fork.

Shortly after the dishes were cleared, a bell tolled. Rising, the women shuffled off — all but the friendly one who had opened the door.

"I'm Sister Mary Margaret." Pausing in the doorway, she explained over the tolling bell, "It is prayer time."

Nodding, Beth stood beside Joanie, uncertain as to what they should do. No questions had been asked about their unexpected appearance, and neither Beth nor Joanie had offered any explanations. Now what? Bear and Walt were surely close by. It wasn't safe to go outside just yet.

The nun smiled. "If you like, you may wait in the library." A giggle escaped her. "It's very quiet and comfy there."

Silently, Beth took her sister's hand and followed the nun to a shelf-lined room. Well-worn sofas, a multitude of reading material, and comfortable overstuffed chairs welcomed the weary travelers. Morning sunlight poured through a bank of eastward-facing windows. A birdcage contained two lively parakeets that were splashing in their water dish during their morning ritual. The room looked safe; a peaceful haven.

"When we finish, I'll bring you a fresh pot of tea." The sister stifled another giggle and left in a soft rustling of black.

Hesitantly stepping to the birdcage, Beth studied the little feathered creatures. "Isn't this the strangest thing you've ever seen?"

"Birds in a cage." Joanie nodded, her eyes roaming the friendly room. "I didn't know there were this many books in the whole world."

Beth's heart broke. She'd begged to learn how to read and write, but Walt had forbidden it. Ma had secretly taught Joanie when she was sick at home, but Beth was always in the cotton fields.

"You don't need to know nothing but how to

pick cotton," he'd said. *"Don't need no fancy learning to put fanciful ideas in your head."*

Fancy learning wasn't her intent. She just wanted to pick up a book and know what the letters said.

Joanie sank to a sofa, coughing.

The long night had been exhausting, and though grateful for the escape and refuge, the strange surroundings added to the feeling of nearly being overwhelmed. Beth eased over and dropped onto the seat beside her. She was bone tired. If she could just close her eyes a few moments, she was sure her powers of reasoning would return. Joanie scooted closer, resting her head on Beth's shoulder. The plan had worked. They were free. All she had to do now was get Joanie medical help — and keep out of Walt's clutches.

"What's next?" Joanie asked.

"We do what we planned. We'll sleep in barns during the night and travel during the day. If we keep to ourselves, we'll not be noticed."

"But we have very little money. And Trella? What will she do?" Joanie reached down to pull her Bible out of her knapsack. The years had left the book worn and ragged.

"She'll follow the plan. I'm sure the

soldiers will keep their word and see her safely to the next town. Once she's there she will have to find work and make a life for herself and her baby. We have to take things one day at a time and stick with the plan, Joanie. We can't be fainthearted now."

Beth refused to spend the remainder of her life ruled by a spiteful uncle. Though last night Joanie had considered admitting defeat and going back with them, in the light of day with a full stomach Beth felt confident that in the end she was smarter than him. She could escape his tyranny, and that was all that mattered. Eventually he would give up the search, assuming they were helpless females who would be the cause of their own deaths.

He'd be wrong.

Joanie's drowsy voice broke into her thoughts. "I wish we could have stayed with the soldiers. Pierce and Gray Eagle are kind —"

"They are men. There's no such thing as *kind* men. How many times do I have to remind you?"

"I know, but actually, those men are good. If we could have stayed with them, I'm sure we would have been safe."

"Maybe. Or perhaps they were deceiving us." Yes. Deceiving them. That was the more likely case. All three soldiers had been courteous, much as Beth hated to acknowledge it, but they could have planned on taking the women on up the road and then turning on them — as men did — doing unspeakable acts. She and Joanie were better off now. They were on their own.

"Joanie, you need to pray."

A part of Beth knew they needed Joanie's faith right about now. Especially in light of her own doubts that lingered on the edges of her bravado. It couldn't hurt to put in a word for Trella too.

"You always say it's a waste —"

"It's not for me. It's for you and Trella. I can take care of myself."

Joanie disagreed with that last part but didn't say anything about it. "Do you think Trella is in real danger? Would Uncle Walt spend a lot of time looking for her?"

"I doubt it. What's another slave to him? Eventually he'll be forced to go back to his own doings."

"You don't really think he'd make you marry Bear."

Beth shivered at the unthinkable thought. "I don't know what he's capable of doing." Her uncle's spitefulness had no limits that she could discern. She wouldn't put anything past him. That was another reason why she didn't intend to hang around. Lately Bear had been looking at her extra long, skimming her slim figure and admiring her waist-length golden hair.

Joanie's eyelids were drooping. "I'm so tired."

"Rest. I'll keep watch."

"I love you, Beth." Joanie set her Bible on the floor. "I'll close my eyes for just a moment. Then I'll keep watch and let you sleep."

Beth cradled her sister in the quaint room with the strange birds in the wire cage. The little creatures hopped back and forth, one landing on a swing. Feathers fluffed as the bird drank in the morning sunlight.

This was the strangest place she'd ever been — but then, she hadn't been anywhere. She knew a big world existed outside the plantation's perimeter, but what that meant she didn't know. Yet she was willing to face the unknown. If it snatched her life, so be it. It would be a life given in search of freedom, and that couldn't be so bad.

Perhaps the kind sisters would permit them to stay until evening. They could steal away before the moon came up, keep to the woods, and avoid being seen. If they traveled this way for the next few days, they could safely escape Walt and Bear . . .

The parakeets chirped. Warm sun shone through the windows. Ham and eggs rested easy in her full stomach.

Life was going to be better. Beth felt it in her bones.

Much better. And if God did exist, as Joanie and so many of the pickers declared, and He knew the hearts of all men, then He would help and not constantly hinder them.

TEN

Waking with a start from a sound sleep, Beth's eyes roamed her unfamiliar surroundings. The parakeets still swung on their perch. The sun had climbed a little higher. She shook the fuzz out of her head and realized how much the short nap had refreshed her. Joanie still snoozed on her shoulder, the faint sound of blocked sinuses creating a whistling sound.

Though she wished they could stay until nightfall, now that she was thinking more clearly she realized that she and Joanie would probably put the convent in danger if they stayed. *The sisters must still be in prayer,* she thought. *We can't burden these strange women with our problems.*

Gently nudging her sister awake, she whispered, "Joanie, wake up. We need to leave."

Joanie stirred. "Are the sisters done?"

"I don't know, but we have to leave before

they return."

Awake now, Joanie stretched. "That wouldn't be polite. We have to stay until they get back. We should explain our situation."

"No. We can't involve them. Walt may be waiting nearby. He would use the sisters to his advantage."

"He will take us first. He wouldn't dare bother these good women."

"We will outwit him." She eased Joanie from the sofa. "I have a plan."

Hushed halls echoed their footfalls when they opened the library door and peeked out. Not a mouse stirred. Eyes darting toward the kitchen area, Beth pulled Joanie into the hallway. A polished oak stairway led to the second floor.

"Their bedrooms must be up there."

Joanie emitted a soft gasp. "Beth! We can't intrude on their private quarters."

"We won't. Well, not much. We just need to borrow a few things."

"No. I'm not going to —"

Beth cut short her protests and pulled her toward the stairs. Within moments they had slipped into one of the rooms. The space was massive, with a huge bed centered along one wall. A rocking chair sat in front of a window beside a small table, which held a lamp and an open Bible.

Joanie's eyes roamed the simple furnishings as Beth made quick work of her mission. She quickly searched the oak wardrobe and took out two long black dresses.

Joanie's eyes widened. "Oh, Beth! We can't!"

"We can and we must." It was the only sensible disguise. Walt would never stop two traveling nuns. Even he wouldn't be so disrespectful.

"It's sacrilegious!"

Beth turned. "It's what?"

"Sacrilegious."

"What does that mean?" Religious talk, no doubt, but she'd never heard a cotton picker use the fancy term.

"It's offensive to God."

Fleeting doubts gave Beth pause. She didn't really believe in this God — but neither did she want to anger Him if He did exist. But if He was as loving as Joanie insisted, why would He be offended? After all, they were trying to prevent harm to His people.

"We haven't time to argue." She pushed a dress and wimple into her sister's hands. "Put this on."

"Oh, Beth! This is awful!"

"Do you want Walt and Bear to find us?"

"No . . ."

Beth carefully straightened the closet so it wouldn't be readily apparent that she'd been in there and closed the door. "Then get dressed and be quick about it."

Without taking their clothes off, the women pulled black material over their heads. Beth's garment was so large it would have fit two of her, but as the black cotton rustled and swayed with every move a close fit didn't matter. She picked up the wimple and quickly secured it.

Turning, she found Joanie dressed, looking as innocent as the driven snow. "You make a nice-looking —"

"Sister," her sister supplied. "I feel miserable."

Taking her arm, Beth ushered her toward the door. "We'll only use the disguise a short while, I promise. We'll launder the garments and bring them back if we can. And I'll leave enough money to replace both gowns. That should make them happy."

"Wait!" Joanie held up her hand.

Beth glanced at the door. "I know you are uncomfortable with this, but we have to go, Joanie. The nuns will be back soon." She had no idea how long a person could pray, but even as she spoke the bell started to toll again. She could only imagine the sound must mean they were close to whatever came next on their schedule.

Joanie silently handed Beth the money from the knapsack. She peeled off some bills and laid them on the table by the window. Then she turned back to her sister.

"We need to go *now*," Beth said again firmly. Opening the heavy door a crack, she nodded. The two slipped out in the hallway as two nuns approached.

"Keep your head low," Beth murmured.

"I'm scared."

"So am I."

They passed the sisters in the wide vestibule, never meeting their steady gazes.

Walking faster, Beth pulled Joanie along beside her. So far, so good. They were only thirty feet from the front door now. If they could make it to the entryway, they would escape Reverend Mother's eye.

Reverend Mother paused when she rounded a corner and saw two back skirts disappearing out the front door. No one used that entrance. It was reserved for visiting guests and dignitaries.

She shook her head, certain that within the day one or two sisters would be in her office complaining that they were missing habits and wimples.

Closing her eyes, she prayed softly, "Grant these two free spirits safety, Father."

She had no knowledge of their problem or what had brought the young women to the abbey. She only knew for certain that nothing was by accident. She glanced at the closed door, smothering a grin.

Spunk. Those two had spunk.

Laughing quietly to herself, she walked on. There was something about spunk that never failed to put a smile on her lips.

Adjusting her cumbersome wimple, Beth parted the brush and peered out. Nothing stirred in the mid-morning air. There was no sign of Bear or Walt.

Blackbirds flew overhead. Squirrels scrambled along tree limbs.

"All clear," Beth whispered.

Stepping onto the rutted road, they both paused. "We'll only walk a short distance and then we'll go back to the thicket." It was a daring move, but Joanie was already gasping from her allergies to the vegetation, and the heat didn't help. Once she had a breath of fresh air they would return to the woods for safer travel. From that point, Beth wasn't certain of their next move, only that for now they had to keep moving. She had no idea how far they would need to walk to reach a settlement. She had no idea if there even *was* a nearby town. She'd heard Pa speak of purchasing goods and food supplies each month at a mercantile. If they could find one of those, they could at least get a few things.

She wasn't overly fond of showing themselves in public, but between the choice of returning to a life of slavery with Walt or finding a community to get what they needed, she decided the risk for freedom was worth it.

The women walked down the road, sweating beneath the heavy black robes. How did those nuns wear these hot outfits every day? Did sweating make them godlier? Beth laughed at the thought. If that were true, picking cotton in the hot sun made her an angel!

And if there was anything she wasn't, it was an angel.

ELEVEN

Pierce reined up when Gray Eagle lifted a hand. The Indian's coal-black eyes assessed the road. "Women's footprints — or children."

Dismounting and removing his hat, the captain wiped sweat from his forehead. "Could be children on their way to play in the creek."

The scout shook his head. "Women." He pointed to the dusty trail. "See. The hems of their dresses brush the ground."

Pierce's eyes roamed the heavy undergrowth. "If I recall, there's an old abbey nearby. Most likely some of the sisters out for an early morning walk."

Gray Eagle dismounted and knelt beside the dusty tracks. His fingers lightly brushed over them. "Do these sisters wear heavy boots?"

The captain shook his head. "I'm not Catholic. I don't know what they wear."

"They don't," Gray Eagle said. "These are our hummingbirds."

Pierce scanned the area and replaced his hat. "Beth and Joanie were wearing boots, but they were also wearing men's clothing if you recall." His thoughts shifted to Beth. He had a hunch that woman could change like a chameleon. Quiet women made him edgy. "We'll follow the trail a while longer. If we can't find them, then we've done what we can to help." Leather creaked as he remounted. His patience was wearing thin. He didn't mind helping when it was needed, but these two were a little too independent.

Turning from the road and back to the thicket, Beth forged a path. Soon they came across a bubbling stream, where they dropped to their stomachs and drank their fill of the crisp, cool water. Joanie's coughs shook her frail body. Surely if Bear or Walt were close by they would hear her. The thought had no more than left her mind than she heard the sound she had been dreading — hoofbeats.

Joanie lifted her face from the creek bed.

Beth saw tears forming in her eyes.

"It's them," her sister whispered.

The riders grew closer. This time they really would need a grizzly to help because

Joanie simply didn't have the strength to outrun them. Getting to her feet, Beth's eyes searched the undergrowth. Walt and Bear might recapture them, but she intended to put a sizeable knot on each of their heads before she surrendered. "Joanie," she whispered. "Hurry. Help me find some kind of a weapon."

Joanie slowly got to her feet, coughing. "I can't . . ."

"We have to gather some large rocks. Something I can throw."

Joanie's eyes met hers.

"Do as I say." Beth paused, noting the pale color of her sister's cheeks. "If you're able."

Gingerly, Joanie moved alongside her. The women worked to fashion a pile of rocks as the riders drew closer. Her uncle would likely be so angry he'd take the bull whip to her right there, but Beth didn't care. She'd make him wish he'd forgotten all about her.

Hunkered down and waiting for the best shot as the riders approached, she could only hope they hadn't already spotted the black robes and wimples, but common sense told her the wish would be as effective as spitting into the wind to put out a fire.

"I can throw," Joanie wheezed.

"I'll do the throwing. I don't want him to have any reason to beat you too."

"It won't matter if I throw or not."

Beth knew she was right, but that didn't stop her from hoping to shield Joanie from another thrashing.

"Joanie," Beth said as her pulse kicked into high gear.

"Yes?"

"If you're sure there's a God, it would be real smart to ask for a little help right now."

Nodding, Joanie closed her eyes and Beth saw her lips move. She caught snatches of the conversation. "He shall cover thee with his feathers, and under his wings shalt thou trust: his truth shall be thy shield and buckler . . ."

The two riders drew even with the women, and she heard them suddenly rein up. They were close, but she dared not lift her head to look at them lest they see her.

"Enough praying. Start throwing," Beth murmured.

The women stood up and let fly.

Yells rang out as rocks found their mark.

"You may want us, but you're going to have to come get us!" Beth yelled. She threw a sizable stone that produced a substantial curse. Shame on Uncle Walt's language!

Granite ammunition flew. Men's angry

116

shouts drew closer. Oh, they would be in for the beating of their lives, but it was worth it to hear Bear's cries of pain.

TWELVE

A good-sized rock came close to grazing Pierce's temple and he flinched. The woman had already hit him in the leg and the stomach. Time to end this. He slid out of the saddle and stalked into the undergrowth. Beth let go with another rock, obviously determined to meet the enemy head-on. Turning, she grasped a handful of smaller stones, whirled blindly, and looked ready to fling them at her tormentor. Obviously, she wasn't going down without a fight.

Pierce blocked her arm midair. She paused, staring into his blue eyes. His tone puzzled her, calm as still water. "What are you doing now, Miss Beth?"

Fear, then elation, filled her face as she realized he wasn't her cousin or her uncle. She paused, allowing the thought to sink in. Her hand released the load she was clutching. The stones skipped off his boots.

"It's you!"

Gray Eagle rode up, dismounted, and pried rocks out of a wide-eyed Joanie's grasp. Her incredulous look suggested she was as surprised as anyone her prayer had been answered.

The scout wiped a trickle of blood off his forehead. His dark eyes calmly assessed the two women.

Pierce let go of her arm and turned Beth's hands palm up as if checking to make sure they were empty before he released her. "Do you care to say why you two are hiding in the bushes, dressed like nuns, and hurling rocks at people?"

Joanie started to answer but he stopped her, pointing his finger at Beth. "I want her explanation."

Lowering her eyes, Beth refused to look at him. He'd only have harsh words for her, and rightly so.

Joanie started to answer again, but he shook his head and pointed at Beth. "Why are *you* throwing rocks at people?"

Biting her bottom lip, she figured she'd have to say something. It didn't seem wise to anger him any further. "We thought you were Bear and Uncle Walt. They took us at gunpoint from the stream and . . ." Her voice trailed off before she added, "A bear

119

saved us."

"Bear saved you."

"Not Bear, bear. *A* bear."

"A bear?"

"A black bear wandered into their camp and went after Uncle Walt. He took off one direction and we ran the other. That gave us the chance to escape. We thought you were Uncle Walt and Bear coming after us again."

Shifting stances, Pierce glanced at Gray Eagle and then back to Beth. "I think we have a communication problem."

Joanie interceded. "She doesn't like men."

"I figured that out." He focused on Beth. "The *truth,* please."

Beth fixed her gaze on a passing bird. She needed to get out of this fix, no doubt about that, but if she told him the truth, she would have to tell him about running from Walt because he would make her tell him where Pa hid the deed. Not to mention that he'd force her to marry Bear. He would steal the deed for himself, and she'd be doomed to a life of picking cotton, and Joanie would be dead. Best to keep quiet about the deed and stick with the plan of her and Joanie traveling alone.

Summoning a smile, she met the captain's eyes. "We appreciate your thoughtfulness, sir, but we . . . we don't need your assistance from here on out. You've been helpful enough. Though we would appreciate it if you would inform Trella we've had a change of plans and won't be meeting up with her."

Pierce's gaze skimmed their habits. "Why don't you come along and tell her yourself?"

Beth straightened her wimple, aware of his cool stare. Of course he would have questions, but she owed him no explanation.

"Do the sisters at the abbey know you're wearing their clothing?"

She refused to answer. She crossed her arms over her chest and pursed her lips.

Finally Pierce sighed and turned to Joanie, who shook her head. "We planned to launder the garments and return them. And we left money to cover the losses —"

"So they don't know you're running around the countryside posing as nuns."

"No, sir." Joanie said, her gaze dropping. "They didn't know that we . . . um . . . borrowed their clothing. Though they may know by now."

Beth tugged her sister's skirt, wishing she would just keep silent. "We have to go. Uncle Walt is looking for us —"

"He's not close by."

Beth glanced at her sister. Expectancy lit Joanie's eyes. "Can you be certain?"

Gray Eagle spoke. "We've covered every inch of this area, Miss Joanie, looking for you. Most likely your uncle has given up and ridden home."

"He won't give up," Joanie said.

Beth swallowed, knowing her sister was right. Even Joanie's prayers couldn't accomplish that hope.

The captain's eyes returned to Beth. "Cat got your tongue?"

Beth drew a deep breath. Disrespectful man. She reached for her sister's hand. "We're leaving now. If you would be so kind as to give our friend the message?" She nudged Joanie into a walk. The two women set off, Beth aware of the men's eyes on their backs.

"Don't you think we should at least let them take us to the next community?" Joanie whispered.

"We'd only be asking for more trouble —"

"Oh, ladies?" Pierce called.

The sisters turned simultaneously.

"I feel obligated to tell you that though your uncle isn't in the area, we did run across that rascally cousin — Bear, is it? He's a couple of miles down the road, in case you're interested."

Mounting up on their horses, Pierce and Gray Eagle turned in the opposite direction and started moving off.

"Wait!" the women chorused. Beth shot Joanie an exasperated look. "See why I don't trust men?" she hissed. The brute wouldn't be satisfied until he forced his help on them. "All right. Tell him we'll ride with him to the next community. But that's where we'll part company. We'll ride no farther." Surely she could put up with the impossible man a few more hours.

"You tell him." Joanie crossed her arms over her chest, coughing.

Beth hardened her look. "You know I don't deal with men. You tell him."

"No. You tell him."

Heaving a betrayed sigh, Beth stepped around her and walked back to face the captain, who had stopped and turned his horse around. Their gazes locked. She cleared her throat. "We'll go with you."

He flashed a white grin. "I thought you might."

She had no intentions of engaging in a sparring match with him. "Sir —"

"Sir?" He quirked a brow.

Lowering her head, she amended, "Captain."

"How about Pierce? That's my name."

"Sir," she repeated, "if you would be so kind as to escort us with our friend and her baby to the next community we would . . . thank you."

Sobering, he said quietly, "We'd be most pleased to do that, Beth." He glanced toward the thicket. "But first I recommend that you return the sisters' garments. They don't have clothing to spare."

Eyes downcast, Beth said quietly, "Yes, sir." She sighed deeply. Once again she found herself at this man's mercy.

A circumstance she was bound to regret.

THIRTEEN

Gray Eagle took Joanie back to camp, and Pierce and Beth headed back to the abbey. Before parting company, Joanie had gladly taken off her black gown and wimple and handed them to her sister.

Beth was not happy about the arrangement. From behind Pierce on his horse, she said, "This is so unfair. I would have returned the gowns eventually."

"Why do I doubt that?"

"Take me back to camp," she demanded. How could she face the sisters after they had been so kind to her and she'd returned that kindness by taking what didn't belong to her? But she'd left money. Surely that wasn't considered stealing. In a quiet voice she said, "I can't face them."

"Oh, but you can," he corrected. "I think the good sisters are due an apology."

"From me?"

"Did Joanie take the gowns?"

"Partly." That wasn't exactly true.

"But mostly it was your idea."

"Mostly," she conceded. She didn't care what he thought about her. "We needed a disguise."

"So you helped yourself to the nuns' habits."

Beth ignored his goading. He wasn't worth the effort. Somehow, she and Joanie would escape him and the others and then be on their way. Joanie couldn't last forever traveling in this heat, and while the men appeared helpful, they were a headache.

The two rode in silence until Beth decided to speak her mind. She could do that; he hadn't taken a whip to her yet. And so what if he struck her? It wouldn't be the first time a man hit her. "I don't feel I've done anything . . . much . . . that requires me to apologize to the nuns." Her cheeks warmed at the thought of standing in front of those lovely women and admitting that she had stolen their clothing.

"You think not?"

"No. I refuse."

"Okay."

"I mean it. I won't make a fool of myself, and you can't make me."

"We'll see."

"Don't 'we'll see' me, Mr. Montgomery."

"We'll see."

He was so aggravating! Before she knew what she was doing, she had doubled her fist and whacked him across his shoulders — broad shoulders. Incredibly muscular shoulders. And then her life flashed before her eyes. He was the first man she'd ever talked back to, much less struck.

Stiffening, he said in a tight tone, "Beth, I feel compelled to warn you that my patience is not limitless." He shifted closer to the saddle horn.

"And mine isn't either. We don't need your help. We were doing just fine on our own."

"You were singing a different tune when we picked you out of that burning field. And when I didn't turn you over to your uncle and cousin when we met them on the road."

"I needed your help then," she admitted. Her conscience pricked her. How could she be so ungrateful? She sighed. "I do thank you for intervening, both times, but now that Walt and Bear aren't in sight, we can carry on from here."

"Really?"

"Really."

"That's good to know. Just think of this as my kind way of intervening again — on your behalf. You said you eventually planned to return the nuns' clothes, didn't you?"

She couldn't really argue with that. It was the truth, but she didn't know how she would have accomplished the task.

He shrugged. "Just being helpful."

It irked her that she didn't have a good argument. She pursed her lips and set her gaze straight ahead, refusing to say another word.

They approached the convent, and before Beth knew what happened she was standing in front of Reverend Mother.

"Well, Beth. How good to see you again so soon." Reverend Mother smiled.

"I'm . . . sorry, ma'am. I borrowed two gowns —"

"You *took* two gowns without permission," Pierce corrected.

Shooting him a miffed look, she modified her confession. "My sister and I helped ourselves to a couple of gowns from a wardrobe closet. We left money . . ."

Reverend Mother's eyes looked pointedly at the stolen garments.

"And I planned to wash both garments and return them . . ."

The nun's eyes skipped to Pierce.

"I will repay the cost if any harm was done," Pierce offered.

"That won't be at all necessary. We have

ample cloth." She focused on a quivering Beth. "Would you like to keep the gowns?"

Beth's gaze dropped. "No, ma'am. But thank you."

"Why don't you both come in out of the heat."

The sister stepped aside, and Beth and Pierce entered the cool foyer, but not without her mouthing the words to the annoying man beside her. "See? She isn't upset."

Pierce crossed his arms over his chest and pasted a smug look on his face.

It was enough to make Beth want to smack him again.

Fourteen

The nuns told Beth that washing the robes would be sufficient penance for the offense. They provided a rain barrel and soap and let her launder both garments. Then Reverend Mother insisted that Beth and Pierce stay for dinner. They couldn't exactly refuse. And then, once the enjoyable meal was complete, Beth set to work washing dishes.

"How did you say your parents died?" Sister Mary Margaret asked.

Beth wished she had inherited some of Joanie's skill with words. She'd never developed the art of deceit — not that Joanie had a deceitful bone in her body, but she had a knack for speaking the truth without being entirely truthful, telling a person what was good about them without having to add on what rubbed her the wrong way. Beth felt somehow that she couldn't tell this woman they were running away from kin. She was afraid the nun wouldn't understand that

Walt and Bear were vicious men. "Ma passed last week. Pa followed shortly afterward."

"And what was the nature of their illnesses?"

"The fever took them. It all happened so quickly."

Mary Margaret wiped a dish and set it aside. "Do you have other siblings?"

"No. It's just me and Joanie."

"What do you intend to do now? Have you worked in the cotton fields all your life?"

"Yes, ma'am, but Joanie knows how to read and write." Beth dried a skillet. "She's sickly with asthma. Our ma was a schoolteacher before she married Pa. She taught Joanie how to read and write — though my uncle never knew. Because my sister couldn't pick every day, Ma educated her in the basics. She figured that the asthma would prevent her from working in the fields permanently, and she wanted her to have the means to survive when she was older."

Beth set the skillet aside. She'd tried to converse with Joanie's adeptness. Everything she'd said was true, but not exactly as she told it. She hadn't mentioned the fire or who had set it. If anyone ever found out that the fire wasn't accidental, Walt would surely make her life more miserable than it was. The truth certainly wasn't as simple as washing out a robe and eating a free meal.

The nun gave her a sympathetic smile, and yet Beth's pulse still quickened and fear gripped her soul. There would be no future unless she and Joanie took their destiny into their own hands.

Sighing, Mary Margaret said, "Captain Montgomery seems very nice, but I would feel better if you had a female chaperone. I would offer to go with you, but Reverend Mother doesn't like for me to be away. I could ask one of the other sisters to ride with you to the next town, but I fear most of our order are old now and not up to long trips."

"I appreciate your kindness," Beth said, "but the captain and his men have been most respectful, and we're hoping there's a settlement nearby."

The sister paused. "We don't go into town much. We grow most of what we eat, and the Indians who are close by shoot our game for us. We have a milk cow, and we keep a few pigs that we butcher in the fall. Our hens supply us with plenty of eggs. The Cherokee also bring us our flour, coffee, and sugar. I've never questioned where it comes from."

Oh, to have such luxuries at the tips of your

fingers, Beth thought longingly.

After the dishes were finished, Reverend Mother asked to see Beth in her office. Rays of sunlight filtered into the room through high windows. It was another peaceful, inviting place. Sitting at her desk, Reverend Mother reached for a pen and wrote something on one sheet of paper and then another. Because she couldn't read, Beth had no idea what the words said.

Reverend Mother handed Beth both pieces of paper. Smiling, she read the simple inscriptions aloud. "This one says, 'God bless Beth.' " She pointed to the other one and said, "This one says, 'God bless Joanie.' "

Beth was so surprised that she caught back a sob. God bless her? How could He bless her when she wasn't sure He existed? And if He did, He sure wouldn't hold with her ways. "Thank you," she whispered as she stuffed the sheets into her pants pocket. She'd give Joanie hers the moment she got back to camp. It would make her feel . . . blessed.

"Do you and your sister have anything to wear other than men's clothing?"

"We each have a dress and a change of underthings and nightclothes. That's all."

The nun shook her head. "I wish I had more to give you, but we have nothing to offer but the gowns you took —"

"We can't take your clothing, Reverend Mother. I mean, not again. You've already been too generous."

Her wish to be generous, after all Beth and Joanie had done to them, seemed inconceivable. Yet she could think of no reason for the offer. The woman had nothing to gain by giving away the very clothes on her back.

Were people really that kind?

Reverend Mother walked Beth to the back door and watched as Pierce helped the beautiful, if boyishly dressed, young woman onto his horse.

Lifting her hand, she waved as the strange duo rode off.

Spunk.

That girl certainly had more than her share. Her face sobered. The girl had more than her share of trouble too, but something about Beth's story didn't ring true.

Something most worrisome.

Pierce and Beth rode into camp by mid-afternoon. Trella ran to greet her friend. "I was so worried about you!"

"I'm fine." Beth slid off the back of the captain's horse and reached out to pat the baby. "How's she doing?"

The proud mother beamed. "She's fine. Got me a *fine* little girl."

Joanie also came up, breathless, and broke in. "What took you so long? I was beginning to worry."

Beth fished in her pocket and took out the notes. "Reverend Mother gave me these. One of them is for you."

"For me?" Joanie's face broke into a grin after she read the message. "How sweet of her."

Draping their arms around each other, the three women walked to their pallets. For Beth, it had already been a long day.

Later that afternoon Joanie reached for her knapsack and rummaged through it. "Beth, have you seen my Bible?"

Her sister glanced up. "No. Where did you put it?"

"I don't recall. I remember having it with me when we were at the abbey . . ." Her breath caught. "Oh, goodness! I must have dropped it when we ran away."

"Joanie!"

"My Bible," Joanie moaned. "I've lost my Bible!"

"We have to find it. The deed to our

135

property is in it. Think. Did you have it after we left the abbey?"

When Joanie burst into tears, Beth softened her tone. "It's okay. Maybe the captain will let us retrace out steps so we can try to find it."

"He will." Joanie nodded. "I know he would do that for us."

FIFTEEN

After settling the horses for the night, Pierce walked back to the fire and joined the gathered group.

"Okay, ladies. If we're going to get you to the next town safely, we have to have some rules."

"Sir . . . Captain?"

"Yes, Joanie?"

"I've lost my Bible. Could we retrace our steps to look for it?"

"Joanie, I wish we could, but we'd only be inviting trouble." Pierce sobered. "Do you have any idea where you might have left it?"

"No, sir. I had it at the abbey, but I can't remember if I took it when we left the nuns."

"Do you have your knapsack?

Nodding, she said, "Yes. And my Bible should have been in it, but it's not. If not at the abbey, it might be in the thicket where you found us."

"I have a vague sense of the area, but to look for a book in the thicket . . ." He shook his head. "I'm sorry, Joanie. I'll ride back that way in the morning, but you'll have to remain in camp."

Beth reached out to comfort her. "It'll be okay. We can get you a new Bible, and I suppose we can apply for a new deed."

"Ladies, we have to focus on the immediate threat," Pierce said, calling their attention back to the matter at hand.

Beth's nose turned up at his tone, but she kept silent.

"That means we stick close." His gaze held Beth. "No riding ahead or behind. We stay together."

"How far away is the next town?" Trella asked.

Glancing at Gray Eagle, Pierce remarked, "You're familiar with this area, aren't you, Gray Eagle?"

He nodded. "I was raised nearby."

"You're Cherokee?" Joanie asked.

Another short nod. "They are my people."

"Do you have family here?"

He shook his head. "There is much distance between here and my family, but I have traveled these parts many times during my childhood."

"We passed a town about forty miles back.

Should be another one coming up, I imagine." Pierce's tone gentled. "I wish we could offer more."

"You've been so kind already," Trella said softly. "If you'll just help us to get away from Walt and Bear, we'll look after ourselves."

"Are any of you trained to do anything other than pick cotton?" Preach asked.

Beth and Trella shook their heads. Joanie said, "I can read and write a little. Enough to get a job and support us, I hope."

"No disrespect, ma'am," Pierce said, "but you're in no condition to work."

Beth noted Joanie's spine stiffen. "I can work. I do it every day — when my cough doesn't interfere."

"Well." Pierce adjusted his hat brim. "I wish I could offer more, but you ladies appear to be intelligent women. I'm sure you'll find a way to manage." He focused on Beth and smiled. "Isn't that true?"

She looked away without answering. He did love to goad her. A long tense moment passed, but the only sound heard was that of the baby beginning to fuss. Beth glanced at the child. Her face was red, and she scrunched her tiny brow.

"Is she okay?" Beth asked Trella, glad to not have to talk to Pierce. She reached over to smooth the tuff of coal-black hair.

"A bit fretful." The young mother's mahogany features sobered. "She doesn't sleep much. I don't know. Doesn't seem quite right." Then she sighed and added with a smile, "But I ain't ever been a mama before, so what do I know?"

The quiet voices and peaceful camaraderie around the fire relaxed everyone. "Coffee smells good," Pierce said, reaching for a cup.

Preach sprang to his feet. "I'll get that for you, sir."

"Why don't I pour us both some?" Pierce removed his hat, and Beth noted the thatch of thick blond hair that curled at the base of his neck. Suddenly, the baby burst out in a crying fit. Pierce turned to focus on her. "What's wrong?"

"Don't know, sir. She's done this two or three times today." Trella reached to gather the child into her arms as the crying grew to frantic sobs. Once the baby held its breath until Beth felt faint.

"Make her stop that, Trella! That's not good for her!"

Pierce started to pace, keeping an eye on the squalling infant.

"I don't know how to stop her! She has a mind of her own." Trella gently jostled the baby on her shoulder, trying to soothe her.

Heads turned. Pierce moved forward.

Trella automatically drew back, and Beth braced herself to see whether he would strike her for allowing the baby to draw such attention. Trella said placatingly, "I'm trying to keep the baby quiet, sir. Honest I am."

Pierce's smile was kind, and he seemed relaxed, not angry. He said gently, "I know you are, Trella. Why don't I watch the child so you can grab a few moments' rest?"

The black girl stared blankly at him.

"Go on," Preach encouraged. "I'll spell the captain in a bit. Lie down for a while. We'll wake you when it's time to feed her."

Tears welled in the girl's eyes. "You . . . you'll take care of my baby whilst I sleep?"

Preach nodded. "Go on. She's in good hands." He smiled. "I have younger sisters. I know what I'm doing."

Backing away, Trella remained focused on Pierce and Preach. When she hesitantly backed to her pallet, Beth stepped forward. "I'll take the child."

Pierce reached out and drew the infant to his chest. "You take care of your sister."

"She's coughing again. What can I do to stop it?"

"Wet a cloth and put it across her nose and mouth," Gray Eagle spoke, pointing toward the line of sycamore trees thick with leaves. "This time of year is hard on her affliction."

Beth left to do as he said. On the surface, the scout appeared to be kind, but she'd seen many a man turn mean when angered. Pierce hadn't lost his temper yet, but just the same she didn't intend to go all soft and think that he might, just might, be a caring soul.

Captain Montgomery simply hadn't been mad enough yet to show his true colors.

SIXTEEN

Stars shone and the moon shed its soft light through the shielding row of sycamores. Pierce had miraculously silenced the infant, who now slept on folded blankets near the fire. Trella hadn't moved since she'd fallen on her pallet two hours earlier.

Breaking camp and going on ahead had been discussed, but Pierce didn't favor the move. He almost seemed inclined to let Walt catch up. "Your uncle knows we wouldn't risk camping in the same place, so we'll use his miscalculations to our advantage," he told Beth when she questioned his motives. "We'll get a good night's sleep and then move on early in the morning." His eyes had fixed on Gray Eagle. "Agreed?"

The scout nodded. Beth noticed that, though he didn't speak often, he spoke precise English and his eyes and ears appeared tuned to every snap of a twig or rustling thicket.

The night before last Pierce had given Beth his bedroll, and tonight he said he and the other men would be just as happy sleeping again on the hard ground again. She might have wished she'd been able to wash the captain's bedding, but she was too weary to mind the musty smell. Her head touched the blanket and her lids closed, but before she fell fully asleep, Trella's infant made a whimpering sound — the sound a child makes moments before it's about to burst into full-blown tears.

Trella sat up and received the baby from Pierce, holding her against her shoulder, whispering soft words. Beth watched her. She had a natural way with the child. Other pickers said the infant's father was one of the field bosses. Unwedded mothers abounded on the plantation. Uncle Walt loved to brag about *growing* his help. Children were sent to the fields at a young age to spend sixteen hours in the blistering heat. When the sun sank, they lugged bulging sacks to the cotton shed, where a stern taskmaster would weigh the day's work. If the child produced his quota, he would eat supper. If he fell short, he would be sent to bed with only a dipper of tepid water in his aching stomach.

Beth suspected that Trella's infant was

sired by Toole Madison, a giant of a man who oversaw the black workers. Like Bear and Walt, Toole ruled with a whip. Scarred backs glistened in the hot sun as the pickers dutifully tried to please his heartless soul, and many of the women had fallen victim to his wicked desires at night.

The newborn's cries grew louder. Beth heard the men on the other side of the fire tossing and turning.

The moon crept higher in the sky. Beth dozed fitfully, awakened every few minutes by the baby's shrieks. Trella now paced back in forth in front of the fire, trying to hush the fussy infant.

"What's wrong with her?" Joanie asked. The effort to speak brought on another coughing spasm.

"Maybe's she's hungry."

"Trella nurses her every two hours. The baby acts as though her tiny belly cramps with hunger pangs."

Another five minutes passed. Joanie's cough persisted, and the baby's cries mingled with the sound of croaking frogs. Finally Beth rolled to her feet.

Pierce did the same. They met up by the fire. A tearful, exhausted Trella said to them, "Maybe she's takin' sick. I can't get her to stop crying."

Beth reached for the infant. "I'll see if I can pacify her." She accepted the small bundle and began to softly coo. The newborn's hysterical cries grew even more insistent.

For the next few minutes, Beth and Pierce passed the infant back and forth, trying to appease the child.

"That's a hungry cry," Preach noted.

"I feed her constantly," Trella said. "She nurses, but she seems hungry minutes later."

Gray Eagle stepped from the shadows. "Your milk does not console the baby."

"I don't know what more I can do." Trella swiped at the tears rolling down her cheeks. The new mother's pain and exhaustion reflected in her tone. Beth's heart went out to her.

Gray Eagle turned and walked away. Beth watched him, wondering what he was up to.

Pierce carried the baby to the stream bank, bouncing the infant on his shoulder. Everyone was wide awake now. Beth knew they were making enough noise to wake the dead. If Walt and Bear were in the vicinity, there was no doubt they would find them.

Gray Eagle reappeared and walked directly to the baby, inserting the tip of a small bag into her mouth. The infant suckled hungrily.

Joanie coughed.

Turning on his heel, Gray Eagle went to the young woman, knelt, and held a cup of lobelia tea to her lips. Within minutes the camp was filled with only the sounds of nature's soothing tones. Frogs croaked. Cicadas sang.

Dropping to her pallet, Beth absorbed the heavenly reprieve.

Pierce passed by her after handing the baby back to her mother. "What . . ." Beth caught herself. She shouldn't be asking questions, but curiosity got the best of her. "What did he do?"

"What I should have done hours ago. He made the baby sugar water."

Beth's cheeks warmed. Why hadn't she thought of that? The field workers often wrapped sugar in small cloths to quiet their babies.

Exhaustion overtook her, and she lay back down as Gray Eagle moved around the fire to his blanket. She noted the look of satisfaction on his face as if he were pleased to have helped the infant and mother and soothed her sister's cough yet again.

For a brief moment Beth wondered if she could be wrong about men.

Seventeen

The camp fire burned low. Across the way the women were silent and still. Pierce poured a cup of coffee and handed it to Gray Eagle, who had come back from a quick perimeter check of their campsite. "Are the women asleep?"

"The little one too."

Shaking his head, Pierce took a sip from his own cup. He'd rather fight a skirmish than try to quiet a newborn. The odds for success were better. "What are we going to do about the baby?"

"She needs nourishment. The mother's milk does not please."

"So, where do we find a wet nurse in these parts?"

Sitting down cross-legged, Gray Eagle studied the flames. "I have not been here for many years, but when I was a child there was an encampment not far from here."

"Are you sure they would welcome us?"

The conflict had settled down many years ago, but resentment toward the white man and his ways still blossomed. Pierce didn't want a war party on his hands with three women and a child to protect.

"They are my people," Gray Eagle confirmed with a nod. "These are their summer grounds. At first light I will ride ahead to see if the camp still exists. If so, I am certain nursing mothers will be there who can feed Trella's child."

"I suppose that is best, though I don't like the thought of further delaying our return home," Pierce said with a sigh.

He longed for sight of his land and the opportunity to make peace with his father. He could taste his mother's blueberry pies — thick and rich with a crust so light it melted on his tongue. He smiled as a wave of homesickness swept over him.

Gray Eagle turned his cup in his hands. "The one called Beth? She is talking to you now?"

"Not if she doesn't have to." Pierce's grin widened. "She doesn't favor men."

The scout's black eyes danced with merriment. "She is very silent around you."

"You noticed? Can't imagine why. I go out of my way not to step on her bustle." He paused. "She doesn't speak often, but she is

149

spirited." *Spirited.* That was a kind characterization. "And ornery as a spiteful mule."

"Is there a woman waiting for you when you return?"

Shrugging, Pierce said, "There was a girl when I left home five years ago. She was pretty young — fifteen. She said she'd wait for me, but I don't know . . . I hope not." He flashed a grin. "I was telling Preach earlier that I can't even recall her name."

"You do not love her?"

"Love?" Pierce chuckled. "My friend, I was nineteen at the time. I loved all the women." He sobered. "If she's waited all these years I suppose I'll have to give serious thought to settling down and maybe starting a family. It would please my parents greatly to have grandchildren." In ways, he wished there was someone waiting for him. A pretty young thing who would share his life and grow old with him. "But what about you? Got a woman waiting for you somewhere?"

Gray Eagle shook his head. "I am like the wind. I blow here and then there. I have no woman waiting for me."

Pierce winked. "I bet many a young maiden has had her eye on you."

"Many women do not think clearly."

Conversation ebbed as each took a sip of

his coffee. Pierce glanced at the sleeping women again and then turned back to his friend. "You have said that your mother was a captive."

"Yes. That happened many years ago when the wars still raged between my people and the white man. She was a missionary's daughter. Her family was massacred during a raid. She was taken to the chief and he married her. She was young with a privileged background. She taught me to read and write. She wanted me to be like the white man, but she couldn't change the color of my skin or the love in my heart for my father."

"Is your father still alive?"

"He was killed during a buffalo hunt."

Pierce nodded, remembering Gray Eagle speaking of how his young father was trampled to death when he was caught up in a buffalo stampede. Shortly afterward, the new chief offered Gray Eagle's mother her freedom as a condolence gift. She declined and lived among the tribe until her death seven years ago.

Tossing the remains of his coffee into the fire, Pierce noted, "We'll have an early start in the morning. We'd best get some shut-eye."

Nodding, Gray Eagle set his cup aside. "I

will leave at dawn and return when I have located the site of the Indian summer camp. They may or may not be there. The war had destroyed most of this land and displaced many."

"While you are doing that, we'll keeping moving forward toward the next town — wherever that may be. You shouldn't have a hard time finding us on the road."

For Pierce, either the next settlement or the Cherokee camp couldn't be close enough. He'd rather fight a war than face a hungry infant . . . or women dressed in nuns' clothing throwing rocks at him.

Wearily, he settled on the hard ground and pulled the brim of his hat over his eyes.

The fire cracked and sizzled. Overhead stars as numerous as Abraham's descendants twinkled.

Rolling to his left side, he focused on Beth. Her eyes were closed, and he could just make out her long lashes brushing her freckled cheeks. Warmth spread through him at the sight. He flicked the irritating reaction aside. But an annoying thought kept him awake. What if a woman like Beth had waited for him? Would his kids have those feisty wrinkles across the bridge of their noses or her thick hair and sparkling eyes?

152

He rolled onto his back. A man could do worse.

Suddenly his future wasn't as clear as he'd assumed a few days earlier.

EIGHTEEN

By mid-morning on the following day, Gray Eagle appeared atop his steed. Reining to a halt, he faced Pierce, who was leading the procession. Not a single community had yet come into sight, though they had made a late start and hadn't gone far down the road.

After Gray Eagle departed for the Indian summer grounds, Pierce had left the women in Preach's care while he went to look for Joanie's Bible as he had promised. Unfortunately, though he had made as thorough a search as possible, he wasn't successful. The little party broke camp and headed out as soon as he returned with the discouraging news. Now they were eager to hear what the Indian scout had to say.

"The camp is still there."

Relief rippled through Pierce. "How far?"

"We can get there well before noon."

"Is there a wet nurse willing to help?"

"Two are available. The summer camp is

now filled with the old and dying, but some daughters and recent widows have come with aging parents. Two gave birth this spring."

"Good enough, as long as someone is able to satisfy the child."

The traveling party rode with purpose now. Beth carried the baby to allow Trella some respite from the infant's crying. Every man and woman in the group felt the child's hunger.

A couple of hours later Gray Eagle came to a halt. "I'll ride in first. The chief is expecting us."

Pierce stayed back with the rest of the riders as Gray Eagle walked his mount through a stand of poplar trees. From here the village was just visible. Thirty or so lodges, with cone-shaped roofs made of bark and walls covered in long grass, were dotted here and there. Beth's heart hammered. She'd never been near an Indian other than Gray Eagle. She'd seen them passing on the road, their bodies decorated with colorful paint and feathers. The pickers said they were warriors spoiling for a fight with the buffalo hunters, but they never bothered the slaves.

She glanced at Pierce. Did she dare trust that this man wouldn't lead her and Joanie into danger? Despite the stories she'd heard about earlier settlers, and the prices they paid when they encountered savages, she found herself developing a certain amount of respect for this Union army captain. The thought sent a shiver down her spine. She and Joanie still had far to go before they would be completely safe. She couldn't go all soft on men just yet.

Trella was holding her baby now, and Joanie rode behind Beth, her head resting on her sister's shoulders. Her coughing increased. Between the coughs and the baby's cries, Beth wondered how long it would be before the men abandoned them beside the road.

She eyed the tall captain. She couldn't claim that he hadn't been kind and exceedingly patient so far, but she knew that could change. It always did with men. She could *not* let her guard down — not for a second. Just the same, she eased her horse closer to him. He glanced over at her and met her eyes with a wicked grin that sent her heart thumping. How could that be? For once it wasn't thumping with fright.

"What's going on? Is it safe?"

"Ma'am." The captain's look chastised her. "Believe me when I tell you that I have no desire to see my scalp hanging from an old warrior's pony."

She focused on the little village ahead of them. "I can assure you, sir. *You* will not witness the sight."

His grin widening, he acknowledged, "I stand corrected. I don't want to witness *your* scalping."

"I didn't say I wouldn't watch yours." She nudged her horse forward a little.

"Feisty little wren." He moved his horse ahead of her, as though to keep himself between her and the village for now. Her eyes took in the strange dwellings. Aging women wearing long deerskin dresses moved across a stream that went down the center of the grouping of dwellings. Others bent over low-burning fires, while still others cleaned animal skins stretched on tall wooden frames.

Though their activities looked peaceful enough, Beth still felt anxious. Would they turn on the uninvited group and leave their scalps hanging on a lodge pole? They were of the older generation. Perhaps . . .

A second, different kind of shiver slithered down her back, and almost involuntarily she turned again to the captain. He spoke low and comfortingly. "Relax, Beth," he said as if reading her mind. "These are Gray Eagle's people. They're friendly."

Just then the scout returned and told them

they could move ahead. Beth kept her distance, allowing the others to ride in before her. When they reached the clear stream, they paused, and a young boy dipped a cup of cold water for Joanie. The small, compassionate act touched Beth, easing her immediate fear, yet she remained watchful, ready to gallop away with Joanie if the situation called for it. Ahead, a man stepped from a lodge. He was dressed in bearskin trousers, shirt, and moccasins. His long black hair streaked with gray lifted in a slight breeze. In the past he most likely had been a proud warrior, but the years had bent his once strong frame, and the hot sun had weathered his features. He was old, and his step was uncertain. Standing in front of his tent, his faded eyes focused on the new arrivals.

Swallowing, Beth crowded her horse next to the captain's mare.

"If you get much closer, you might as well ride with me," he said under his breath.

She eased her animal back somewhat, allowing him room. Gray Eagle made a motion with his hand that Beth took as a sign of peace.

Nodding, the chief took in their ragtag party.

"We come as friends," the scout said.

The chief's eyes moved, silently assessing each rider.

Shifting in his saddle, Gray Eagle indicated the squalling infant. "The child cries from hunger. The mother's milk does not comfort her."

The chief's glance skimmed mother and infant. After a moment he pursed his lips and tilted his head, indicating a large tent facing the north.

Dismounting, Preach approached Trella's horse and took the child from the tearful mother's arms.

"Will he allow us to stay?" Trella asked.

Nodding, the chief's eyes pivoted to a woman who was tending a fire. "You are invited to rest. Eat."

Beth picked up her reins and turned her mare, now following a young boy who ran ahead of the group. He led them to a field rich with green grass. Sliding off the horse, Beth lifted her arms to help Joanie down. Her frail body shook with coughing spasms. When the party returned to the camp, Beth caught an exchange between Gray Eagle and a young dark-haired woman with large, soulful eyes as they spoke in their native tongue, smiling.

Joanie leaned on Beth, and they made their way to assigned sleeping pallets in a lodge across the village. "He must know her well," Joanie whispered.

"So it would seem."

The scout glanced their way and offered a smile to Joanie, whose cheeks flamed a dark red. Beth tugged her forward, breaking the connection. He was indeed a fine male specimen, but she hoped her sister didn't for one minute think there might be a love match in the making. Gray Eagle had been tender to Joanie, but he'd been just as kind to Trella. She couldn't read romance into his manner. Every one of the men in their group had acted in a polite fashion. Beth eased her sister onto the comfortable pallet in the airy space.

"He is quite handsome, isn't he?" Joanie asked. Beth paused to meet her gaze. "Does the thought disturb you?"

"No. I think he's very handsome," Beth said reluctantly.

"He's really nice too. Don't you think?"

"He's a savage, Joanie."

Closing her eyes, Joanie took deep breaths. "Doesn't matter. I know that no man will ever love me."

Beth fussed with the pallet. "Why would you talk such nonsense? You're a lovely woman —"

"And a very sick one." Joanie reached in

her pocket for the piece of paper Reverend Mother had sent and pressed it to her chest.

Beth recited the simple note's message to herself: *God bless Joanie.* She knew the words gave her sister great comfort.

Joanie lay back and closed her eyes. Beth dampened a soft cloth from a jar of water on a stool near the lodge's entrance and returned to wipe her sister's flushed forehead. She had no idea Joanie thought in such hopeless terms. Did she really believe she would never grow old? Never know love? Never have children? The thought saddened her. Beth would never seek love, but that was her choice. Joanie deserved to be loved.

"Don't be so morbid," Beth scolded gently.

"What man would want to listen to this?" Joanie purposefully coughed. "For the rest of his life?"

"A *good* man." Beth tenderly wiped flushed cheeks and runny eyes.

"You say yourself there is no such thing."

"What do I know?" Beth wrung the cloth dry. "For me there isn't, but if you believe in this God you talk about, then perhaps He has different thoughts on the matter." If Joanie's God did exist, wouldn't He provide a true love for her? A man who loved her —

someone who wouldn't let a thing like asthma turn him away?

"I do talk to Him about it. Daily." Joanie sighed when Beth set aside the cloth and lowered her back to the pallet. The sounds of camp life drifted around the sisters. Meat sizzling over an open fire. Women's soft voices talking among themselves as they worked to prepare the noon meal. Children darting back and forth at play, their infectious laughter filling the summer air. And yet fear grew in Beth's heart. They were safe for the time being, but what would happen when they reached the next town and the captain and his men finally did ride away?

The image of her uncle's angry face filled her vision. Walt would find them. Of that, Beth was as certain as the fragrance of perking coffee in the air.

And they would have no man's protection.

NINETEEN

Joanie was asleep when Beth awoke. Though it was the middle of the night, the moonlight was bright, calling Beth outside the lodge. She felt stiff from travel and thought a short walk might help her relax. Moving quietly through the sleeping village, she paused in front of the large tent where she'd seen an Indian woman enter earlier in the evening, carrying Trella's baby. Her eyes searched the immediate area, and when she saw no one she parted the canvas and stepped into the dim interior. Two nursing mothers sat before a low-burning fire, infants suckling at their breasts. One glanced up when Beth entered, her eyes questioning the newcomer.

"I thought I might help?" she said softly. She couldn't nurse the child, but she could care for Trella's infant once she was fed.

The young mother silently shook her head, but her eyes indicated the infant. For one of the first times since she was born,

163

the baby slept in peaceful contentment, with Trella sleeping soundly beside her. Beth studied the nursing mother, one of the prettiest women she had ever seen. Hair as black as a raven's wing hung to her tiny waist. Her expressive coffee-colored eyes were welcoming without her saying a word. She patted the mat beside her, inviting Beth to sit.

Beth complied, settling on the bearskin rug cross-legged in the same fashion as her host. Smoke curled through the opening at the top of the lodge. The fire cracked. An occasional burp sounded from one of the infants being fed. Beth had never experienced such serenity. Her life had been filled with angry shouts and painful whips. This oasis was like a refreshing stream on a hot summer's day. No one spoke. Beth wouldn't have understood the Indian language, but she felt the thread of womanhood — the invisible bond of like minds as she sat in the dome interior and listened to the babies' noisy suckling. She never allowed herself to think of motherhood. She knew it would never come to her.

Witnessing men's cruelty had stripped her of all desire to marry or have children. Her sister's wish to fall in love confused her. Joanie had lived inside the same anger and

fury. She had witnessed Uncle Walt's meanness and the way he had dominated their
pa. Beth didn't doubt that Joanie's man was
out there somewhere waiting, but love in
her life? She couldn't imagine falling in love
with a man.

Until that moment.

A moment when she sat among women
who she hadn't known existed until a few
hours earlier. She should be frightened by
their strange ways, but their eyes were kind.
Beth felt protected here. Her gaze shifted to
the tent flap when it lifted, and she saw that
Captain Montgomery was motioning her
outside.

Smiling regret to her hosts, she stood and
moved to the lodge opening, shaking the
creases from her pants.

"What do you want?" Drawn from fanciful thoughts, she couldn't bring herself to
speak with complete civility to him.

"Good to see you too."

She tempered her response. "It's the
middle of the night. Was there something
you needed?" She started back toward her
sleeping lodge.

He turned to walk with her. "No. I saw
you walking through the village, and thought
I should make sure *you* didn't need something. What were you doing in the lodge?"

"I thought I might help."

He cast a questioning eye in her direction.

"I thought I could help care for Trella's infant while she's resting. The poor thing is exhausted."

"Is she ever going to name the child?"

"I'm sure she will — eventually." Nothing had been mentioned about a name, and events had happened so quickly that naming the baby had been the last thing on the escaping women's minds. "It's been a difficult few days."

"It will be even more difficult when you reach a community."

She let the observation pass. She knew that what lay ahead would not be easy. The two strolled slowly through the camp, keeping their voices low.

"I'm not afraid," she finally said. She didn't want him thinking she was one of those fainthearted ninnies who flinched at the sight of hardship.

"You wouldn't be here if I thought you were in danger." He nodded. "The real danger is still out there looking for you."

"I know."

"Then I don't have to worry about you slipping off to some nunnery when my back is turned?"

"No." Though for the life of her, she

couldn't imagine why he would want the aggravation of caring for a band of ragtag runaways.

"Good, because we're going to be leaving shortly."

Her heart shot to her throat. Leaving? They couldn't leave them alone among savages.

"The men and I have been talking. It looks like the baby will have to remain here for a few weeks, and that's a real delay. Also, Joanie needs the rest. I think it's best that Gray Eagle, Preach, and I ride on. But before we go, I'll arrange for one of the men in the camp to escort you, Joanie, and Trella to the closest settlement as soon as the baby is able to tolerate cow's milk."

"You're leaving us?" She stopped dead in her tracks. "Why can't Joanie and I come along? We won't —"

The captain held up a hand, halting her words. "Beth, Joanie is in worse shape than the baby. Surely you can hear that when she breathes."

Beth couldn't deny the truth of what he said, yet the thought of being left behind while the men moved on frightened her. "But we can go to a town, get medical help —"

There was that hand again. "She needs

rest. You won't leave her, and Trella's baby won't survive just now without a wet nurse." Even in the dim light the compassion she saw in his eyes nearly undid her. Beth looked away. Of course she wouldn't leave her sister. Joanie was all she had left in this world.

She turned to meet his gaze again. How could he be certain that these Indians wouldn't turn on them once he rode away and hold them captive — or worse?

"You can't leave."

"I am leaving," he insisted, leveling a look at her. "But maybe if you told me the true nature of your flight from your home, I might be able to set your fears to rest."

"I . . . I've told you. We're running away from Uncle Walt."

"I understand that. What I don't understand is why the desperate plight? Where are your folk?"

"Dead."

"Brothers and sisters?"

"Only me and Joanie. Please, Captain —"

"I've asked you to call me Pierce."

She crossed her arms over her chest.

Meeting her stubborn gaze, he shook his head. "You're a hard one to figure out."

"I wouldn't try, Captain. But . . . you can't leave us here. You just can't."

"Is it that you don't like men in general or you just don't like me in particular?"

She stiffened, waiting for a blow. Though he was smiling at her, Uncle Walt often smiled before he was about to strike. So did Bear.

"Well?"

"I . . . don't have anything against you personally. In general, you're all right. I don't trust other men."

His eyes assessed her. "Care to say why not?"

"No, sir." She kept her eyes straight ahead and her response respectful.

"You never told me your last name."

She didn't dare reveal that. Uncle Walt was well known around these parts, and there was no telling what kind of connections the captain might have to men her uncle knew. For some reason, beets flashed through her mind and she seized one upon that.

"Beet . . . smoth." She steeled herself for his response. Joanie said lies were the devil's work, but because Beth didn't know the devil or the Lord, she guessed it didn't matter.

"Beth Beetsmoth." He tasted it on his tongue. "That's your name?"

"Yes, sir." She didn't meet his eyes.

"Beth and Joanie Beetsmoth."

"Yes, sir."

He shook his head and they walked on. "Why don't I just call you Pickled Beets?"

He was mocking her now, but she couldn't let him shake her. Or leave. "Fine. Anything that pleases you."

He paused. "All right. What other concerns do you have about us riding ahead?"

"Well . . ." Could she voice her true feelings? She felt somewhat safe in his presence. And yet . . . she couldn't quite bring herself to tell him all that had brought her and Joanie to this point, so she opted for a diversion. "Please just wait a few days. By then the baby will be stronger and we can find a way to feed her cow's milk."

"You're really wanting me to stay?"

"I . . . well, I . . ." Her brow furrowed. "It's just that I don't know if we can trust these people."

"And if I stay, what am I supposed to do?" His tone altered, almost intimate now, and she resented the implication.

"The wait shouldn't be long. Trella's baby will be thriving soon, and then we can all move on together."

"What if your optimistic outlook doesn't pan out and we're delayed here for weeks? You have to understand my position, Miss

Beetsmoth."

The name rankled and she gritted her teeth. If she was going to cooperate with the man, she'd have to level with him. Sighing, she said, "My name is Beth Jornigan."

"Jornigan. That has a nicer ring than Beetsmoth."

A smile crept to the corners of her mouth. "Thank you, Pierce." His given name came out before she thought about it, and she nearly choked when she realized she'd said it.

"Pierce, is it? My, my. I think I like this Beth Jornigan better that the Beetsmoth woman. She was a might testy." They paused before the large ceremonial lodge, and his tone grew serious. "Tell me the truth, Beth. What are you really hiding from?"

She considered him, knowing she had to come clean or there was no way he would stay. At the very least, she had to make him better understand why she wanted to run. Some log benches were next to the path. She gestured to one and they sat down.

"My uncle is a terrible man. You surely saw that. He and my cousin are ruthless." She took a deep breath as she prepared herself for what she would tell him next. "Walt often made Joanie work long hours in the cotton fields, even when she was sick.

When Pa and Ma came down with the fever, he took no pity on them. Ma died, and Pa followed soon afterward." She swallowed. Now the half-truth got tricky. Exactly how much did she tell this man? Could she trust him with even a part of the secret? His next question opened the door.

"Why were the brothers at odds?"

At last the moment she'd been dreading. "I'll tell you the truth," she ventured, hoping the morsel she'd decided to offer up would be enough to satisfy his curiosity. "I didn't know anything about the Trail of Tears — when President Jackson moved the five tribes to Oklahoma. I don't have the learning that Joanie has, but I hear things and I remember them. My great-grandmother married a Chickasaw warrior. She fell in love with this man and had two children by him. As the head of the family, my great-grandfather was forced to the reservation; my great-grandma chose to go with him, keeping her family together.

"Years ago we had a wealthy white cousin who owned the plantation, and, because he had no children, upon his death he bequeathed it to Pa's father. Before my grandfather died, he gave the deed to Pa for safekeeping. Because he was the second son and his older brother was a bully, he hid that deed, and Walt knew that, but Pa was stubborn and refused to tell Walt where he put it. Because of Pa's mulishness, my family lived at Walt's mercy — picking his cotton and tending his fields in exchange for very low wages and meager shelter. Pa was a good man, Pierce, I won't deny that, but he couldn't stand up to his brother. And he refused to take us away, which would have spared us the misery we endured all those long years." She sighed as she finished her tale. And while all of that was true, she had deliberately left out one important detail. Pa had told her the night before he passed where the deed was hidden. He said that if he didn't make it till morning that Beth was to somehow get the deed and take Joanie away from there, someplace where Joanie could get the medical treatment she so desperately needed.

Pierce's brow furrowed. "Your pa could have used the deed to take care of your sister?"

"He could have; but like I said, he wasn't willing or able to stand up to his older brother." Tears swelled to her eyes. "Don't blame Pa. Uncle Walt overwhelmed all of us. He threatened constantly to give Joanie or me to one of his cruel overseers, but Pa told him that if Walt ever let a man have his way with us that he'd never find out where the deed was hidden, so I guess, in his own way, Pa did stand up to him."

"Did someone ask you to set fire to the shanty?"

She bit her lower lip. She trusted him only to a point. A watchful point.

Memories of the night Walt appeared and searched the shanty with Pa and Ma at gunpoint would never leave her. And his search had been useless. Pa would never have hidden the deed anywhere Walt might have found it.

"No. It was my idea to set the shanty on fire — but *only* the shanty. I wanted to hurt Uncle Walt, and burning one of his buildings would make him angry. I also thought he and Bear would be so busy putting the fire out that Joanie and I would have time to escape them for good. I never meant for the cotton to burn, but a wind came up —"

"I recall."

The blazing inferno could have burnt down the whole plantation for all she knew, and she wouldn't be sorry. Of course, that would make Walt and Bear even more furious.

"That's quite a tale you have there, Beth."

She felt his assessing eyes on her. He wasn't a fool. She'd told the absolute truth

— almost. She hoped it was enough to convince him that he was obligated to keep them from Walt and Bear's greedy hands.

"If you leave, Uncle Walt and Bear will find this village and take us again. And he'll force me to marry Bear."

"Marry your cousin?" Pierce shook his head. "They won't find the village, and even if they do you will be safe here. The chief won't let anything happen to you or the others."

"I'd still rest easier if you'd agree to stay for at least a little longer." But even as she said it, she knew it was a terrible thing to ask. How many times over the past few days had she heard the men talking about home, fresh-baked bread, and warm apple pie? Asking him to stay was selfish, but the thought of not having him around scared her witless. She'd grown used to that cocky grin.

The same grin that broke across his features now. "Miss Beth, I do believe you'd miss me."

Miss him! Personally? That notion was ridiculous. She stood, and for a moment she was not sure how to respond. She'd miss his protection and nothing more. Then tensing, she said, "Go or stay. It doesn't matter to me, but Joanie's welfare does. She needs to see a real doctor, and if you make us stay here that can't happen. You'll have her death on your hands, Captain Montgomery, not me. I've tried my best to get her help, but now *you're* standing in the way. Go on, leave. Ride away. I just hope you can sleep at night." She turned and stalked on, shooting a scathing look over her shoulder.

"Gray Eagle's knowledge of herbs is good," he said, easily catching up to her and walking beside her again. "I'm sure the camp medicine man will help her."

"Poof!" She couldn't rightly deny that the lobelia provided temporary relief, but Joanie needed more.

"Oh, my. The lady is talking like a saloon brawler."

"You . . . you mind your own business!"

"I'm trying to, but you keep interfering."

She'd never met a man who could argue in a calm tone.

They approached a cook fire, where fragrant aromas from supper still lingered in the air, and he relented — something a man was also not noted for. "I'll talk to Preach and Gray Eagle and get their opinion. If they're willing to stay, I'll keep you happy."

She whirled. "Keep me *happy?*"

He didn't blink. "Isn't that what you're

asking?"

She turned and walked to the fire.

"Either way, Beth, I have to warn you. My friends are good men, but we're all itching to get home. I can't promise more than they are willing to give."

Beth paused, holding her hands to the comforting warmth of the low-burning coals. She couldn't quite bring herself to end her conversation with Pierce, though she didn't want to examine why. She said, "You seem pretty familiar with all of this. Do you live in these parts?"

"Born and raised about fifty miles from here." He smiled. "Bought me a piece of land close by, and once I check on my folks I plan to live there and make it my home."

The thought of this soldier settling down to farm a piece of property surprised her. For once they had something in common. "I bought us a parcel too," she said. "As soon as Joanie is able, we'll be living on our new place."

The thought brought tears to her eyes. Their place. They would never be beholden to Walt again.

Pierce paused to consider her. She felt awkward, crying under his gaze. She swiped at her tears. "Do you have brothers and sisters?" she said.

"A brother, Jeff."

"Then you know the love I feel for my sister."

"Yes, ma'am. I know that love, and I'm willing to do all I can do to help you get to safety, but I'm mighty anxious to claim my property. I'm tired of trouble. And fighting. I want to get home, sit on my land, drink sweet tea, and let the world go by."

"What's sweet tea?"

"Tea — with sugar."

"Oh. Walt never let us have sugar. And we never had tea."

"You didn't have sugar on your table?"

"No."

Shaking his head, he paused and reached for the coffeepot. "Can't imagine a world without sugar."

"I can't imagine one with it."

Straightening, he met her gaze again, sympathy in his eyes. Beth looked away.

"I'll talk to the men," he said kindly. "Chances are they'll see the wisdom of your request."

Wisdom. No one had ever accused her of being wise, least of all a man.

TWENTY

The light of the moon still claimed the sky when Pierce roused the other men from their sleeping bags. "Sorry to wake you, but we need to talk."

Instantly alert, Preach and Gray Eagle rolled from their beds and walked with Pierce downstream, away from the quiet village and listening ears.

"What's going on?" Preach asked.

"We have a problem, gentlemen." Briefly, Pierce shared Beth's request for the men to stay. "I know we have an agreement to ride home, but there is no denying all three women have a need for protection. And it seems we're the logical choices."

Preach squatted and tossed a pebble into the stream.

Gray Eagle said quietly, "What is the problem, exactly?"

"Yet another delay," Pierce said simply. "One that could be lengthy. How far do we take our protection role?"

The men's eyes focused on him.

"We could saddle up, ride out, and leave the women to fend for themselves. We don't owe them anything but respect, and I think we've fulfilled that duty."

"Or?" Gray Eagle asked.

"Or we stay with Trella and the Jornigan sisters as long as it takes to make sure the uncle and cousin have given up their search and gone home."

The other two were silent.

Pierce sighed. Shaking his head, he said, "Preach, at first light you can saddle up and leave if you want. You could be home in a couple of days. Gray Eagle and I will stay back and help the women with this matter." His gaze centered on Gray Eagle. He'd seen the way the scout looked at Joanie — but then again, Preach couldn't seem to keep his eyes off Trella and the baby. If his guess was right, all three would willingly sacrifice a few more days — even weeks. Who knew when this situation would end?

Preach stood slowly and said thoughtfully, "It could get ugly. How do you intend to stop this chase? I thought you were through with violence."

"I was, but circumstances changed my mind. That and the longer route." He gave them both a pointed look. "If we'd never rode this way we would be home by now. Me, sitting on my land. Eating pie."

"Drinking sweet tea," Gray Eagle mocked.

"Drinking sweet tea," he said ruefully. "Preach?"

"Captain?"

"Does God have a sense of humor?"

"Yes, sir." The black man flashed a white smile. "Sometimes folks don't laugh, but I shore enough think He's got one."

Pierce glanced at Gray Eagle. "How do we solve Beth and Joanie's problem?"

Shaking his head, Gray Eagle asked, "How do you stop evil men from anything?"

"I've had my fill of killing," Pierce said.

"Maybe it won't be necessary."

"How so?"

"It is my experience that men like Walt and Bear usually do themselves in either with stupidity or carelessness."

"Or greed."

"Greed." Gray Eagle nodded. "What's the one thing Beth's uncle wants?"

"Beth and Joanie. Probably Trella too, once he realizes she's with them," Preach observed.

"I'm not so sure. I had a long talk with Beth a little while ago," Pierce said. "Walt and Bear would undoubtedly like to keep their hold on Beth and Joanie, but what they really want is the deed to the plantation that their pa hid."

Gray Eagle lifted a surprised gaze. "Do you know where this deed is hidden?"

"No. I was pushing it just getting Beth to divulge that much. She didn't volunteer its whereabouts."

"But she knows," Preach guessed.

Pierce nodded. "She knows. I'd stake my boots on it." His gaze shifted to the left. "Are you in or out on this?"

"I'm in." Preach flashed a guilty smile. "I can't let those two varmints hurt Trella or that baby, not if I can stop it. Brutal men have made those three women afraid of their shadows. They think all men are alike, including us."

Gray Eagle added, "In many ways we are alike, but I will fight to the death for Joanie and her health."

Pierce nodded briefly. "Same here — for Beth."

Gray Eagle stiffened. "I did not mean to imply I have any romantic interest —"

"Hey, I just meant I didn't want to see Beth get hurt." Pierce held up his hands. "I don't have any personal interest in her. When I settle down, it'll be with a woman who can at least tolerate a man."

"No, sir." Preach grinned. "Wouldn't want to set on the porch and drink sweet tea with that woman."

"Any woman," Pierce corrected. "At least, not right away."

"What if you happen to recall the name of the girl you left behind?"

Pierce shot Preach a dark look.

"Same goes for me," Gray Eagle said, clearing his throat. "Toward Joanie. Just looking after her health."

Preach pulled their attention back to the matter at hand. "It seems to me we should all three stay. None us got to be home any certain time, have we? We've been gone five years."

Pierce was glad to leave the topic of his romantic interests behind. "So we are agreed. The three of us will stay and help the women to fight this battle."

The other two nodded.

Reaching for a stick, Gray Eagle drew a large circle in the sandy river's edge. "Any ideas on where to start?"

"We know Bear is still in the area," Preach said. "And if that other bear didn't eat Walt, without doubt he will be back as well."

"We're going to have to draw them out and put them on the defense." Pierce scratched his unshaven chin.

"The only thing that will draw them out is bait," Preach said.

Pierce shook his head. "We're not using Beth for bait."

"Or Joanie," Gray Eagle noted.

"Well, we're sure not using Trella and the baby." Preach adjusted his hat on his head.

"Walt doesn't care about Trella," Pierce noted, "or he would have tried to get her last time. The only bait that'll work is Joanie."

Gray Eagle glanced up. "No way."

"Walt knows that if he took Beth, she would never tell him where the deed was hidden. But if he had Joanie, Beth wouldn't be able to stand it. He will use her loyalty to her sister against her."

Gray Eagle shook his head "No. I will not stand by and allow Joanie in harm's way."

The captain's eyes hardened to flint. "Do you *ever* want to get home?"

"Joanie stays with me." Gray Eagle held firm.

"We'll have her back," Preach argued.

"It's the only way." Pierce straightened. "If we have any hopes of getting home in the near future, this feud has to end." He removed his hat and swiped a forearm over his eyes. He knew the matter was far from settled. "Now we just have to figure out how to draw Walt to the bait."

"I think all we have to do is wait," Gray Eagle said as though he'd changed his mind and decided to go along with the plan. "Uncle Walt is restless. He's tiring of the game. He'll make his move soon. Then we get him." His jaw clenched.

"Relax." Pierce touched the scout's shoulder lightly. "You're nothing to her but a nurse, Pricilla."

Gray Eagle brushed the hand away. "Do not call me Pricilla."

"That's what you call me when I'm acting like a sissy."

"Then we'll put Beth out as bait and Joanie beside her. Priscilla."

"You been smoking that lobelia weed?"

"Gentlemen." Preach stopped the friendly ruckus. "We got more important things to do."

Pierce rubbed a hand over his jaw. "If Gray Eagle's right, Walt will set the pace. He'll form the plan, or the bargain, depending on his demands. We play along. Take it step-by-step."

They all agreed. Battle plans by necessity were often formed on the spur of the moment. It wasn't the ideal approach, but it was the only viable one at the moment.

Gray Eagle met the captain's eyes. "Can

you find out where the deed is hidden? We'll need to know in case we're separated."

"I'll try to pry it out of Beth." Might be like dragging a dead horse to water, but he'd get the information from her.

Gray Eagle said quietly, "All right, then. We're agreed. We return to camp and wait for Walt's next move." As they set off for their tent, he turned to Pierce. "Do we tell the women?"

Pierce nodded. "They'll need to know."

"I will speak to Joanie to see if she's willing to participate. Excitement worsens her condition. The lobelia is helping, but it is not enough."

"They'll be scared," Preach warned.

"It's up to us to relieve those fears." Glancing over, Gray Eagle said, with irony tainting his tone, "Aren't we the ones who sought peace and quiet?"

"That was the idea."

Chuckling, the three men matched strides to camp, where all was quiet.

As their laughter faded, a keen sense that this was no laughing matter settled in on Pierce. Though their plan seemed the only viable option, they were putting the women in the direct path of danger.

A danger Pierce wasn't anxious to revisit.

TWENTY-ONE

"Yes." Beth faced Pierce later that morning. "I know where the deed is hidden, but why should I tell you?"

"I don't care where it is, Beth, but your uncle does."

Looking pretty as a rose, she turned back to the wash she was hanging. She'd put on her dress today and had washed and brushed out her hair. She was lovely and feminine to his eye. Five days away from the hard work of the cotton fields had renewed her youthful features. Lines of stress had eased from her face, and the gaunt look of starvation had faded a bit. This morning she looked rested and healthy. "What Walt wants doesn't concern me."

"It concerns everybody, Beth. The men and I have been talking. We're going to end this feud one way or another so that you don't have to live in constant fear."

Tears welled up in her eyes and she

blinked. "And so you can leave us. You're free to do that —"

"I'm not. Not until we settle this ruckus."

Lifting surprised eyes, she met his gaze as if she couldn't believe he meant to help her, that he truly wanted to help.

He briefly explained the men's conversation from the night before and their decision. He, Gray Eagle, and Preach would stay.

The more he talked, the more overwhelmed she felt. Never ever had any man, let alone three men, come to her rescue. Of course, it wasn't just about her. Joanie and Trella were also the recipients of their kindness. But the men were offering to free her and Joanie once and for all from her uncle's tyranny. The thought made her head spin.

"You would do that?"

He met her uncertain gaze. "I'll tell you what I will do when you tell me where that deed is buried. From this point on, we have to anticipate any move your uncle might make."

For a second time a voice spoke in her head. *Beth, you either trust this man or let Joanie die and you live in fear the rest of your life.* The thought resonated inside her. She said, "The deed is buried less than a hundred feet from Uncle Walt's house."

A snort escaped Pierce. "You're not serious."

She nodded. "There's a deep ravine — a canyon, actually, that runs beside the main house. On the opposite bluff are all sorts of caves. Pa hid the deed in the third cave to the right when you face it from Uncle Walt's front yard."

"Right under his brother's nose."

"Like I said, Pa didn't try to fight Uncle Walt. He outwitted him. The box is safe until someone goes to fetch it. I suppose if there is no other means to help Joanie, then I'll do it."

"Jump a canyon?"

"I know the situation isn't the best, but I'll figure it out when the time comes. Pa risked his life to hide that deed. He had to attach a good, strong rope to a hickory tree at the edge of the canyon and swing across. He said if the branch had snapped or the rope had given way that he would have fallen to his death."

"But Walt would most likely risk the chance."

"I believe he would. He isn't known for good sense. He's known for his cruelty and having his way, no matter the cost."

"Why not tell him? Let him take the risk? He'd be sure to go after it, and if he didn't

189

make it, then you and Joanie would be free of him."

"I've considered it in my weaker moments, and the notion sets right — but I couldn't be part of a plan that might very well end up killing a man." She'd worried the idea over and over in her mind, but she couldn't lower herself to Walt's level.

Pierce nodded his understanding. "Still . . ."

She stiffened. "And what if he made the jump successfully? Pa did. Then Walt would have the deed, and with it he'd buy up more land, more slaves . . . well, now I guess he'd hire more workers, but it would only continue what he's started. Nothing good would come of it, and he would only put more people under his abuse. No. I can't, Pierce. I'll never tell him. Not ever."

She had a valid point. And a big part of him admired her selfless attitude. She hadn't gone seeking the deed herself. Instead, she'd sought a simple life with her sister, choosing only to escape Jornigan's tyranny when perhaps she could have had so much more.

"Can you draw me a map of the caves?"

"Yes . . . but what are you going to do?"

"We're going to play this by ear," he admitted. "We don't have a specific plan,

190

but one will become apparent. Right now, we're waiting for Walt to make his next move, which we figure will be any time." His features tightened. "Beth, I don't want to include you in on this, but I might have to. I won't let you or Joanie get hurt. You'll have to trust that whatever I say or do will be in your best interests."

He could see the hesitancy — the war raging in her eyes. Trust a man? Was she capable of complete trust? "I . . . don't know."

"You'll have to trust me, Beth, if we're going to end this chase."

"Pierce . . ."

He answered her objection before she voiced it. "I'm not like the other men you have known. And I promise I won't walk away, nor will I allow anyone to lift a hand to you. I . . . we . . . will do this together, but it would make it a mite easier if you'd cooperate."

Swiping at hot tears, she avoided his eyes until he gently tilted her face to meet his. "Will you help me?"

Nodding, she drew a deep breath and said, "I will."

At that moment, he was taking this woman's plight dead serious, and he should. Without thinking about it, he bent and

191

pressed his lips to hers.

She didn't move. She just watched him with open eyes.

He lifted his head. "What?"

"You . . . kissed me."

His features softened. "So I did. You must be pretty kissable, Beth Jornigan. I haven't kissed a woman in years."

He lifted his hat and then strode off.

TWENTY-TWO

Nodding a greeting to the lone Indian woman tending the cooking fires late the next morning, Beth checked on Joanie, who had gone back to bed after breakfast. She'd had a poor night, her coughing waking Beth continually. Sitting beside her sister's pallet, Beth allowed her fears to surface. Her sister couldn't endlessly go on praying for each breath.

Praying, the one thing Beth hadn't tried in order to help her sister . . . well, except for the one time beside the road when Preach struggled to keep Joanie alive. She had prayed then, sort of, and Joanie had found breath again. Until this moment she hadn't made the connection, but it was surely Preach's prayers that had brought Joanie through yet another breathing crisis and not her clumsy attempts at talking to God.

Beth's gaze roamed the camp, where others were setting about their morning rituals. Did these people pray? The thought intrigued her. Some of the pickers prayed out loud. And the nuns? As they had washed dishes together, Mary Margaret told her a tolling bell summoned them to prayer morning, noon, and evening. What summoned the pickers? What made Joanie drop to her knees to lift her face upward with such assurance? Beth had been deeply entrenched against that God for so long that she'd never given the issue of prayer much thought.

She was beginning to think that everyone but her prayed. Pa and Ma did, but they never had family prayer. Pa was always so worn out at night that about all he could do was eat and then drop into bed. Bowing her head, Beth tested a prayer on her tongue. "Lord. God. You." She shook her head. She didn't know the first thing about asking something from someone she couldn't see.

Joanie slept soundly at last, so Beth rose and roamed the camp. Oddly enough, others took no notice of her but simply went about their business as though she belonged there. Meat sizzled in heavy skillets. Coffee perked.

When the sun climbed higher, she ventured deeper around the camp's perimeter, keeping the captain's warning in mind. She was not to wander far away. She was to wait until Walt found them. Captain Montgomery. Her lips still tingled from his kiss. When she even thought about his brashness she shivered. She had enjoyed it. Far too much.

The gurgling stream wound deep into the woods. She followed the trail, listening to bird calls and the sound of river life. Bright yellow butterflies flew overhead, darting here and there. She wasn't in the habit of taking notice of her surroundings. From sunup to sundown she had bent over sacks of cotton, striving to meet both hers and Joanie's daily quota. Joanie picked all she could, but there were hours where she sat in the hot sun and simply struggled to breathe. Beth's hand reached out lightly to capture a butterfly. Handling the insect carefully, she examined its unique beauty. How did such a creature, so intricately formed, come to be on this earth? Lifting her palm she gently nudged the insect to flight. Nothing this beautiful should be restricted. Deeper and deeper she wound her way downstream, losing all track of time.

An unfamiliar sense of freedom empowered her. Her world had been limited to the plantation, but here another world existed.

A world of towering trees and blooming wildflowers. Here she could almost forget her former life. Almost.

Memories flashed of earlier conversations with Pa after working thirteen hours under a stifling sun with little water to quench their thirst.

"How can Uncle Walt be so cruel?"

"It's not our place to judge, daughter. He might not be punished here on earth, but he will one day stand before God, and then he'll have a powerful lot of explaining to do."

Beth had let the thought skip through her mind all that day. Perhaps there was a God and Walt would answer for his meanness. That only seemed fair. But long ago Beth had come to realize that life wasn't always fair. Not in her eyes.

Locating a large rock, she brushed it clean and sat down, pulling her knees up to her chest. She had nothing to do but sit and admire the beautiful morning and enjoy the scent of blooming flowers, the sight of little rabbits skipping across the path, and the sun's warmth as she sat in partial shade. Her body didn't ache from bending over all day, and her head didn't hurt from the blistering sun.

Glancing up at the sky, she noted with surprise that it was close to noon. She'd been gone longer than she had intended. Joanie would probably wake soon and wonder where she had gone.

Beth started back to camp, lightheartedly picking her way through the thick vegetation that grew along the banks of the stream. When a hand clamped down on her shoulder, she whirled, her heart in her throat as the captain's warning came back to her.

Stay close to the camp.

TWENTY-THREE

Joanie's sleepy gaze met Gray Eagle's when he touched her shoulder.

"The sun has been up for hours," the young man said softly.

Sitting up, she looked around and asked, "Where's Beth?"

"Somewhere about. She is safe."

"Oh." She glanced up at him and smiled. The scout had become a familiar, secure sight. He was always there to give her cold water when a relentless spasm refused to ease. He would offer her small sips of lobelia tea, and soon the cough would temporarily ease.

Extending a hand, he helped her to her feet. "Come. I have some lunch for you."

"I'm not hungry. I'm afraid I don't have much of an appetite."

"I have noticed. You are small, like a baby bird."

She smiled shyly and he kept her hand in

his as he led her through camp to the main fire, where a steaming plate of meat awaited her. After helping her to a seat on a pallet, he brought a gourd filled with water and placed it beside her. "Eat."

Smiling, she took a bite of the meat and found it quite tasty. "Where are the others?"

"Around." As he made himself comfortable beside her, she studied his tall, lean frame. His nut-brown skin was taut and firm from hours in the hot sun. His long jet-black hair was secured with a leather scrap. He wore bearskin pants, but his broad, muscular chest was bare in the heat of the day.

No wonder the camp maidens couldn't keep their eyes off of him. Joanie struggled to concentrate on her meal. "It's not like Beth to wander away."

"You will be together shortly. I checked on Trella, and the baby is doing well this morning. It won't be long before the little one can leave the wet nurse."

A long silence stretched between them. Joanie picked at the meat, her appetite lacking as she tried to think of another topic of conversation. "You scouted for the South?"

He nodded.

"Exactly what does a scout do?"

He met her curious gaze. Leaning closer, he whispered, "We scout." A glint of humor filled his eyes.

Color heated her cheeks. "And by 'scout' you mean . . . ?"

"We were actually called 'pickets.' We were responsible for keeping our unit from ambush on both the front and rear flanks." He smiled, meeting her gaze. "My position was that of raven spy."

"Raven?"

He pointed to his neck. "From this day forward, Joanie Jornigan, you will know us when you see us, and recognize us if you see us on the trail. I'll be scouting the front with this tied around my neck." He tugged on the raven-feathered choker circling his dark throat. "My brother scout will have a strip of wolf skin tied to his neck. He is scouting the rear. Another will be wearing fox skin around his neck, and he will be watching our left."

"But . . . the war is over."

"So it is said, and yet there are battles to be won."

"You speak flawless English."

With a flash of even, white teeth, he nodded. "My mother was white; my father, Cherokee. My mother taught me both the white man's and red man's ways." He

200

paused to look at her. "You said you were educated?"

She nodded. "Somewhat. My mother was a schoolteacher before she married my father. Because my illness wouldn't allow me in the fields many days, mother taught me at home."

"And your father?"

She lifted a piece of meat to her lips. "He worked for my uncle Walt in the cotton fields."

"Was he an educated man?"

"No. Not Pa. And because we lived in Uncle Walt's shanty, and he didn't care for books, when he caught Ma with one he would rip it into pieces with his meaty hands and make her burn it. Women with knowledge were dangerous, he always said. No woman on the plantation would ever learn to read or write, but Ma defied him by teaching me."

The hue of his eyes deepened. "I value books as priceless treasures."

"You learned this from your mother?"

Nodding, he said softly, "Now that the war is over, I wish to fulfill my mother's desire and become a doctor."

"A doctor?" Joanie had always wanted to be a nurse. She knew it would never happen, but it was a nice dream.

He met her eyes. "It is my desire also. To help my people."

Joanie drank in the exciting thought. Money was always scarce in their home, and from what she'd read, an education — the kind Gray Eagle was talking about — would be very costly.

"I have a friend," he said, as though he read her thoughts, "whose father owns many plantations, and he has agreed to sponsor my education."

"How soon will you start?"

"Soon. When I return home."

"You have known and fought with Pierce and Preach?"

He nodded. "I met Pierce many years ago, and though we ended up fighting for different sides, we became friends. When word of the war's end finally reached us, Pierce and I agreed to ride home together. We bumped into Preach along the way, and he decided to join up with us." He shifted. "You are weary. You should rest and not talk. The coughing will start again."

Joanie knew he spoke the truth, though she felt as though she could talk to him all day. But the exhaustion deep in her bones was even now pulling her back to sleep. They made their way back to the lodge where she and Beth were staying, and he helped her settle again onto her pallet.

He was kind, and his medicine made her body relax. A sense of calm floated over her, and she was barely aware when he drew up the light blanket. She felt the warmth of his eyes on her — a gentle, caring warmth.

A welcome tenderness.

TWENTY-FOUR

A squeal escaped Beth when she came face-to-face with Sister Mary Margaret.

Grinning like a mule eating spring grass, the friendly nun greeted her. "Beth! I thought you and Joanie had moved on from around here."

Pressing her thumping heart back into her chest cavity, Beth tried to clear the light-headedness that was close to overwhelming her. "Sister! You scared the daylights out of me."

The nun's features fell. "Forgive me."

"Not intentionally," Beth corrected. She knew instinctively that the good woman wouldn't harm a fly, but her sudden appearance had completely unnerved Beth. She'd thought for certain that she had strayed too far from safety and that Walt or Bear had found her alone.

Mary Margaret's smile swiftly resurfaced. "What are you doing here?"

"I could ask the same of you."

The cheerful sister giggled. "The Indians make their summer camp on our land — well, the Lord's land — but the order owns it. We've never said a word to them. It's just an honest mistake. And they don't hurt a thing. I think I shared with you that they are actually very helpful."

Now that her heart had settled back in her chest, Beth lowered her hands. "What are you doing here?"

"I fear I am easily diverted. Father, forgive me." Swiftly she made the sign of the cross. "I was working in the vegetable garden this morning, but the day is so lovely that I chased a butterfly much farther than I intended. When I looked up, I spotted you and could hardly believe my eyes." Her gaze roamed the area. "Where is Joanie?"

"She's with the Cherokee."

Mary Margaret turned curious. "Why?"

"It's a long story, Sister."

"I have time for a story." She offered an encouraging grin.

Mentally sighing, Beth relayed the details, reminding her of the circumstances of their departure and the birth of Trella's baby.

"Trella's milk apparently wasn't rich enough for the infant," she went on, "so after we left the convent, the soldiers suggested that we locate a wet nurse for the child. The Indian village was the closest settlement we could find."

Mary Margaret laughed softly. "A wet nurse would have been difficult to find at the convent."

"Yes. Very unlikely, though we hadn't considered the idea until Pierce mentioned it."

"Yes. The kind man who came with you on your second visit." Mary Margaret smiled and then seemed to instinctively reach for a strand of beads hanging from her belt.

Beth watched the nun's nimble fingers trace each bead as she whispered in soft tones. When she finished, Beth hesitantly asked, "Were you praying?"

The sister opened her eyes. "Yes." She smiled. "You are not Catholic?"

"I'm not anything."

Mary Margaret's eyes widened. "You most certainly are. You're God's child."

"I don't believe that. But Joanie prays, and she does it differently. She either bows her head or gets down on her knees beside the bed and just talks." She focused on the beads. "You touch beads."

"My rosary."

Beth studied the strand in the sister's

hand. "Joanie doesn't have such a thing. Does that mean her prayers aren't heard?" *This praying stuff is so complicated! Believing in a special, loving person you'd never met to take care of your needs no matter what?* Beth shook her head. She wished she had such faith.

"My goodness, no!" the nun said. "God hears all prayers — unless a man's heart has been hardened — but He hears all of His children's prayers."

His children? Now, there was another mystery. God didn't sire her; Pa did. And Pa hadn't loved her unconditionally. She got in trouble plenty of times for little things.

The sister's explanation still didn't account for the variances she'd seen in how people spoke to the Almighty. Her explanation made no sense to Beth, but the sister seemed convinced that every sort of murmuring or tolling of bells or whispering over beads reached a higher source. Beth furrowed her brow.

"How is Joanie?" the sister said.

Beth was a bit startled at the change in topic. She wanted to get to the bottom of this puzzle.

"Is she doing better?"

Beth sighed and said, "Yes, one of the men

traveling with us has been giving her lobelia tea."

The sister snapped her finger. "We should have thought of that. Sister Patrilla is our herbalist, but she's very old and sleeps late. If you had remained after morning prayers, I'm certain she could have helped."

"I'm sorry. You all were very kind, but at that time we felt that we had to leave."

The nun nodded, the wide straw brim of her hat bobbing with the motion of her head. "It is good to know that you're nearby. Will you stay a few days?"

"Yes. At least until Trella's baby can take milk from a cow."

The sister's infectious laugh filled the quiet meadow. "That sounds as though it could take a while, though I wouldn't know. I was an only child."

Grinning, Beth thought she would have liked to have known Sister Mary Margaret as a child, though in many ways her personality was still childlike. Trusting. Joyful. Beth found that she'd formed an instant bond with the merry sister.

"I should be going. They will wonder where I went," Mary Margaret said.

"Oh, me too."

The sister giggled. "I have rows and rows to plant and care for. It's my second planting this year, and Reverend Mother thinks I'm a bit of a scatterbrain." She glanced up, shading her eyes from the hot sun. "It will be time for lunch soon." She turned back. "May I tell the others I've seen you?"

Beth hesitated. She didn't want to put the convent in danger. If Walt and Bear came upon them, there was no telling what they would do if they knew the nuns had befriended her and Joanie.

"I would appreciate it if you wouldn't."

Nodding, the sister pretended to button her lips. Then she giggled. "I'm here every day. That is, any day I'm not off chasing butterflies and it doesn't rain. If you want company, walk to the garden." She turned and pointed up the hill, where rows of flowering vines could be seen. No one else was there.

"Do you work alone?" Beth asked.

The plot seemed to be quite large. It looked to be a back-breaking chore for one person to manage.

"Yes, but it's no problem. I'm the youngest in the order. The others are old and feeble, so I take on the heavier tasks. This patch is string beans and turnips. I leave the peas, tomatoes, and squash in other locations easier to reach. Don't be afraid to visit me here. No one else will see you."

Beth thought of all the long, blistering days, months, and years she'd toiled in the cotton fields and of the barbs that had left her hands raw and bloody. Beans and turnips would be heaven. She turned to meet the nun's face. The least she could do would be to help out while she was here. She accepted the offer.

"I'll come back tomorrow."

"Wonderful!" Mary Margaret set her wimple more securely in place. "I pray that God will shower you with blessings this beautiful day." She winked. "But not rain. I have to get those turnips hoed."

"Thank you." Beth wanted to return the lovely wish, but before she could be asking God for anything, she needed someone to convince her He was there. And prayer? That was downright confusing. It seemed to her that praying wasn't as simple as getting down on her knees beside the bed and talking. Maybe she needed some smooth wooden beads.

She made a mental note to ask Pierce what he thought of the matter. He seemed knowledgeable and, so far, she thought, he'd been honest with her.

Skirting the bank, she headed toward camp, aware she'd been gone a few hours. Joanie would undoubtedly be wondering where she was.

Hoofbeats sounded on the road behind the line of heavy thicket. Beth stepped in closer to the tangled vegetation. Most likely it was a passing farmer who'd pay little attention to the stream, but she couldn't be too careful. The realization that she was alone again quickened her pace. She wished the captain were with her — but as soon as the thought crossed her mind, it irked her.

Then the crack of a gunshot shattered the silence.

Beth's hands came up to cover her mouth. Bear? She hadn't heard or seen anything of him for days, though Pierce had said he was still in the area.

Dropping to her knees, she hugged the riverbed, crawling deeper into the dense brush. She should have known her cousin would never give up. He was as deranged and greedy as Uncle Walt. A second shot rang out, the bullet grazing a thatch of weeds not far away. He was outright trying to kill her, and Pierce and Gray Eagle were nowhere around.

She pulled herself along on her belly, determined to survive. The sisters would hear the shots and come to investigate, wouldn't they? Or the Cherokee? If she could elude the oaf five more minutes, help would be on the way.

A third shot rang out. Squeezing her eyes shut, she eased though the thicket. Her heart pounded so loudly that she feared Bear would hear its erratic thumping and immediately spot her.

When she paused to catch her breath, she heard the sound of heavy boots thrashing now through the brush. Pressing close to the ground, she shut her eyes and lay as still as a corpse.

The footfalls ceased.

Beth could feel her cousin's beady eyes roaming the area, searching for her. How had he found her? The vegetable patch couldn't be seen from the road. She had taken great pains to heed Pierce's order to stay off the main path. Now he would be angry with her. She winced, trying to quiet her breaths so Bear wouldn't hear her.

Silence. No footfalls. Or gunshots. Just silence. Where was he? Towering above her, waiting for her to acknowledge his presence?

Opening one eye, she studied the ground. No shadow appeared. A meadowlark flittered in and out of the brush above.

She stayed immobile until she thought she'd burst, terrified to move, but finally she couldn't remain still a moment longer. She hadn't heard a sound for more than fifteen minutes. Perhaps he'd given up and moved on. She sat up, her eyes sweeping the empty meadow. No one was there. She waited another few minutes, but still no one appeared.

Finally, drained of emotion, she got to her feet. Neither a nun nor an Indian had come to check out the source of the gunshots.

Bending, she dusted grass and twigs off the front of her clothing and then again hugged the river bank as she started back to camp.

Glancing to the right, she spotted a small clearing, and her heart beat wildly in her chest. Bear, wearing Pierce's blue uniform, bent over a large deer, field dressing the animal. How could he have gotten the uniform? Her hands flew to her mouth as realization dawned. Of course! Bear had shot Pierce and taken his clothing!

At least he hadn't spotted her. He'd been shooting at the fresh meat.

Suddenly, pain from years of abuse and ill-treatment rose to the surface. She couldn't just leave — she wanted to get even. If she could surprise the brute and knock him out cold, she could have a little retaliation for some of the misery he caused both her and Joanie. Her heart also ached for the poor captain lying wounded —

maybe even dead — somewhere.

Glancing around for a large rock, she located one and picked it up. Bear was still bent over the deer, his knife slicing through the hide. No doubt he thought he was the only person around. He was so involved in his work he probably wouldn't have heard a train approaching.

Lifting the rock above her head, she took aim and swung, striking a blow against the back of his head. He toppled like a felled oak.

Anger drained, she stood back, realizing she might have killed him. She shuddered. That certainly wasn't her intention. Creeping close, she checked his pulse and detected a strong steady beat. Good. She exhaled a long sigh. Bear was ornery, but she didn't want to be the cause of his death. He'd have a head as swollen as a watermelon for a few days . . . her eyes skimmed the motionless form and rested on his shirt and trousers.

How could he have overcome the captain? Pierce was a formidable man. The thought of him sprawled somewhere caused heat to fill her cheeks. She ought to give her cousin a knot on the other side of his head!

Rolling him face up, she gasped. Pierce? A dot of blood oozed from the blow she'd inflicted. "Pierce?" she said, trying to bring him around. She lightly tapped both cheeks. "Captain? Pierce?" When there was no response, she raced to the stream, tore off a strip of cloth from her petticoat, soaked it in the water, and raced back. Removing his hat, she bathed the man's face with the fabric and apologized, "I'm sorry. I'm so sorry. I thought you were Bear."

Coming around rapidly, Pierce opened his eyes.

"Oh, thank You, God." That brought her up short. Had she just acknowledged God? Tingles flooded her.

Slowly sitting up, he rubbed the rising knot on the back of his head. "What . . . happened?"

"I . . . you've been unconscious." How could she tell him she had deliberately struck him?

"Out cold? I was cleaning a deer . . ."

"I know. And . . . and . . . what a fine deer!" She turned to admire the prize. If she diverted his attention to something else . . .

He focused on her. "Beth, what are you doing here?"

Clearing her throat, she crossed her arms and said in a stern tone, "Well, what are *you* doing here? You are supposed to be . . ." She didn't know where he was supposed to be. Just not here.

He rubbed his head, wincing. "Gray Eagle and I were on the way to cut wood when my horse threw a shoe. I told him to ride on. Then I spotted the deer and thought the sisters would enjoy some fresh meat." He turned to her and said, "Seriously, Beth. What are *you* doing here, alone and outside the camp?"

She cleared her throat and glanced away before meeting his eyes. "I took a walk and ran into Sister Mary Margaret. She takes care of the abbey's bean and turnip garden." She pointed to the patch up the hill. "I told her I'd come back tomorrow to help." She was chattering now. Definitely chattering.

He slowly rose to his feet, still rubbing the injury. For the moment he appeared to have forgotten to ask how the blow had occurred.

She said, "Do you have an extra knife?"

He glanced at her. "Why?"

"I'll help you."

"You can dress a deer?"

The question was almost comical. Pa had had a weak stomach, so she, Ma, and Joanie had dressed all the fresh kills. "I can," she said. "As well as any man."

"I'd appreciate the help. I'll get you a knife." He walked toward his horse on unsteady feet. Beth waited beside the deer

216

as a sense of regret moved through her. Regret that Bear hadn't gotten what was coming to him. Regret the captain had taken Bear's punishment.

The feeling fled as dread crowded her throat. She would have to tell the captain she had struck him. How would he react?

Pierce returned carrying a second skinning knife. Together they set to work cutting away the hide. Beth's feelings confused her. On the one hand, she was relieved it was Pierce and not Bear she'd encountered. On the other, she didn't especially like the emotions the captain caused in her. Squishy, girlie feelings. And always the sense that she was safe in his presence. She'd never been around a man like that before. He was kind and generous. Never mean to her. How could that be?

Stripping the hide from the carcass, she set it aside, knowing the Indians would value the gift.

"Pierce?"

He glanced over. "Yes?"

"I . . ." She drew in a deep breath and then winced as she finished. "I hit you from behind."

He cut a large steak from the hind quarters. "I figured as much," he said, with no trace of malice in his voice. "Care to tell me why?"

"I didn't know it was you."

"So you go around knocking strangers out cold with rocks? I know you have a thing about men, but I didn't know you carried it this far."

"No . . . it wasn't . . . I thought you were Bear."

His knife instantly paused. "Has he been around this morning?"

"Not that I know of, but you warned me to be cautious. So I had it in my head that he might be . . . and I was being cautious."

"You darn near killed me!"

"I wasn't going to kill you — or Bear, even. I just wanted to teach him a lesson. Give him a knot he wouldn't forget."

Pierce touched the back of his head again with his probing hand. "Job accomplished."

"I'm truly sorry." She met his eyes. "But was it hard enough? I mean, if it had been Bear instead of you? Because he has been a thorn in my side since the day I was born."

"Oh, indeed. You taught him a lesson he won't soon forget."

She flashed a grin. "Thanks."

"Glad to be of service."

They worked in comfortable silence for a while before Beth picked up the conversation again. "If you're from around here, why did you fight for the North?"

"I believed every man had a right to freedom. I still do, but I'm starting to see my father's wisdom . . ." His voice trailed away as if he were in another time, another conversation. Then he looked back at her and continued his work. "A man is only free if he can afford to feed his family and keep a roof over his head. The plantation owners fed, clothed, and housed many people. Some slave owners were tyrants, but others were like my father. Honest. Good to their help." He paused again, the blade of his knife glinting in the sun. "I'm not sure I did the blacks any favors, and I know I hurt my father deeply. I regret that so much."

Beth's family had never spoken about the war. She imagined they didn't know much about it. Uncle Walt employed hundreds of slaves. Beth's entire childhood consisted of working acres of cotton — known in these parts as white gold — right alongside them.

"What about you?" he asked. "Life seems to have been pretty hard on you so far."

She'd spent her whole life just trying to survive. How could she have feelings about it one way or the other when so much of it was outside her control? She regretted Joanie's struggle; she regretted Ma's death and that the two of them hadn't been better friends. Ma was closer to Joanie than her. She supposed it was natural. A mother always took to her wounded sheep.

Beth wasn't wounded. She sometimes thought she was the strongest person in her family — at least in will. She worked the fields, ate her meals, did her chores, and wasn't afraid to fight Uncle Walt and Bear. She'd accepted her fair share of lashings for her independent streak.

Come dark she'd drag herself up the ladder to the loft she shared with Joanie, and she would fall asleep almost instantly listening to her sister softly read from the Bible by the moonlight filtering through the small window. She'd never had time to think about war and death. Images of the fire danced before her eyes and she sighed. "I suppose I've had a few regrets as well."

"What are your regrets, Beth Jornigan?"

Beth shifted to the back of the animal, cutting at the meat that remained there. "I regret that my ma married my pa."

"Oh?" His blade paused again.

Nodding, Beth kept working.

"Okay. There's still more to your story than what you've told me. Do you want to tell me what's really going on?"

She refused to meet his eyes. "We're field

dressing a deer."

"Come on. I'm not a fool."

"It's none of your business." Because he treated her as an equal didn't mean she should lower her guard. He'd been thinking of riding off and leaving her here, with strangers, while he went home to his nice quiet land where he planned to build a house, sit on the porch, and drink sweet tea. She had her land too, and she was going to taste sweet tea someday. She glanced at the still swelling knot on the back of his head.

Actually, he was fortunate to be alive. She'd struck him hard.

Shame washed over her, but she almost didn't recognize the emotion. She'd experienced it so few times in her life. Then, for the life of her, she didn't know why the words popped out of her mouth, "Ma would have been far better off if she hadn't married Pa and brought me and Joanie into the world."

His features remained calm. "You love your sister. Think of what life would be without her."

"I wouldn't be here either."

He paused to face her. "And that would be one fine shame."

Color crept up her neck and she lowered her head and concentrated on her work.

"I'm sorry," she murmured. "Please . . . don't tell anyone I said such a thing . . ." She lifted her head and pleaded with him with her eyes.

"I won't tell anyone, but I would like to hear why you feel you'd be better off having never been born."

In for a penny, in for a pound. How many times had she heard her mother repeat the old adage? Now that the worst was out, she might as well complete the thought. "Pa was good and honest, but he was a weak man. He couldn't stand up to his brother — or anyone else, for that matter. He just buried his head in work and didn't think about tomorrow."

"In a sense, that's what the Good Book teaches."

She paused, meeting his blue eyes. "Do you pray, Pierce?"

"Yes, ma'am. Don't you?"

"Not really. Though I tried it this morning and . . . it wasn't so bad."

"Go on."

She lifted a shoulder. "There's not much to tell. Pa and Uncle Walt never saw eye to eye, but Walt wouldn't let up on Pa. He constantly threatened him and us with all sorts of harm if he didn't tell where the deed was hidden. Pa knew that Walt knew men — men of importance who were even meaner than him — and if Walt ever got his hand on that deed, he'd see that Pa was cut clean out. Pa couldn't fight him, but he could sure be mule stubborn."

"Sounds like a case of like father, like daughter."

She stiffened and concentrated on her work. "I'm nothing like Pa."

"Oh, I don't know about that. I've seen a hint or two of uncertainty in you, but you do take good care of your sister."

She felt him move to her side.

"Look. I'm not making light of you, but for the life of me I don't know why your pa would stand by and let your uncle run roughshod over him or your family."

"Pa had his flaws." She glanced over. "I'm sure you wouldn't know anything about that. You're strong. Independent."

"I thank you, ma'am, but I'm as faulted as the next man." He winked at her, and her stomach jumped. "When you and Joanie reach your piece of land, how do you plan to build lodging?"

"Can't say for sure. I'm pretty good with a hammer and nail. Actually, we haven't talked much about it. Everything happened so fast. Ma, then Pa dying, the fire."

"How did Trella get mixed up in this?"

"Well, right after Ma died the three of us worked together in the fields that afternoon. Trella overheard me and Joanie talking about running away if Pa went too, and she begged us to take her along. She was close to having her child, and Uncle Walt — well, you've heard enough about Uncle Walt. We both knew he would work her till she dropped, and when the baby was born he'd likely take it away from her." Her tone dropped. "Trella isn't married."

"I figured as much."

"She feared Uncle Walt so badly that she said she would do anything to escape him. It was a risk we were willing to take. We all knew if he caught us he'd . . ." She shuddered at the lengths he would go to punish them.

Pierce reached over to rest a hand on her shoulder. "Your uncle needs a horsewhip taken to his back."

Biting back tears, she let the soothing words wash over her. No one had ever listened to her fears, much less offered such words of kindness. The hand resting on her shoulder was like the touch of . . . of an angel. "Neither Joanie nor I was afraid to strike out on our own because we both knew it was Joanie's best hope."

"You pa wouldn't even fight for his ailing

daughter?"

Shaking her head, Beth said, "I never understood why he wouldn't, or why Ma kept quiet too. I guess they were afraid of Walt. Afraid that he'd set us out in the cold. As long as Pa knew where the deed was hidden, Walt wouldn't throw him off the plantation."

Pierce reached for his knife and went back to work. "He could have retrieved the deed and taken your uncle to court if he tried anything funny."

"Walt had a lot of crooked friends in this area, a judge, even, and Pa didn't have the money to defend his rights. And though Pa was given the deed, he was still the second son."

"Beth —"

"Please. Can we . . . can we not talk about this anymore? It does no good. What's done is done, and Joanie and I just have to make the best of things now."

He looked as though he wanted to say something else, but then he apparently decided to honor her request and went back to work beside her in silence.

As they continued to tend to the deer meat, she watched him from the corner of her eye, berating herself for her impulsive tongue. Why had she told him so much about her life? She felt exposed. Now he probably wouldn't be so quick to keep his promise to see them to safety. Or risk a second kiss. The thought of that brought heat to her cheeks.

Now for sure she and Joanie would have to leave. The moment she got back to camp, she'd get Joanie and they would say they were taking a walk. Nobody had bothered her this morning. Most likely no one would bother her tonight. Once they were near the fields, they could hide in the long corn rows. Nobody would find them. Eventually they would find the main road.

The image of Uncle Walt filled her mind. He was likely still out there. Her teeth worried her lower lip while she worked. She had looked forward to working with Sister Mary Margaret in the turnip patch. And Joanie was so well tended by the Indian women . . .

Oh, why had she opened her big mouth? Because of her, she and Joanie would have to be on the run again. Her heart ached.

She knew better than to trust a man.

The afternoon light was waning by the time Beth and Pierce delivered the fresh kill to the nuns. Reverend Mother was delighted with the gift. She unlatched the door to the smokehouse and helped store the bounty as the captain built a fire to preserve it.

The sunset was a sight to behold as Beth and Pierce returned to camp. His horse's saddlebags contained the deer hide.

Nestling close to the captain's back, Beth drank in the last of the perfect day. Golds, pinks, and oranges painted the sky. The hot sun cooled to a warm breeze. Joanie ran to meet them, her eyes filled with concern. "Where have you been?"

Pierce helped Beth down from the horse, and she embraced her sister. "I'm sorry to cause you alarm." She told Joanie about the events of the strange day. Then, easing her aside, Beth examined her sister's pale features. "What about you?"

Joanie bent and rested her head on her sister's shoulder, her words disheartening. "The cough has worsened."

Gray Eagle stood to the side, his dark eyes focused on Joanie. Beth met his gaze for a moment, not sure what to make of the man's attention.

Surely the Indian didn't have designs on her ill sister. But if Joanie was interested . . . and he was interested . . . she shook the image of the unlikely pairing aside.

Joanie couldn't be that fanciful.

Twenty-Five

Pierce looked up as he loosened the saddle strap and watched Gray Eagle approach.

"I was concerned," the Indian said.

Flashing a grin, Pierce put his worry to rest. "After I stopped to take care of Sue's shoe, I spotted a deer. Beth had been taking a walk in the woods, and so she helped me field dress it for the nuns. I thought they might enjoy a fresh venison roast." He hefted the leather off the animal. "Sorry about not helping you cut wood."

Gray Eagle stepped closer, lowering his voice. "Joanie is very sick."

"Has the lobelia tea run out?"

"The herb is not enough."

Pierce shook his head. "Do you know of an alternative? We're not even sure there'll be a doctor in the next community." Doctors were scarce in these parts. He hadn't wanted to dash Beth's hopes, but he knew the war had depleted the supply. Even if they got the women to the next town, there wasn't any assurance there would be anyone there who practiced medicine.

"This is my fear as well. I'm going to speak to the chief."

"And ask what?"

Gray Eagle didn't answer. Pierce studied him for a long moment. The man was clearly torn about something. He had seen the same emotion cross the scout's features more than once this week.

"There is one course of treatment I would like to try, but I would need his permission."

With a short nod, Pierce said, "It goes without saying that whatever you can do to help her, you should do it."

The village had settled down for the night. Smoke curled lazily from the low-burning cooking fires. Overhead, a summer storm drew close. Lightning illuminated the building thunderheads. Pausing before the chief's dwelling, Gray Eagle gathered his thoughts. A woman standing by the entrance turned to greet him. Gray Eagle asked to speak to the chief.

Moments later the old man appeared. When Gray Eagle spoke in his native language, the chief stepped out of the house and the two men walked to the river.

"The coming rain will be good for the corn," the chief said.

"Yes. It has been dry this year."

"You speak your mother's tongue." The chief's observation was not a question. Gray Eagle had visited the village many times in his youth. His great-grandmother had lived among this tribe.

Smiling, the younger Indian said, "I am the son of Walks-with-Sun."

"Yes, I remember your mother. She was good woman."

"I have come to make a request of you."

"Speak."

"The young woman, Joanie?"

"The Coughing One." Already the women of the tribe had given Joanie a name.

"She is very ill. May I take her to the river?"

The chief's faded eyes focused on the stream next to them.

"Not this river," Gray Eagle said when he saw the direction the chief's eyes had taken. "The Healing River."

The chief remained fixed on the path. "You ask a great favor."

"I would be deeply grateful if you would consider my request."

The men walked in companionable silence. Overhead, night birds called to one another as the storm moved closer. "It is peaceful here," the chief observed.

"I find great harmony in this place," Gray Eagle admitted.

"You have fought in the war?"

"Yes."

"And you have won?"

"No. The North won."

The older man glanced over and a smile surfaced. "But you gave them a good fight."

"The best I had."

"Perhaps you knew my good friend, Stand Watie? His Indian name is Takertawker. Do you know the meaning?"

"Stand!" Gray Eagle broke into a grin. "We fought together at Bird Creek. I believe the name means to stand firm, immovable." Stand was immovable all right, and more. He had been ready to support his convictions at any cost.

"My good friend is a most honorable man," the chief said. "We met as young men. He came with family to the new territory many years ago."

"Some say he was the only Indian to garner the rank of brigadier general," Gray Eagle said. "Others say Ely Parker, a Seneca, also shared that great accomplishment."

The chief appeared lost in memory. "My friend Stand grows old and gray, like me."

"He has a lot of fight left in him still." Gray Eagle glanced over. "As I am certain you do as well."

"Not so much anymore. Time is a ruthless thief." He smiled. "Your mother would take pride in you."

Gray Eagle recalled the quiet woman who had loved and raised him in the community of his father's people. "It is my wish to make her proud."

"You have not taken wives?"

"Haven't had the time. I've been too busy on the war front. I think I'll follow my mother's ways and take only one wife. It seems to me that the more wives a man has, the more headaches as well."

The chief's laughter boomed. Gray Eagle smiled with him.

Finally the chief said, "Your father, Dark Horse, was also a great warrior. He made the Cherokee stand tall against the enemy."

They walked on as thunder rumbled in the distance, two tall men, regal in their heritage. Gray Eagle's loose black hair blew in the wind.

The chief said, "This request you ask of me. The woman means much to you?"

"I barely know her, but I have . . ." He paused to consider. "Yes," he finally admitted. "My heart takes great pity on her. I

232

would like to help ease her pain. I fear that she will pass if she doesn't get help."

"To pass to the great beyond would not be a bad thing."

"No, not bad, but she is tender and young. My hope is that she will have many more days and years on this earth."

The chief crossed his arms over his chest as he stopped walking. He turned his proud profile toward the thunderheads, deep in thought. After a few moments he said, "Your request is granted."

Relief filled Gray Eagle. "Your mercy will not be forgotten."

The chief's tone sobered. "The Great Spirit has given the red man this river."

"The water is healing."

Again, the wise smile appeared. "Only the Great Spirit heals. It is true that this river and its hot springs bring much relief to those who experience it, but the river itself holds no power."

Only this small tribe knew of the hot springs' existence. Gray Eagle's mother had told him the legend many long years ago when she was dying. The springs had not helped her illness. A mighty Cherokee warrior had come across the hot bubbling waters spouting from the ground. His favorite wife, one whom he loved beyond all others, had been very ill. The couple lingered at the fascinating pools. Later, she pleaded to remain there, to soak every day in the strengthening water until she was healed. Her husband eventually built a village close by. The secret remained in the tribe for many years. No outsider soaked in the pools without the chief's permission.

Turning, the chief extended his hand. Gray Eagle removed his knife from its sheath and sliced a piece of skin off the end of his thumb. Bright red blood flowed. Handing the knife to the chief, he did the same. The two men touched thumbs, blood mingling.

The bond was sealed.

Twenty-Six

In the stillness of the quiet evening, Preach cradled the light bundle in his arms. Trella's infant was beautiful, with glossy black hair, olive skin, and dark soulful eyes. It had now been almost a week since she came into the world, and still she remained nameless. Just a tiny bundle of lungs and black hair. "She sure is something, Trella."

The proud mother sat on the pallet, her eyes fastened to her child. "She's precious. A true gift from the Almighty."

Preach cooed at the baby and was rewarded with a brilliant smile. It might have just been from a gas bubble, but the sight of it warmed his heart. He sighed contentedly at the babe before he handed her back and then took a seat beside the mother. The sweet sound of laughter on the far side of the camp drew their attention. "I'd have never thought the red man had so much good in him," Preach mused.

"Why? Have you fought the Indians?"

"Fought beside 'em. There's good and bad among them all, but I figure they have a beef." The hue of his eyes darkened. "The white man took the red man's land. He found more. The white man took his food. He grew more. The white man took his pride. He developed integrity." His gaze lifted to meet hers, measuring her. He changed the subject. "I've been thinking, Trella. You haven't mentioned your baby's father." His eyes skimmed the infant, and he decided the child was more black than white. "Is he looking for you?"

She shook her head. "I . . . I don't know who the baby's father is."

Preach quickly averted his gaze. The personal nature of her answer was too abrupt. He barely knew her, but the haunted look in her eyes had him wondering.

"I'm not a loose woman, Preach."

"No, ma'am." The thought hadn't entered his mind. He knew too well how it worked on the plantations. She was scared. It didn't take much speculation to identify her fear.

"I don't know the baby's father because . . . Walt Jornigan passes his help . . ." Her guarded tone became angry. "We're passed around like candy at Christmastime."

"Trella . . ." The winsome young woman wasn't many years from the innocence of childhood, and he felt his protective nature surge. If Jornigan were here right now . . . "I'm deeply sorry to hear that. You did the right thing by running away."

Moisture filled her eyes. "I'm not a good person, Preach. Not like you. I hate Walt Jornigan, and the Good Book tells us not to hate."

"The Book tells us not to hold hate in our hearts," he agreed. "But the good Lord was human in all ways, and He understands our feelings. He don't intend for us to let our emotions eat us alive." He managed a smile. "You're free of Walt and Bear Jornigan now. The past is behind you." She was young and strong, and she was free now to make a new life for herself and the child.

Sighing, she toyed with the light woven blanket shielding the baby from a soft breeze. "I'm not gettin' my hopes up. He'll find me. He won't let his women workers get away."

"He won't find you. Not if I have anything to say about it." He didn't have much say, but he knew Pierce and Gray Eagle would hold fast. They wouldn't allow harm to befall the Jornigan women, and he would

237

do everything in his power to keep Trella safe.

Glancing up, she asked, "Are you married?"

"No, ma'am. I signed up to fight when I was twenty-one. Haven't had time since then for a wife and kiddies, but now that I'm going home, I'm getting a longing to settle down." A wide smile lit his face. "I want to take over my papa's flock. He's a man of the cloth, but he's getting older. What about you? You won't stay with the other women once you reach the town, will you? Do you have kin elsewhere?"

Lifting a thin shoulder, she said quietly. "I lost both Ma and Pa and my grandparents when I was twelve. I was purchased by Walt shortly afterward. I've picked his cotton and done his bidding every miserable day of my life since then." She released another long sigh. "But I want more for my baby. When I heard Beth and Joanie planning to make a break, I begged them to let me go with them."

"That right?" The girl had a scrappy side to her, but she didn't seem bitter.

"Every woman we left behind was desperate, Preach. Have you ever been desperate?"

"No," he admitted. "Can't say that I have. I had a good upbringing. My pa pastors a

238

small white community. The town always treated us like one of their own."

Her gaze grew warm and sweet. "You were one of their own."

"True, but black people aren't always treated that way." His gaze followed an Indian woman who walked by, carrying a large basket of freshly picked berries.

"You seem young for a preacher."

"Well, truthfully, I've never known a time when I didn't know the Lord. Pa saw that his kids understood the Almighty's love and grace for every soul." He chuckled. "Maybe there were a few times when I didn't serve Him like I should have, but I've always known His presence. Carried me and thousands of others through this war. Pa and Ma are slowing down. Figure I'll take over the pulpit, and they can set back and rest a spell."

"That's a wonderful thought." A moment passed. She fussed with the blanket. "Preach . . ." she finally said, hesitating.

His gaze returned to meet hers. "Yes, ma'am?"

"I haven't named my baby."

"I'd noticed. Is there a reason?"

"I can't think of a good, strong name to give her. I want her to be different than me. I want her to be able to hold her head up with pride and be a fine lady."

Gazing at the infant, Preach tried to imagine the child grown, dressed in beautiful clothing. The woman he saw looked a whole lot like her ma — lovely bone structure, warm eyes. Though Trella had been mistreated, she was still a mighty fine-looking female.

"Would you help me?" she asked.

He glanced up. "Name your baby?"

"Yes, sir. I figure a man like you — a man with spiritual goodness — would know what to call her."

"I've never thought about naming a child," he admitted. He gazed at the sleeping infant and the name Esther came to mind. She was an upstanding example of a godly woman in the Bible. "Esther."

"Esther? Are you speaking of Queen Esther in the Bible? The woman King Ahasuerus chose for his wife?"

"Yes, ma'am." He gazed at the infant. "This one's a queen if I ever saw one." He gave a firm nod. "If she were my child, I'd name her Esther."

Trella studied the child, her eyes gently taking in every inch of the bundle. "Esther. That is a nice name."

"What's your middle name?" Preach asked.

240

Biting her lip, she gave the question thought and then said, "I don't have one — leastways one I can recall." She paused, meeting his concerned gaze. "Do you believe in miracles, Preach?"

"Yes, ma'am. Can't say I ever witnessed a full-blown one, but I believe God can act if and when He wants."

Her head bobbed. "Me too. I prayed day and night that someone would rescue me. I never lost faith that one day the good Lord would answer my prayer."

"And He did."

"Yes, sir," she said. "Not in my time frame, but He sent you along, and that's all that counts."

Preach's heart lurched. Any one of the thousands of soldiers returning from the war could have been on that road that day, but her words gave him pause. Common sense should tell her that life was never going to be easy, and yet she had faith. His pa convinced him in his youth that everything that happened had a purpose, but had he seen such an expression of belief as this before?

"I surely do appreciate the compliment, but I'm not a miracle or an answer to your prayer. I can't do anything other than see that you and Esther get to the next town safely."

"That's miracle enough for me," she said. "I was certain I would never leave the plantation and that I'd go on having men's babies and pickin' cotton the rest of my life." Her eyes rested on her sleeping infant. "But God thought otherwise."

Shaking his head, Preach said softly, "Do you have a last name?"

"I did — once. It was Jones."

"Trella Jones."

Lifting a shoulder, she added, "I remember someone calling out to my pa one afternoon. The man said, 'Have a fine day, Mr. Jones!' "

A smile broke across Preach's mahogany features and his eyes traced the girl's delicate face. She was a rose picked from a thorny field. It angered him to hear of the men who had taken advantage of her. "Your pa must have been real likeable."

"I can't say. I was young when he died — they all died. Pa caught the ague, then Ma, and then Grandpa and Grandma. I remember how sickly they were, out of their heads with fever for days. I was an only child. I also recall that Ma was quiet as a moth. She never uttered a word unless she was spoken to."

"So you take after her," he teased. "You and Beth contribute less to a conversation than any women I've ever met."

She lay back on her elbow. "Well, I never saw the need for small talk. Guess I am like my ma." She glanced over and met his dancing eyes. "I'm talking to you."

"You surely are." He smiled happily. "Are you enjoying the conversation?"

"Indeed." She was silent a moment, and then she said, "And so is Esther. She hasn't been this content since she was born."

Settling back himself, Preach shared a compatible silence with Trella and little Esther.

Esther. He gazed with love at the newborn. A fine name if he did say so himself.

TWENTY-SEVEN

Joanie opened her eyes when a warm hand settled on her shoulder. "Gray Eagle?" she said when she realized who it was.

"I'm sorry to awaken you," he whispered.

Sitting up, she covered her mouth and yawned. "I was just dozing." She learned long ago to close her eyes and try to lie still, willing the coughing spasms to stop. Eventually sleep would come.

He extended a brown hand. "Come with me."

Beside Joanie's pallet, Beth stirred. "What . . . where are you taking her, Gray Eagle?"

"She will be safe with me, Beth. Go back to sleep."

"But —"

He gently nudged her back to her pallet. "We will be gone just a short while. Sleep."

Dropping back to the pallet and closing her eyes, Beth murmured, "You're a man.

How do I know I can trust you?"

Grinning, Gray Eagle gathered Joanie in his arms as he would a bride. "Have I behaved like a man in your presence?"

Beth rolled to her side, saying in a sleepy tone, "There's always the first time. I'm watching you."

Secure in his strong arms, Joanie wondered where Gray Eagle was taking her at this hour. Thunder rumbled overhead and lighting streaked the sky. He walked with sure, confident strides, moving quietly through the sleeping camp. It hurt to draw a deep breath. She was so tired.

"Where are we going?"

"You'll see."

She thought to argue, but she placed full trust in this scout. She studied his profile as the moon moved in and out of rain clouds. Strong forehead, chiseled nose, eyes as dark as the night, nut-brown skin painted deeper by the sun. He was handsome — and maybe five or six years older than her.

"Gray Eagle?"

"Yes?"

"Do you belong to someone?" The question was a most improper one. She knew at least that much about courtship.

A grin turned up the ends of his mouth.

"No, ma'am. I am alone in this world." But the expression in his eyes seemed to say something else. Exactly what, Joanie couldn't tell.

Gray Eagle left the village carrying her in his arms. They were wrapped in silence for a few minutes, and then the sound of gurgling water reached her ears.

"Are we going to water?" Perhaps he thought she needed a bath. Her cheeks flamed.

"We are."

Resting her head on his wide shoulder, she simply tried to breathe, longing to ask more but her insides were so sore from coughing. One day she would fail to catch her breath — she knew this. Ma had warned of it, but she was all too happy to be summoned by the Father. Thoughts of long days running through fields of flowers and breathing easy didn't frighten her. She looked forward to the time when her body would be made whole. She had one last duty here on earth. She had to pray long and hard enough for God to soften Beth's heart and open her eyes to His existence. Walt had made it hard for anyone to believe in anyone, especially a kind God.

"Close your eyes."

"Pardon?"

"Close your eyes."

Her lids fluttered shut. "Is this a game?" *A rather odd one,* she thought.

"This isn't a game." Her body shifted with the pace of his footsteps, her eyes closed. She couldn't imagine what awaited her. Did he want her to meet someone? Perhaps a good friend? Her heart skipped a beat. A woman? One he cared deeply for? Perhaps the woman who had so warmly welcomed him to camp? Her thoughts went back to the day they entered the Indian settlement and she noticed the lovely woman with long black hair. In her mind's eye, Joanie saw again the way she'd smiled at Gray Eagle. The way they moved to the side to speak in soft tones.

The sound of bubbling water was quite loud now. A clap of thunder boomed in the distance, and she stiffened. "Gray Eagle — we shouldn't be in water —"

Her words faltered as he lowered her. Down. Down. Her breath caught when her body was engulfed in the warm spring. Settling her gently on the bottom of the pool, he whispered softly against her ear, "Open your eyes."

Her lids slowly opened. She was sitting in a large body of bubbling water. Jaunty spurts surrounded her. Her eyes roamed the moonlit area with awe. The hot water closed around her, and her aching body thistly drank in its comfort.

"Is this heaven?" Perhaps she had died today, her lungs finally giving out.

Chuckling softy, he whispered. "No, but I believe pools like this will be up there."

"Do you believe in God?" she asked, surprised by his response.

"Yes. My mother taught me about the One who lives on high."

"I thought Indians believed in a Great Spirit —"

He stopped her. "They believe in a higher source."

"Oh, Gray Eagle." His name escaped her lips as the soothing water swirled around her weary body, calming aches and pains. The bubbles were like prickly fingers dancing across her chest, touching sore spots and soothing them. "Why haven't I been here earlier?"

"You cannot come here alone, Joanie. Nor can you bring Beth or even speak of the waters to her."

"But —"

He placed a quieting finger across her lips. "This river belongs to the Indians."

"But —"

He shook his head.

"Beth has tried so hard to find help for me. Will this water cure me?"

"Only God heals, but the water will help you. Its heat will soothe your body, and the steam may quiet the cough. You must thank God for this. The chief granted me special permission to bring you here. It was a very great favor. My people call it Healing River."

"Then it does heal."

He shook his head. "The water comes from hot pools beneath the earth. It is not mystic water — but it is God given. Some find relief; others do not. I brought my mother here when she was ill. The waters did not help her."

She touched his face. "I'm sorry." She pictured him as a small boy, running through the camp, pushing a hoop with a stick as she'd seen the children do. He had grown strong and powerful. He'd become a proud Cherokee man who fought for his government, even though his government had stripped his ancestors of land, buffalo, and, for many, their spirit.

The rain finally came, a light shower dancing on the waters. Steam surrounded her. Joanie groaned with pleasure. "I don't want to leave." For the first time in . . . well, ever . . . her body was at rest.

"We do not have to leave."

"It's raining."

Chuckling, he eased down bedside her, clothes and all, steadying her body with his right hand. "Are you afraid you will get wet?"

Her laughter rang out — a sound foreign to her own ears. "No, but if it starts lightning we'll be —"

"Cooked? Like meat on a spit?"

More giggles. "You have learned the white man's language quite nicely."

"I am watching the sky closely. There is no need to fear." Sobering, he spoke softly. "Remember. You are not to speak of these pools to anyone."

She nodded, knowing how difficult it would be to keep this miracle quiet. "The nuns don't know about it?"

"Well, yes. They do. Sister Earlene and Sister Prue are two of the oldest. They are permitted to soak in the waters to ease their aching joints."

"Then this isn't exactly a secret."

"The pools are known to exist, but nobody but the Indians and sisters know their location."

Joanie reached out to him and they latched hands. For a long moment their eyes met as the light shower splattered the water with diamond-shaped drops. "Thank you, Gray Eagle."

His gaze locked with hers, he said, "You are welcome, Joanie Jornigan."

Beth opened her eyes at daybreak. Chirping birds chattered happily overhead. When her hand automatically reached over to Joanie's pallet, she noted that her sister was back and sleeping soundly. Odd . . . her shirt sleeve was damp. Where did she and Gray Eagle go on their mysterious walk? Shading her eyes from the rising sun, she realized she'd overslept. Easing to her feet, she tiptoed away. Joanie hadn't coughed once during the night.

"Thank You, God —" She caught herself. Those thanks were coming easier in the past few days. Yet her gratitude seemed properly earned. She couldn't remember a night when Joanie's hacking cough hadn't kept her awake. If thanks were due, they would belong to God. For some reason, that thought didn't bother her as much as it once did.

Smells from the cooking fires reached her. Her stomach growled with hunger this morning. She smiled with the knowledge that she wouldn't have to go hungry, that a simple but satisfying meal would be provided her. Joy filled her heart at the beginning of this new day.

After breakfast, she helped the women wash utensils and straighten pallets and then, dressed again in trousers and a shirt, she walked downstream. Sunlight topped the rise. She didn't want to miss helping Mary Margaret in the vegetable garden.

The friendly nun glanced up when Beth emerged from the riverbank thicket. Smiling, she waved to her. "Good morning!" she trilled.

"Good morning!"

The sister's smile was broad when Beth joined her, ready to work. "I was hoping you would come!"

"I would have been here earlier, but I overslept. Joanie had a really good night. She didn't wake me like she usually does."

"Praise be to God!" Mary Margaret handed Beth a hoe. "Let's work close so we can talk."

Grinning, Beth took the implement and followed the good sister to the long, flowering rows. It felt actually good to work again. Until now, Beth had always spent seven days a week in the cotton field. She was starting to feel like a worthless slug, doing virtually nothing day in and day out.

Conversation flowed easily as the women

hoed. Reverend Mother had the sniffles this morning, Sister Mary Margaret informed. Sister Grace had dyspepsia. The convent had enjoyed the fresh venison last night, and all sent their gratitude to Captain Montgomery.

The mere mention of the handsome captain sent Beth's pulse racing. For the life of her she didn't know why. Well, she did. He was unlike any man she'd ever met. Kind, helpful, and nonjudgmental. If all men were like Captain Montgomery, she might understand why Joanie hoped to find true love one day. Poor Joanie. While she had wanted to encourage her sister, in her heart Beth thought no man would ever want to take on the burden of Joanie's affliction, despite the fact that she would make a faithful and loving wife. She was certainly the best sister in the world — and the only bright spot in Beth's life.

"Sister?"

"Hmm?" Mary Margaret remained bent over, hoeing away. Her sizeable caboose stuck upward, her black skirt swaying with each movement.

"I . . . I'd like to know a little more about prayer."

"Oh?"

"Well . . . I told you yesterday that Joanie

believes in God and in prayer."

"What about you?"

"I don't. Leastways I've never been taught much about God, if there is one."

"There is!" Her joyful laughter rang out.

"How do you know for certain?" Beth stopped working to lean on her hoe.

Mary Margaret paused as well. "Jesus rose from the dead. How much more proof do you need? When He ascended into heaven, He promised to return, and He hasn't come back yet."

"He's coming back?"

"Oh, yes."

Beth checked the sun. "When?"

"We don't know. Even the angels in heaven don't know, and the Lord tells us not to even try to guess when the time will be, but He will come when He's least expected." The sister returned to her work.

Beth took up her hoe and mulled on the thought for a whole row. "So, if one were to believe in God, what is the proper way to pray?"

The nun paused, wiping perspiration trickling down her temples with a cloth. "The proper way?"

"Yes. I've noticed that people do it differently."

"They do?"

"Yes."

"How so?"

"Well . . ." Beth sank the hoe into a stubborn weed. "As I mentioned yesterday, when Joanie prays she gets down on her knees, clasps both hands together, lifts her face, and talks to Him."

Mary Margaret nodded.

"The pickers also talked to God often, just right out loud with their eyes wide open. They would laugh and shout and sing songs to Him. And I noticed that when you and the other sisters pray, a bell tolls. You also touch those beautiful beads." She pointed to the rosary hanging from the sister's waist.

"Hmm," the nun mused, still mopping her face with the cloth. "I hadn't thought about there being a right or wrong way to pray. I believe God hears all prayers if they are offered from a sincere heart."

"You do?"

"God has large ears, Beth, and He hears anyone who speaks to Him in earnest, however they do it. Do you want to speak to Him?"

Beth shook her head and then bent to her task again. A warm blush flamed up her neck. "I was only askin'."

The sister nodded. There was no judgment. She didn't push. She just let her eyes roam the long turnip rows. "My, my. All these turnips."

"What about corn? Do you plant corn too?"

"The Indians provide us with corn, but we plant peas, okra, and lots of other things. Just about everything but corn."

"You seem to have a good relationship with them. You're really not afraid of the Indians?"

Another laugh. "They are good people. We give to them and they give to us. They keep to themselves mostly, unless we ask for their help." She pointed to the far horizon, where a field of corn stalks poked their heads up to the sun. "They are the best farmers around. During the fall they share their hay with us, and just before they leave for their winter grounds, we find cordwood stacked everywhere — enough for a long winter."

"I thought all Indians were warriors, people to be feared."

Mary Margaret shook her head. "Not these Indians. They are growing old and waiting for their Great Sprit to lead them to a faraway land." She paused, thoughtful. "I suppose every one of us could be fearsome if we were angered enough, and the Indians would certainly be a force to contend with if they were riled, but they don't bother anyone. They are peaceful and generous to fault. They lead a good life. We couldn't ask for better neighbors. Many are like family, and we rejoice when they come back each spring."

Beth studied the long rows of waving stalks, not surprised now as she once would have been to hear that her fears were ungrounded. The Indians had welcomed her and her friends. She evidently had much to learn about this world.

Mary Margaret glanced up. "We must get busy. Reverend Mother will wonder if I've fallen in the creek!"

Laughing, Beth chunked out another stubborn weed.

"She doesn't like me to be gone long." The sister sighed. "I tend to do . . . somewhat silly things often."

"Don't we all?"

"Well, yes!" The cheerful nun grinned. "I hope you can join me again tomorrow. I love talking to you."

"Me too. I'll try to be here."

Beth nodded to the women in the camp as she headed straight for Joanie's pallet. How odd these people must find their new visitors.

Joanie sat up as Beth approached. Wiping sleep from her eyes, she studied the sun. "What time is it?"

"Late afternoon," Beth said, lowering herself next to her sister. "Are you just waking up?"

Joanie nodded. "I can't imagine sleeping this long. Have I missed breakfast?"

"And lunch." Beth cocked her head and studied her. "You barely coughed all night."

"I . . . slept soundly." Joanie shook her head. "I've never slept this deeply."

"Where did Gray Eagle take you last night? Your clothing was damp this morning."

Joanie shifted on her pallet, seemingly uncomfortable with the question. "He . . . we went for a walk."

"He was carrying you when he left. Did you go for a swim?"

"No." She stretched. "Well, kind of . . ." She straightened her shirt. "Is there anything left from lunch?"

Beth studied her sister's face. It was rosy with color. She hadn't looked this good in . . . Beth couldn't recall the last time she looked this healthy. "Where did he take you, Joanie?

"Nearby."

"In the camp?"

"Yes."

Joanie had always been like a chattering blue jay, yet today her answers were vague and she chose her words carefully.

"Joanie?"

"Yes."

Beth scooted closer, reaching for her sister's hand. "I've been meaning to talk to you."

"About what?"

"Gray Eagle."

Crimson color flooded the young woman's cheeks. "What about him?"

"You're not falling for him, are you?"

"No!" She shifted slightly on her pallet. "Why do you keep asking, Beth? He's very kind, that's all. And I enjoy his company."

"I see the way you look at him, all sweet and trusting. And the way he looks back, all interested-like."

"Well, what if I do? And what if he is? Would that be so earth-shattering?"

"Yes. Gray Eagle isn't . . . suited for you."

"Why not? Because he's an Indian?"

"No. Because you are ill and require a lot of care."

"I'm not an old grandma." Joanie moved away. "Is there anything to eat? I'm famished."

"Don't change the subject." Beth pulled

her back and looked her in the eye. "Tell me you aren't falling for this man."

"I am not falling for this man. I am not in love."

"Then why are you spending time with him? The moonlit walk with a man you barely know? Permitting him to scoop you up into his arms and carry you? And you surely must be swimming together. That isn't good, Joanie."

"You're questioning my judgment? And it did rain last night. That could account for my damp clothing."

"It could, but somehow I don't think that it does. I'm questioning his judgment."

"He's not like that, Beth. He wants to be a doctor. Did you know that his mother was white and his father full-bloodied Cherokee? Her family was massacred in a raid, and she was taken, claimed by Gray Eagle's father."

"That's horrifying, Joanie. Not romantic."

"I didn't say it was romantic. I meant that his mother was very smart and taught him all she knew. He is skilled and intelligent."

"All very nice, but he isn't the man for you."

Drawing back, Joanie stared at the cold embers of the previous night's fire. "Why are the fires out?"

Beth studied the churning sky. Minutes

ago the weather had been sunny and nice. Somehow the Indians knew another storm was brewing. One stray ember, and the village could go up in flames.

Getting to her feet, Joanie said, "Let's find something to eat before the rain moves in again."

The two sisters moved to the main cooking fire, where a large pot of coffee always sat. Picking it up, Beth checked the temperature with her fingers. "Lukewarm."

"I'll drink it anyway."

Beth moved to a pitcher where heavy cream awaited. She poured a generous amount into the cup and returned to Joanie. "There's cold mush and flat bread."

Shaking her head, Joanie sipped the tepid coffee. "This will do for the moment. Maybe the storm will move on and I can have some eggs."

The afternoon turned dark. Gusting wind rattled the dwellings. Beth and Joanie huddled under a blanket to fight off a chill when the first sprinkles fell. But shortly afterward the sun popped out again and black clouds skittered past.

Relieved, Beth got up to search for a match, planning to start the fire so there would be a nice hot one going for supper. The Indian women were so obliging. Up to this point, they had barely permitted the visitors to lift a hand.

"Where is Gray Eagle?" Joanie asked Beth.

"Hmm . . . not sure. He and Pierce may have gone hunting. Why?"

"Oh, no reason."

Beth turned, certain she heard Joanie catch her words. Studying her sister, she couldn't shake the feeling Joanie was fair to bursting to tell her something but refused. What secret would she hold so dear that she wouldn't tell her sister? Ordinarily Joanie told everything she knew.

Joanie tilted her head and smiled. "Let's talk about you. Do you find Pierce a bit . . . shall we say, intriguing? And handsome?"

"No!"

A giggle escaped Joanie. "Methinks you protest too much."

Beth struck a match and held it to the kindling she'd settled around the cold embers. Tinder blazed. Straightening, she said. "Methinks? What sort of language is that?"

"Shakespeare."

"Who?"

"Never mind. Do you deny the attraction?"

"There is no attraction." Beth banged a skillet over two large rocks. There was no attraction. True, she was starting to trust this man too much for her own good, and she couldn't deny that if it hadn't been for him and his kindness they would still be under Uncle Walt's miserable thumb. The admission was nothing less than painful. She took a deep breath. If not for his compassion — and that of the others — Joanie would surely have died the day they ran away.

"I know Pa should have stood up for us more," Joanie said, "and Uncle Walt and Bear are meaner than a riled bull, but maybe all men aren't the same."

"Those are fanciful thoughts."

"No, really, Beth." Joanie sat up straighter. "Maybe we got a bad bunch. Ma always said to think with common sense, and common sense would say that not all men are bad."

"Every man I've met has been."

"Perhaps we've met the wrong ones until now."

The fire blazed. Beth dipped a wad of grease out of the pot that sat near the fire and shook it off the spoon and into the skillet. "How many eggs?"

"Two, please."

Beth glanced up when a shadow crossed the sun and the wind picked up again. A dark dark cloud was overhead. "Oh, dear."

She wiped her hands and mentally urged the grease to warm. "We were mistaken. The rain isn't over."

Joanie frowned, glancing up. "Oh . . ." Thunderheads ballooned in the west. Her gaze pivoted back to the fire.

The wind suddenly gusted, bending small saplings midway to the ground. Sparks showered around them, going airborne from the campfire.

Beth jerked the skillet off the flame, realizing her mistake. "We have to put this fire out!"

Thunder boomed, jarring the ground. Joanie sprang to help, reaching for the water bucket. They girls were too late. Embers were already skittering and dancing across the village. Squealing, Joanie and Beth stomped madly, trying to extinguish the fiery darts on the ground before they escaped to spiral to the treetops.

Lodge doors opened, and faces peered out. Elderly men and women burst outside to join the fight, making feeble attempts to extinguish the sparks. Burning embers swirled up in the wind and then dropped down on the Council Lodge, and within minutes the building was on fire. Shouts filled the camp. The Indians quickly ran to the creek and formed a water brigade. Pails passed through hands.

After what seemed like forever, Beth glanced up to see that Mary Margaret and Reverend Mother had joined them. How long had it been since the first spark flew from the fire pit?

"We spotted the smoke and came running," Mary Margaret confessed breathlessly. Three of the older nuns stood on the river bank filling buckets.

More tents were ablaze.

A regal-looking woman, perhaps in her eighties, stepped to the opening of a large structure, her weathered features a mask of concern. Beth hadn't seen the woman until now, but by her dress she had to be one the camp's officials. Like a woman chief or something.

Riders appeared, and Beth groaned when she realized they were Pierce and Gray Eagle. With strings of fish dangling from their saddles, they galloped in. The men slid off the horses and grabbed buckets to help fight the fires.

For more than an hour they fought to save the village. The clouds and wind finally moved on, and the sun came back out. When the last ember was stomped away, Pierce leaned against a tree to catch his breath. Beth studied his smoke-rimmed eyes and said, "You look funny." She swiped at the thick soot covering her own cheeks.

He stared at her and then broke into laughter. "You're thinking *I* look funny?"

Giggling, she nodded. "Very funny."

"I was just thinking the same about you." They bent double, though the situation was anything but humorous. Two homes, the main lodge, and various tents had suffered damage all because Beth had started a cook fire.

Started a fire. She sobered suddenly as panic set in. What would the Indians do to her? Her gaze roamed the blackened ground and the sisters' soot-covered faces and singed habits. Many of the village inhabitants wore moccasins with seared soles.

She, Beth Jornigan, was responsible for all this damage.

Instinctively she stepped closer to Pierce, hoping against hope that when the source of the fire became known, this kind, patient, helpful man would save her hide.

Again.

There was no doubt about it. She was going to have to stay clear of matches.

Twenty-Eight

Beth's sudden movement toward him caused Pierce to focus on her. Smoke rose gently around them from extinguished embers. A thought suddenly occurred to him. "Miss Jornigan? You haven't by any chance been near a match, have you?"

She stiffened. "I can explain . . ." But her words faltered when she saw an angry color now dotting his cheeks.

He stalked off, leaving her standing by herself. "You . . ." She caught her tongue. He couldn't walk away and not consider her side of the story! Then again, maybe he could. Prior to now he'd been the perfect gentleman, but she'd known that deep down he was a man. A very perturbed man, at the moment.

Still, she couldn't have him thinking she'd done this on purpose. Running, she caught up with him. "Pierce, I would like to explain my side of the story," she said. "Please."

"And that would be?"

"I did start the fire. That was foolish, but I thought the rain was over and Joanie was hungry. She didn't want cold mush; she wanted eggs — and it's so hard to get her to eat anything — so when the sun came out and the storm seemed over, I started a fire."

"All the camp fires were out. Correct?"

"Yes."

"You didn't think it was strange that *all* the cooking fires were out? That maybe the Indian women had a reason for that?"

"I thought of it. But then, when the clouds moved on . . ."

"You reached for the matches." Pausing, his eyes skimmed her. "Do you have a thing for fire, Miss Jornigan?"

He was upset all right. He was calling her Miss Jornigan now. Her gaze skipped to his side to see if he carried anything that he could punish her with and noted his gun belt. Her eyes focused on the sidearm.

When his gaze traced hers, he shifted. "I'm not going to shoot you, Beth." Shaking his head, he said softly, "I'd like to get my hands on the men who have made you terrified of my gender."

She met his steady gaze. Gender. Had he insulted her? She wasn't familiar with the fancy word. She glanced to the lodge, seeking Joanie.

"Men," he clarified, as if reading her thoughts.

"Why didn't you just say so?"

He turned and walked on but she dogged his steps. "I understand why you're angry, but I honestly didn't mean to burn the village."

"Or your uncle's cotton fields?"

"Or the cotton fields." She winced. He must think she didn't have the good sense God gave a goose. God. If she were a praying person, this would be the ideal time to have a talk with the Almighty. She sure wasn't winning points with the captain. "I know what I did was reckless, and I will apologize to that woman who looked so worried."

"That lady," he said, "has the real power over the village."

"How so? I thought the chief —"

"Don't kid yourself. Cherokee women rule the home. And they fight like warriors. Actually —" He paused to adjust his hat. "They own the homes. That's part of the marriage contract. This particular woman, White Bird, comes from the Blue Clan — wait a minute. Don't change the subject! You are going to apologize not only to White

269

Bird, but also to the chief and the villagers."

She stopped in her tracks. Would the Indians accept her apology and forgive her? Or would they be so angry that they would make her and Joanie and Trella and Esther leave? Beth put her face in her hands. What had she done? How could she have endangered the safety of her sister and friends so recklessly, not to mention the homes of the Indians who had so kindly taken them in?

In her sorrow for her actions she almost forgot that Pierce was standing next to her. Then she felt his hands on hers, lowering them so he could look in her face. He seemed to be over his anger. "I'll stand next to you while you speak to the village."

"You will?"

"I will." His eyes met hers. "You're not going to fight me on the apology?"

"No. I'm in the wrong and I admit it." She turned to walk away but not before she saw his grin.

Cad.

Half an hour later, Beth cleared her throat. Her eyes lifted to meet the crowd before her and then focused on White Bird. "I am truly sorry for starting the fire. It was a mistake. I was just trying to —" She stopped. It didn't matter that she was only trying to feed her sister. These people didn't deserve excuses. Her eyes sought Pierce's, seeking strength from his nearness, and then she went on. "I deeply regret that I've burned part of your camp."

Disgruntled voices rose in the crowd. Faded eyes pinned her before people began turning away. As Beth watched them leave, she asked Pierce, "What more can I do?"

He shook his head, not looking very happy himself. "Nothing but try to fix the problem." He sighed deeply. "You do realize that this is going to delay us even longer. We can't burn down these folks' homes and walk away without doing a thing to help them rebuild."

"It was a *mistake.*" Hadn't Mr. Perfect ever made a mistake?

"My point is that we can't leave. We have to stay and help rebuild."

Her features fell. "How much longer?"

Pierce looked over the smoldering ruins. "As long as it takes, Beth. A week, maybe two."

A relieved sigh escaped her. "A week or two. That's not so bad." The hindrance would mean that Joanie was still one to two weeks away from seeing a doctor, but her cough was better. And another week or two would give Esther a definite advantage.

Gray Eagle approached after talking to White Bird and the chief. His grim features told the gravity of the situation. "The woman may continue to stay."

"Tell the chief we will stay as well and help rebuild," Pierce said.

"I already have. He is pleased." The scout's dark gaze focused on Beth. "Is Joanie all right?"

"She's fine. She's with Trella and the baby in the nursing tent."

Gray Eagle turned to the captain. "May I have a word with you?"

Nodding, Pierce stepped to the side to join him.

"The fire was an accident. The delay in moving on is frustrating, but Beth is sick at heart about her actions," Pierce said. "Joanie wanted eggs."

"I get that she wanted to provide food for her sister, but no Cherokee in camp would have allowed a fire during a storm."

Pierce looked back and noticed Beth's forlorn look. Her arms were crossed in front of her, protecting herself, and a miserable expression was on her lovely face. He shouldn't have come down so hard on her, but she was like a child at times, needing a father's guidance. "She thought the storm was over."

Gray Eagle's eyes fixed on the smoldering ruins. "And we will stay and rebuild. It is another disruption." He met the captain's eyes. "I will stay if you want to ride on."

Pierce shrugged off the suggestion. "I'll stay. I'm here to see this through." It was time to change the subject. There was a question he wanted to ask his friend. "You took her there, didn't you?"

Gray Eagle glanced up. "Who? Where?"

"Joanie. You took her to the heated pools."

"How do you know about the pools?"

"I followed you."

"You followed me!"

Pierce flashed a grin. "I've scouted a bit myself."

"Yes. I took her there."

"Her cough was better last night. Perhaps she wouldn't be coughing even now if not for the smoke."

"Yes. I listened also during the night. She slept well."

"Then a couple of weeks' delay could be a blessing."

A smile crossed Gray Eagle's weary features. "Yes. It could be good. It is as I have heard you say often. It would be good to find a place of complete peace."

"Not on this earth," Pierce corrected,

though he knew he voiced the sentiment often. Then he grasped his friend's shoulder. "The will of God will never take you where the grace of God will not protect you, but don't fall for Joanie, Gray Eagle. You're from two different worlds."

"Not so different."

"Different enough."

"It was not so with my mother and father."

Pierce nodded. "I suppose there's always an exception." He turned to face his friend. "Regarding staying, just now I don't think either you or I could force Preach away from that baby."

Laughing together, the men's eyes shifted back to Beth.

"Agreed," Gray Eagle said. "But please try to keep her away from matches."

TWENTY-NINE

The sounds of saws and hammers were heard early the next morning. Not long after breakfast the burnt structures were razed and scorched deerskin wigwams pulled down. Women scraped hides.

Beth contritely helped other women carry food — berries, fresh fruit, and sliced melons — to the men who toiled in the hot sun.

As heavy as her heart was, she couldn't help but smile when she walked through the village and saw Sister Mary Margaret and Sister Prue turning a jump rope for the village children. The two sisters sang a silly song designed to entertain. Later, Beth spotted the two nuns playing a game of hopscotch with the kids. Shaking her head, Beth grinned. *Thank You, God, that these kind people don't hold the fire against me.* She thought about her silent prayer. Had God heard? Sister Mary Margaret said He did.

She wondered what He thought of her awkward thanks. Did He welcome them? Or did He wonder what had kept her from talking to Him for so long?

By evening the villagers and their guests were bone tired. Gray Eagle sat near the fire, chatting with the chief. Beth watched the exchange, aware that Joanie's eyes never left the handsome scout.

After working hard all morning, late in the afternoon he'd taken her away again, and she returned an hour later, her eyes sparkling like rare gems and her clothes quite wet. She refused to answer Beth's questions as she changed into her dress and hung her pants and shirt up to dry. Emotions clashed within Beth. On the one hand, she was grateful that her sister had the muscular young man's attention. On the other, she was worried sick that Joanie would fall in love, only to be devastated by him. He would go to his own village soon, leaving her more alone than she had been before. Beth wished she could divert her sister's attention away from their growing attraction, but until they reached the next community, there was little she could actually do but keep a close eye on the couple. She went over to the group around the fire and found a seat next to Pierce. His hat was

over his eyes, and he appeared to be snooz-
ing.

"Gray Eagle!" A child's excited voice
broke the peaceful silence.

"Yes, Little Bear?"

The child spoke in his native language.
Beth guessed that he had asked the scout to
tell a story.

Chuckling, Gray Eagle glanced at the
chief, who nodded. "It would please the
children."

Little ones appeared from the shadows,
their young faces and black eyes bright with
anticipation.

Beth leaned toward Pierce and said softly,
"Hey. Wake up."

His drowsy bass answered. "Why?"

"Something's happening."

Lifting the brim of his cap, he focused on
the sight. "The kids want Gray Eagle to tell
them a story."

Beth drew her skirts close and hugged her
knees. "And will he?"

"He will. He tells these legends every
chance he gets." He tipped the brim back
into place.

When she glanced up again she was surprised to see that half the village had
gathered around the fire to hear Gray Eagle
speak.

The scout said, "What story shall I tell?"

"The owl!" a little boy said.

"Ah. 'Why the Great Spirit Gave the Owl Big Eyes.' Is that the one you want to hear?"

"Yes!" the children said in chorus.

Standing in front of the fire, with great relish he began to entertain his audience with the old Cherokee legend.

"The Great Spirit, the Everything-Maker, was busy one day creating animals. He was working on Rabbit, and Rabbit said: 'I want very long legs and long ears like a deer, and sharp fangs and claws like a panther.'

"The Great Spirit said quietly, 'I will make your body the way you want it to be. I will give you what you ask for.' He was working on Rabbit's hind legs, making them long, just the way Rabbit wanted.

"Owl was sitting in a tree nearby and patiently waiting his turn. Seeing that Rabbit got his wish, he said, 'Whoo, whoo, I want a long neck like Swan's, and some red feathers like Cardinal's, and . . . yes, I think I want a long beak like Egret's, and a huge crown of plumes like Heron's.' He blinked his eyes. 'Make me into the most beautiful, the fastest, and the most amazing of all the birds!'

"The Great Spirit did not like distraction when He worked. He said to Owl, 'Be quiet.

Turn around and look in another direction. Don't you know that no one is allowed to watch Me work?' The Great Spirit was then making Rabbit's ears very long, just the way Rabbit wanted them.

"Owl refused to be quiet. 'Whoo, whoo! Nobody can forbid me to watch. I like watching You, and watch I will.'

"The Great Spirit shook His head and went back to work on Rabbit, but Owl kept up his chatter. 'Whoo, whoo! I want to be different!'

"The Great Spirit turned, lifting Owl down from his branch. He stuffed Owl's head deep into his body, shaking him until his eyes bulged with fright and pulling at his ears until they were sticking up at both sides of his head.

" 'There,' the Great Spirit said. 'You are different. You won't be able to crane your neck to watch things you shouldn't watch, and you'll have big ears to listen when someone speaks. I have given you large eyes — but not so big that you can watch Me. You will be awake only at night so you can't watch Me work during the day. And your feathers won't be red like Cardinal's, but gray like this,' and the Great Spirit rubbed Owl with mud all over, 'because of your disobedience.'

"Owl flew off, sulking. 'Whoo, whoo, whoo.'

"Returning to His work, the Great Spirit was about to finish Rabbit, but Rabbit had been so upset by the Great Spirit's anger that he ran off half done. He wasn't finished. Rabbit's hind legs were long, so he had to hop instead of run. Because he took fright then, Rabbit has remained afraid of almost everything. He never got his claws or the fangs he asked for so he could defend himself. If he had been wise, he would not have run away. Rabbit would have looked much different today.

"As for Mr. Owl, he's stayed as the Great Spirit had shaped him in anger — with big eyes, a short neck, and ears sticking out of the sides of his head. And he has to sleep during the day and come out only at night."

The children leaped with glee, shoving to get closer to Gray Eagle as he finished the tale. Three young girls ran to the captain, disturbing his nap. Playfully, he tickled their ribs and tugged their ears. High-pitched squeals filled the soft night air.

Beside her, Beth heard Joanie's longing sigh. "He's wonderful."

"This Great Spirit?" Beth said. "Is this supposed to be God?"

"It is a form of their god. We don't share

280

the same belief, but Gray Eagle believes in God." She turned to smile at her sister. "I think he thinks of Him when he tells his stories. God is very large, Beth. He has made this vast world and all of its people."

Focused on Gray Eagle, Beth murmured, "This faith thing gets more confusing by the moment."

THIRTY

"Look at him, Sister." Beth leaned on her hoe, shamelessly gawking. Pierce and Preach were manning a crosscut saw this morning, taking down a dead oak near the sisters' turnip patch. Arms like steel bands worked the saw.

Mary Margaret raised her head and then quickly lowered it, laughing softly. "I'm not supposed to look, Beth."

"Oh. Sorry." But Beth knew without noting Sister Mary Margaret's soft gasp that even she was getting all moon-eyed over Captain Montgomery. She certainly wasn't alone in her attraction. Beth was supposedly running from men, not toward them. What she needed was someone to shake sense into her.

"Shake me, Sister."

Straightening, the nun frowned. "Why would I do that?"

"Shake me." Beth closed her eyes and

waited. Ma had never taken a switch to her, but when Beth had stepped out of line — as she was now — her mother had gently shaken some sense into her. "I am ogling Captain Montgomery."

"Beth!" The nun laughed again. "Such language. But I'm sorry. I really can't shake you."

"Why not?"

"Because." Heat flushed the cheerful woman's face. "I serve the Lord."

"You don't think He would think I need a good shaking?"

"I don't presume to think for our Father and neither should you." Another giggle escaped. "If it strengthens your faith, the captain *is* difficult . . ." Another snicker. "He's very difficult to ignore, in which case we both need a good shaking. And if Reverend Mother heard us discussing the captain this way, she'd be happy to oblige."

"Please, Mary Margaret. Other than Joanie you're my only friend." Clamping her eyes shut tighter, she pleaded, "Shake some sense in —"

She opened her eyes when she heard horses approaching and watched as a young Cherokee male rode up to the men and paused. His strong tanned body gleamed in the sunlight. Words were exchanged, and then moments later the youth rode off. Pierce and Preach set the saw aside and walked to their waiting horses. Beth frowned as they mounted up and rode after the young man.

"Something must be wrong." She set the hoe aside. "I'll be back shortly."

"Your curiosity is going to get you into trouble," Mary Margaret advised. "By the way, that's a lovely bonnet. Did Sister Prue give it to you?"

"I'm sure you're right, and yes, Sister Prue made me this. She said she thought the sun was too hot." If Sister Prue only knew how hot a cotton field could get.

Running now, Beth crisscrossed the field and made her way toward camp. Sweat rolled from her temples. Loosening her bonnet, she let it slide down her back.

When she arrived, she was met with an unexpected sight. A soldier dressed in tatters and wearing a Confederate gray-and-gold hat sat atop his horse, accepting a cup of water. Pierce and Preach had dismounted from their own horses and were deep in conversation with him.

"You fought in Virginia?" Preach asked.

The man nodded. "On my way home. Got a ways to go yet."

The captain's voice washed over her.

"Then you must have passed through Moss Hill?"

Nodding, the man held out the cup once he'd drained it. An Indian woman refilled it. "Yes, sir, 'bout two days ago." He drained the cup again.

Stepping closer to the horse, Pierce asked, "Did you ride by the Tall Oak Plantation?"

"Yep." The man handed the cup back to the woman and motioned that he'd had his fill. "Couldn't miss a spread that size."

Beth noted the way the captain's face lit with expectancy. "Everything okay up that way?"

The man shook his head sadly. "Nothing's left."

Pierce took a step back. "There's a lot of destruction there?"

"I'd say so. Everything's gone. Tall Oak's been leveled, and everything within ten miles around is burnt to the ground."

Pierce's features tightened, his eyes registering disbelief. "And the folks who owned Tall Oaks? The slaves and workers?"

Shrugging, the man said, "What can I say? When I rode through there was nothing left but ashes. The whole area is a ghost town. A feller I passed on the road said the Union army burnt everything to the ground a couple of weeks before the war ended."

"The plantation owners . . . you're certain the owners didn't survive?"

The man shook his head. "Gone. You have to hold your nose to ride through the area. It's a pitiful sight."

Preach reached over and laid a steadying hand on Pierce's shoulder. "Sorry, Captain."

Beth felt as though her heart were coming out of her chest. Pierce's folks were gone. Pain as real as the agony she felt when Pa and Ma died filled her.

"Are you certain? Tall Oak Plantation. Around fifty miles from here. Two thousand acres of cotton."

The stranger's Adam's apple bobbed as he wiped his mouth on his sleeve. He nodded. "Certain. Did you know the folks?"

"They were my family."

"I'm shore sorry. This war's been a thorn in every side."

No longer able to hold back, Beth walked up to the men and took Pierce's hand. He squeezed hers reassuringly, and she bit back her tears. It must be awful for a man to not be able to cry when his heart was broken.

"Did anyone mention my sister? She's smart. It would take more than a few Northerners to take her down," Pierce said.

The stranger's brow furrowed. "Truth be I did hear mention of your sister. They said she put up a whale of a fight. You'd have been proud of her."

Beth felt the captain sway. "Pierce —" She tightened her grip on his hand. "Can I get you some water?"

Instead of responding he inhaled deeply and then faced the man. "Thanks. I appreciate your telling me."

"Sorry to have to bring you such bad news. Nothing but scorched land there now. If you were headin' that way you might as well turn around. That's a sight no man should witness." He waved at the Indian woman who had brought his water. "Much obliged for the drink. I have more ground to cover before the day's over."

Grim-faced, Pierce nodded. "God go with you."

Touching his forefinger to his hat brim, the stranger turned his horse and rode out of the camp.

Letting go of Beth's hand, Pierce turned and walked away. She hurried after him and fell into step beside him. He seemed to be heading for a place downstream. In the midst of God's creation — soft green grass, low-flying birds, and the scent of honeysuckle filling the air — worry and pain went missing there.

"Don't you have something better to do?"

Taken aback by his curt question, she momentarily lagged behind. She knew he would need privacy. Men didn't openly grieve if they could prevent it. Yet she longed to comfort him.

Still trailing behind him, she tried to match his long strides. Angry strides. And why wouldn't he be angry? He'd fought for the Union and risked his life to preserve the North's beliefs, only to find out that Union soldiers had slaughtered his family. The thought would make anyone mad.

They approached a peaceful clearing, and Pierce paused. She caught up, standing still as a mouse, not sure what to say to him.

"Pierce," she said softly after a few moments. She wanted to comfort him, but she didn't know how to grieve herself. She'd loved Ma and Pa and their death had hurt, but she was able to go on, and that was when she didn't even believe there might be a God to console — not then. Maybe not even now, but the past few days she'd run into a whole lot of people who put stock in the claim of a higher source. She'd plied Sister Mary Margaret with questions and the nun hadn't been put off by her doubts. Rather, she seemed to welcome the conversations, offering kindness right alongside her wisdom. It came easier now to believe

288

there could be a God, a God who actually cared about people. About her. She might not have paradise here on earth, but according to Sister Mary Margaret, life was a short journey on the way to an eternal place, where there would be no more sorrow, death, or suffering.

She clung to the thought as she wrapped her hands around the captain's arm. "If you want to cry, I'll understand."

A muscle worked in his jaw. "I don't want to cry. I want to shoot someone."

Beth stepped back, her hands dropping away from him.

"I said I want to shoot someone." He turned to face her. "And that makes me real mad, Beth."

"Why? I thought you wanted peace. You said you're weary of war —"

"That's what I want," he interrupted. "Deep down that's what I want, but right now . . ." His face turned red, and he sat down roughly and raked his hands through his hair.

Grief was making him talk crazy. "I understand," she soothed. "When a person's had all they can take, they want to reach out and hurt someone. I know that feelin' well."

"You don't understand."

"I do." She paused and their eyes locked.

"I understand hatred."

"Beth."

"Please." She took a hesitant step toward him. "At first I was afraid of you — even despised you — but you have proven to be a . . . a decent man."

It surprised her to realize that sometime in these past hectic days his friendship, and his feelings, had become important to her.

For the first time in her life she liked a man. A man who had lost everything important to him.

Reaching out, he drew her down to him and held her tightly. She rested against the solid wall of muscle, her head tucked under his chin, grieving with him. After a long while, she blinked. "Pierce."

"What."

"What . . . are we doing?"

"We're thinking. In silence."

"But —"

His hold tightened. "Complete silence."

So they thought. In silence. For an extra long time it seemed. Beth wound her arms around him, hugging him and praying, *God, help him to be able to endure this loss.*

Eventually, his hold loosened and he held her away from his chest, facing her. "Beth."

"Yes?" She gazed into his eyes, eyes she could drown in if he permitted.

"Thank you for your compassion."

Nodding, she said softly, "I'm so sorry about your family."

"So am I, but not for the same reasons."

Her head tilted questioningly.

"I don't have a sister, Beth."

Her features crumpled. "Oh, Pierce. I know how you feel. If I lost Joanie —"

"No." He put a finger under her chin and made her look at him. "I don't *have* a sister. I never did. That man was lying."

A soft gasp escaped her. "Lying!"

"Lying. Someone must have paid him to ride in here and feed me a wild story. Walt's or Bear's work, no doubt."

"How could they be so low?" She knew the answer before the words came out of her mouth. Neither man was known for integrity.

"They want us to ride away and leave you and Joanie here."

Beth was still trying to digest the news that the man had lied. He'd been *so* convincing. "That's . . . awful." Her temper surfaced as realization fell. "That's deplorable! And so like Uncle Walt."

She was going to get up and march away when he caught her arm. "Hold on. Where do you think you're going?"

"To find Uncle Walt and Bear and put a

stop to this right now!"

The steel band clamped tighter. "No, you're not."

"I am! He can't do this to good people. I . . . I won't permit it."

"What are you going to do? Surrender to him?"

The notion stopped her cold.

"Think about it, Beth. If you play into his hands, you'll be giving away everything you've worked for — your self-respect and your sister's health. Not to mention the deed to the plantation." His eyes met hers. "Are you willing to do that?"

"No. I can't surrender." They had come too far and risked too much. Joanie was getting better every day. Beth didn't know if prayer was doing the job or if it was simply being out of a home that brought only pain and misery.

He looked to be deep in thought. She felt terrible. She had brought all this on him.

"Pierce, what else can I do? I can't let Walt destroy innocent lives because of me. I have no other choice but to go with him. He'll let Joanie stay here if I agree to tell him where the deed is hidden. I don't want the plantation. It holds nothing but memories of misery and hurt for Joanie and me. I have my own plot of land if I can ever get there."

Pierce tucked a lock of hair behind her ear and just looked at her thoughtfully.

"I'll do what you want if you'll help me keep Joanie out of Walt's hands."

"What about you?"

Resigned, she sighed. "I guess I've always known that I'd pick Walt's cotton for the rest of my life."

"What about Bear?"

"Walt will make me marry him."

Shaking his head, he put his hat back on his head and stood. He held out his hand to help her up. "Not if I have anything to say about it."

As she took his hand and came to her feet, hope surged — and then just as quickly deflated. "That's the problem. You don't have anything to say about it."

THIRTY-ONE

Late the next morning, Beth packed a lunch for four and went in search of Joanie. She found her in the nursing tent with Trella, whom she embraced warmly. "I've seen so little of you since we arrived!" Beth exclaimed.

"I know, and I'm sorry." Trella glanced at her sleeping daughter, who was lying on a soft pallet near the fire. "Esther takes so much time."

Beth stepped over to admire the child. She'd lost her earlier redness, and now her skin was a lovely, healthy-looking hue. "She looks mighty satisfied."

"She is well fed." Trella smiled at the Indian woman who sat alongside her. "Awinita is like a second mother."

Joanie sat next to the fire, peeling potatoes. "What are you doing here? I thought you were working in Sister Mary Margaret's garden."

"I was earlier, but I thought you might like to have lunch together."

Shaking her head, Joanie said, "Thank you, but I'll stay and visit with Awinita. Did you know her name means 'fawn'?"

Beth smiled. "I didn't. Are you sure you wouldn't like to go? I packed your favorites. Cold fried squirrel and fresh berries."

Her sister laid a potato in a bowl. "I'm sure."

Shrugging, Beth said, "All right. I'll tell Gray Eagle you sent greetings."

Joanie scrambled to her feet. "Gray Eagle?"

Wearing her most innocent look, Beth said, "Why, yes. I'm taking lunch to Gray Eagle and Pierce."

"I'll go."

Where did my resolve to keep the two apart go? Beth wondered. She not only was encouraging the attraction, she was actually feeding it. Yet she knew why her reservations about Gray Eagle failed to hold. She'd seen the gentle care he had for Joanie. Always kind, comforting. Every day he and Joanie went for a walk, and every day her health improved. She still coughed a little, but not the wracking spasms that seemed as though they would tear her body apart. His company did Joanie a world of good, and

Beth couldn't begrudge her sister's happiness.

Together they walked downstream to where Pierce and Gray Eagle were working. Rebuilding the village structures from the fire four days ago was in full swing in the bright weather. When Pierce glanced up and spotted the two sisters, he grinned.

Waving, Beth motioned to the loaded basket.

The men approached, their bodies glistening with sweat. Slipping on his shirt, Pierce eyed the packed basket hungrily. "What have we here?"

Gray Eagle sought Joanie's eyes. "Hello, Joanie Jornigan."

"Good afternoon, Gray Eagle." Both had shy smiles for the other.

Beth spread a blanket on the ground in the shade, and then she set out lunch, painfully conscious of Pierce's presence and how much she enjoyed his company. Over the last few days, it was beginning to make sense to her why some women felt that they needed a man in their lives. If all men were like Pierce and Gray Eagle, the world wouldn't be so bad. But fanciful thoughts about the captain and scout were useless. Even if Gray Eagle could overlook Joanie's illness, and Pierce was a different kind of a man than she'd ever encountered in her life, the handsome diversions would eventually be on their away.

Pierce blessed the food and they begin to eat. Beth's mind strayed to her earlier prayers. Evidently God didn't intend to release her or Joanie from Walt. Perhaps she'd been right all along about Him and her doubts about His existence were justified. Yet she hoped He had heard her pleas. What if she'd really listened when Joanie read the Bible to her aloud in the secrecy of their loft on moonlit nights? Clearing her throat, she asked, "May I ask a question?"

Pierce reached for a piece of flat bread. "Shoot."

"It's about prayer."

Smiling, Pierce folded the bread in half and took a bite. Then he asked, "Are you still worrying about the proper way to pray?"

Joanie glanced up. "You are?" She broke into a wide grin. "You're actually thinking about prayer?"

"Thinking of how to pray *properly,*" Beth clarified, worried that Joanie would get her hopes up that she might become someone half as knowledgeable as her sister.

Joanie's face softened. "I've prayed so long for this moment, Beth."

"I've been doing a lot of thinking. And

I'm considering the matter."

Nodding, Joanie's face sobered and she said softly, "You feel the weight as well?"

Joanie felt guilty too? Beth slowly nodded. "Something awful. It was wrong of us, Joanie. We shouldn't have done it."

Gray Eagle rolled to his side and dropped a strawberry in his mouth. His expression said he had no idea what they were talking about, but Beth didn't care. She needed to get this out.

"I never dreamt that burning the shanty would also set the cotton fields on fire. That mean act has made me feel . . . so bad and shameful," Joanie admitted. "We must have put many friends out of work."

Choking on his food, Gray Eagle sat up. When it appeared that he couldn't dislodge the berry from his throat, Beth reached over and whacked his back. His coughing eased.

"Are you okay?" Joanie asked.

"Fine." He rubbed moisture from his eyes. "What did you say?"

"Are you okay?"

"Before that."

Joanie's features turned curious. Beth supplied the answer. "You said we most likely put many friends out of work."

Joanie's hand came to her mouth. "I did?"

Pierce reached for another slice of bread.

"Don't worry about it, Joanie. Beth told me about the intent to only burn the shanty. The fields were just an unfortunate result of that."

"Beth!" Joanie exclaimed.

Beth's cheeks flushed with heat. "I did. I'm sorry." She shot the captain a censuring look. Of course he would tell on her.

"Nobody here is going to say anything to Walt." He flashed a grin. "He had it coming." Pierce stuffed another piece of bread into his mouth.

"You deliberately burnt your home?" Gray Eagle's frown deepened and he turned to Joanie. "Why haven't you said anything to me about this?"

"I . . . I've wanted to, Gray Eagle, but . . . I'm so ashamed of what we did. It was a horrible thing to do." She started crying.

Gray Eagle turned to Beth. "Why would you do that?"

Briefly Beth explained the plan. "We waited all day to leave, but Pa didn't pass until almost the next morning. After we dug a grave and buried him, we closed the shanty door and then burned it. It was mostly pure meanness on our part, but I swear I didn't intend to set the cotton field ablaze."

Gray Eagle shook his head. "You really

are a hazard with fire. You know that, don't you?"

"She didn't mean to burn the cotton field. Or the village," Pierce said, coming to her defense.

"Go on," Gray Eagle said, his eyes focused on Joanie.

"There seemed no other way," Joanie said, wiping her cheeks of tears. "We had to leave, and we figured if Walt spotted the blaze it would occupy his time long enough for us to escape. He would have whipped us if he'd caught us trying to get away."

"And the day your pa died you made your break."

Joanie's eyes darted to Beth. "Yes. We had to."

Beth choked on a bite of meat. Clearing her throat, she met Joanie's eyes. "I confess — it was my idea. Now I see that we have wasted a lot of time and energy, and we'll still be in Walt's hands."

"About this deed your pa hid —" Pierce began.

A soft gasp escaped Joanie. "You told him about the deed *too*?"

"I did." The fact that she'd tell a man anything didn't make a lick of sense even to Beth, but since the fire she hadn't been thinking straight.

"I don't know what she's told you, but it's probably not true," Joanie said.

"Joanie!"

"Well! I think we can trust him, Beth." Her gaze swung to Gray Eagle. "And him too."

Gray Eagle frowned. "Now I'm *him?*"

Color crawled up Joanie's neck. "Sorry. You're more than just *him.*" She reached out and took his hand. "Much more than that."

Eyeing the show of affection, Beth said, "All right. The deed isn't in the third cave. It's in the fifth one."

"This is your way of speaking the truth?" Gray Eagle asked.

"I'm sorry. I really can't decide if you're trustworthy."

"We've delayed our return home. We're rebuilding the homes *you* destroyed. We remain to this day to protect you. What exactly will it take to gain your trust, Beth Jornigan?"

"She trusts us. She just doesn't want to admit it." Pierce leaned back and ate a strawberry. "Would you tell me the truth if I asked why your pa has the deed and Walt doesn't?"

Joanie glanced at her.

Beth sighed. "This is the truth. When our

301

grandpa passed, Grandma knew what a wretch Walt was, so she entrusted the plantation deed to Pa until Walt could grow out of his mean streak. She knew that when she died, if Walt had the deed he'd cut Pa out of the land forever."

"And she did die," Joanie added. "And Walt's still just as mean."

"Your grandmother was a wise soul," Gray Eagle observed.

"She was," Beth agreed. "I don't know how she and Grandpa could raise such an evil man. Pa was good."

Pierce chose another strawberry and ate it slowly, giving her time to continue.

"I didn't think setting fire to our home would bother me," Beth said, closing her eyes, "but every time I shut my eyes I see the flames . . . smell the smoke." She paused and then opened her eyes. "So, you see, you are keeping company with two criminals."

Pierce glanced at Gray Eagle. "I don't know about you, but these are about the two prettiest outlaws I've ever come across."

Gray Eagle focused on Joanie. "Agreed."

"I don't see how you can make light of what we've done." Beth lifted her gaze to meet Joanie's. "I'm serious, Joanie. If I do ask forgiveness from your God —"

"He's your God too if you so choose." She

squeezed her sister's hand. "Ask anything you want in His name."

"And He'll answer me?"

"He promises to supply your needs, not your desires, Beth, but that's still so very good of Him."

"The point is, I do want to know how to pray properly."

Gray Eagle spoke. "There is no proper way."

That only frustrated Beth more. She sighed. "But everyone I see praying does it a different way. I want to know how to do it so God will hear me."

"Well, in the Bible the Lord says to go into a closet, shut the door, and pray," Joanie said.

"A closet?"

"Among other ways."

Pierce rolled to his side and faced Beth. "I'll tell you what I know about faith and obedience. God often spoke in parables — story illustrations, similar to Gray Eagle's stories from his youth. This is a story my great-grandfather told me when I was very young and spiritual matters confused me. He said that God came to a farmer one day, and the farmer was complaining about bad crops, lack of rain, grasshoppers, and how he wasn't sure he had enough faith to see him through the coming winter. Suddenly, a huge boulder appeared before the man, and God said. 'Do you trust Me?'

" 'I trust You, God. It's the weather, lack of rain, and the grasshoppers I don't trust.'

" 'I'll tell you what I want you to do,' God said. 'See this boulder?'

"The farmer couldn't miss it. It was solid granite and towered above him. 'I see it.'

" 'I want you to come out of your house every morning and push that boulder. Push it with all your strength.'

"Because God gave the command, the farmer did as he was told. Every morning he came out of his house and he pushed. He grunted and strained, and the rock wouldn't move. After months of toil, his body grew lean and his muscles were like iron, but the rock refused to budge.

"Eventually the Lord returned and spoke to the man. 'Have you faithfully pushed the rock?'

" 'I have,' the farmer said. 'But I can't move it even an inch.'

"God smiled. 'I didn't ask you to move it. I only asked that you push.' "

Pierce smiled as he met Beth's thoughtful gaze. "That's all He asks us to do, Beth. Push. You're making God too complicated."

He rolled onto his back again, sighing peacefully.

Just then gunshots shattered the silence.

Springing to their feet, Pierce and Gray Eagle ran toward camp with the women close on their heels.

THIRTY-TWO

"What's all the shooting about?" Pierce shouted as soon as they arrived back at the village.

An elderly warrior indicated up the road, where gunfire still sounded. A bullet zinged past Pierce's ear. Gray Eagle raced on ahead as Pierce pushed Beth and Joanie to the ground just inside the perimeter of the camp. "Stay down!" He didn't want to leave them unprotected, but he had to deal with whatever was going on further up the road. Nothing good, that was for sure. "Stay with your sister," he said to Beth. "Be safe."

Gray Eagle rode up, leading the captain's horse by the reins. Pierce leaped into the saddle, and the two men joined a small group of warriors inside the entry gate.

"What's going on?" Pierce called to the Indians.

"Someone is shooting into the camp."

The riders moved out, and it only took

seconds before they caught sight of the culprits, who by now had stopped shooting. Walt and Bear listed in their saddles, with the younger man drooping over the horn.

Pierce's jaw firmed. "It figures. They're drunk."

"Why do they shoot into our camp and threaten our women and children?" a nearby Cherokee warrior asked.

Pierce turned to Gray Eagle for the proper term. "What is the Cherokee word for idiot?"

He answered in the native tongue.

The Indian's face lit with understanding. Then he looked at the bearded stragglers with disgust before moving away.

"These two aren't going to give up. I might as well see what I can do." Gray Eagle nudged his horse a bit closer.

From their appearance, Walt and Bear — dirty, unshaven, and with matted hair — had continued their search for the Jornigan sisters. Pierce wrinkled his nose as an unmistakable odor wafted toward him. The nuisances were soaked in whiskey fumes.

"Greed." Gray Eagle shook his head. "These two have no concern for anyone but themselves."

Pierce agreed. "We can't hand the women over to them, and we can't move on with our lives while these two roam free." Shifting in the saddle, he studied the distance, letting out a humorless laugh. "My land is somewhere around here. I could be free of this and drinking real coffee — not that harsh chicory stuff we've had over the years — but real coffee each morning. Eating peach pie swimming in heavy cream for dessert at night."

Gray Eagle met the captain's eyes. "They only want Beth and Joanie."

Shrugging, Pierce said, "Well, they will meet their Maker trying to get them out of my hands."

Gray Eagle nodded. "Or mine."

Pierce walked his horse closer to Bear. "Drunk as skunks," he confirmed after he had leaned over to check the now-unconscious man's pulse.

"Don' touch my boy!" Walt slurred.

"This one too." Gray Eagle straightened in the saddle and studied the nearly senseless lout. "How long do you suppose they've known where we are?"

Shaking his head, the captain said, "Hard to say." His features darkened. "You don't think they've been to the abbey?"

Gray Eagle turned his horse. "I'll check on the sisters." He rode off in a cloud of dust.

Pierce stared at the miscreants. It took a lot to rile him, but these two were pushing his limits. Glancing at his sidearm, he realized he could put a stop to their chase right here and now. Shifting in the saddle, he debated with himself and then shook his head. He'd had enough killing. He didn't need two more deaths on his conscience.

Bear and now Walt snored, mouths agape.

Sighing, Pierce caught the bridles of their horses and led them down the road for a while. Far enough away that the drunks wouldn't immediately know where they were when they awoke. Then one by one he hoisted Walt's and Bear's dead weight out of the saddle and dragged them to a thicket, wading through a patch of poison ivy.

He hated the plant as badly as cold winters without a coat, but there was a certain irony that he didn't miss. A smirk tilted the corners of his mouth.

Stepping carefully, he dumped Walt in the itchy weed, and then moved to haul Bear to an even larger bed.

Twenty minutes later, he stood back and surveyed his work. Both men were now in fetal positions, hands and feet secured, in a sizable patch of poison ivy.

The second part had been tricky but worth the effort. He'd located a large beehive, and then with determined finesse, he'd taken out his pocket knife and made a long pole from a hickory stick. He managed to work enough honey from the hive to make a face cream for Beth's uncle and cousin. He'd heard honey was good for the skin. No, wait a minute. Maybe that was milk.

Straightening, he searched the fields. Speaking of milk, too bad a cow wasn't nearby . . .

So what else could he do to strongly hint that they ought to give up and go home?

He worked another ten minutes, smearing thick honey on the snoring men's faces — he even dropped a taste or two on their slack tongues. They twitched and tried to swat his stick away but never woke up.

After wiping his hands on the grass, he picked up the men's firearms, careful to check their clothing for any additional ammunition or weapons.

Overhead, bees buzzed.

Walking back to the road, he stored the guns in his saddlebags. Then he grabbed the reins of the two horses and his mare and turned back to admire his work. If this didn't quench a man's doggedness, he didn't know what would.

His gaze focused on the sleeping men.

310

They were clever enough to shed the ropes once they sobered up, but they would be mighty uncomfortable for a few days. And they'd better have their running boots on. They were going to need them.

Shaking his head, he mounted. Pity some folk had to be so worrisome.

Gray Eagle was back at the camp when Pierce returned. He nodded to the captain. "The nuns are fine. They said they haven't seen Walt and Bear around."

"That's good to know." After seeing to the horses, the men fell into step.

"What did you do with them?" Gray Eagle asked.

"Not much. Walt and Bear were sleeping it off when I left."

"You didn't end the matter?"

"Wasn't in the mood."

Gray Eagle sent Pierce a questioning look.

"Short of killing them," Pierce said, "I don't know what to do. So I tried a little friendly persuasion."

"We can't let them shoot into camp."

"No, we can't. But unless it's self-defense, what can we do?"

The men met questioning gazes as they walked. Beth ran to greet them. "What did you do with them?"

"Gave them a little comeuppance," Pierce said. "Don't worry about them."

Was that appreciation he saw? Affection? *Careful, Montgomery. Those big eyes are getting to you.*

Gray Eagle smiled at Beth. "Where is Joanie?"

"She's on her pallet. The excitement aggravated her cough."

Grim-faced, Gray Eagle excused himself and walked away.

Beth walked along beside Pierce. "What did they do? Walt and Bear?"

Pausing, he turned to face her. "They didn't *do* anything. I believe our lunch was interrupted. I'm starved. Is there anything to eat?"

"Um . . . sure. I'll fix you something."

"Thanks. I'll be back shortly. I want to clean honey off my hands."

"Honey?"

"I'll be back shortly," he said again with a wink. He watched her walk off and wondered if he should have done more to keep Walt and Bear from her and Joanie. He could have ended the matter there and then, but that would mean leaving, and he was getting sort of comfortable in his misery. If the pests rode into camp and demanded Joanie in exchange for Beth's knowledge of

312

where the deed was hidden, he and Gray Eagle would do what needed to be done.

He'd had his fill of the game.

THIRTY-THREE

Joanie opened her eyes and met Gray Eagle's affectionate gaze.

"You are a beautiful woman, Joanie Jornigan."

"I've been thinking about you." She sat upright on her pallet, fussing with her hair "When you didn't come back right away, I started to worry."

The scout sat cross-legged near her bedroll. "I have been chasing — what is the white-man's term? Fools?"

Grinning, Joanie reached for his hand. He had strong, long fingers hardened by the elements. She drew his right hand to her nose and breathed deeply of his scent. "Fool is an unflattering term."

"I can think of nothing pleasing to say about your uncle and cousin."

She started to reply when she was seized by a wracking cough.

His face darkened. "The cough has returned?"

With a sigh she held tightly to his hand and summoned a sense of humor. "Gunshots tend to make it worse." She smiled. "I'm okay. Really I am."

"It is time for our walk."

Joanie laughed when he stood and scooped her up into his powerful arms.

Her eyes scanned the camp, looking to see if anyone noticed his action. "You're making a scene." His strength easily held her slight weight.

"So I am." Carrying her straight through the camp, he acknowledged curious eyes with an English greeting. "Good afternoon. Lovely weather."

Mouths dropped open. Women smiled shyly behind their hands. Gray Eagle didn't seem to care one bit. He walked proudly, as if proclaiming his love in the action. Joanie gazed at his face adoringly. *Do I love you too?* The answer came before she had a chance to finish the thought.

Joanie's breath caught when Gray Eagle waded into the pools of bubbling water and gently lowered her into heavenly relief. Closing her eyes, she lay quietly and allowed the heat to ease her aches. The vapors opened her head and lungs, and the cough and wheezing gradually subsided.

"Better?" he asked after a good half hour. Concern filled his voice. His compassion made her light-headed with emotion. She had fallen in love with this quiet man — this man who was far kinder and more handsome than any man she had ever read or dreamed about. His touch brought goose bumps. The intensity of his dark eyes was as sweet and rich as thick molasses. *Beth.* She couldn't allow Beth to know the depths of her feelings for him. She would never approve the relationship. If eyes could speak, his would whisper that he also felt the growing bond.

Slipping away from her, he floated on his back in the water, smiling. "I know now why these springs are so revered."

"Heaven must be a little like this," she mused.

He smiled. "Yes. I believe it must be."

"Gray Eagle."

"Hmm?"

"Tell me a story." The children's eyes had lit with excitement when Gray Eagle had spoken to them the other night. His deep voice had carried through the camp, sweeping the listeners away as he told the owl legend.

"Wouldn't you rather relax?" His drowsy tone indicated his preference — to simply enjoy the water.

"I understand if you're too tired, but I love to hear your stories. You had everyone enthralled with your tale of the owl and rabbit."

Paddling back to her, he settled on the shallow pool's bottom. "They are not my stories. They are the stories of my ancestors."

"But you chose the white way."

"I chose both ways," he confessed. "The legends and stories are part of my heritage, as well as the Bible."

She reached to lightly trace the outline of his rugged features. "Tell me a story of your youth."

Grinning, his gaze locked with hers. "You know how to direct my thoughts."

Smiling back, she whispered, "I'm very devious."

His eyes sobered. "You are so beautiful. Like a firefly, lighting my life. You rest lightly on my heart."

Color tinged her cheeks. "That's the nicest thing anyone's ever said to me."

He moved closer, hovering so near that she could feel the heat of his breath against her cheek. "May I kiss you, Joanie Jornigan?"

She had never been kissed before. Her

heart skipped one, two beats, and she nodded. "After the story."

Chuckling, he settled on one elbow, his
gaze locked with hers. "What kind of story
would you like to hear?"

"I don't know. Is there one about creation?"

"Genesis."

Grinning, she settled back. "I'm familiar
with that one. What is the Cherokee belief?"

"Far too complicated to explain in one
sitting, but there are legends . . ." He eased
closer again. Steam rose above their heads.
"I will tell you a legend my father told me
many times."

Joanie smiled and lightly touched his
cheek.

He closed his eyes. When he opened them,
he began.

"Earth is floating on water like a big
island, suspended from four rawhide ropes
fastened at the top of the sacred four directions —"

"Sacred?"

"Shh . . . do not interrupt. This is my
legend," he teased more than scolded, and
then he continued. "The sky's ceiling is
made of hard rock crystal, and this is where
the ropes are tied. When the ropes break,
earth will come tumbling down and all liv-

ing things will fall with it. Then it will be as if the earth had never existed, for water will cover it. Maybe the white man will be responsible for this act."

When she was about to ask a question, he shushed her again with a finger to her lips. "Legend says that in the beginning, water covered everything. Though living creatures existed, their home was up there, above the rainbow, and it was crowded.

" 'We have no space. We need more room,' the animals said. So after a while they formed a plan and sent Water Beetle to look around.

"Water Beetle searched the waters for days but couldn't find any solid footing, so one afternoon he dived to the bottom and surfaced with a little dab of soft mud. Suddenly the mud spread out in four directions and formed this earth. Someone Powerful then fastened earth to the sky ceiling with ropes.

"The earth was flat, soft, and moist back then, and the animals were eager to live on it. They continued to send down various birds to see if the mud had dried and hardened enough to hold their weight. But the birds always came back to heaven and said that there was no place to land. They must wait longer.

319

"Grandfather Buzzard decided to go down and take a look for himself. Flying very close to the ground, he saw that the earth was still soft, but then he swooped lower over what would become Cherokee country, and he discovered that the mud was getting harder. By that time Grandfather was tired and spent. When he flapped his wings, they created a basin where the tips touched the earth and mountains in between.

"The animals watched from above the rainbow with amazement. Mother Blue Jay said, 'If he keeps on, there will only be mountains!'

" 'Come back,' the birds called. 'Come back!' "

He smiled. "That's why there are so many mountains on Cherokee land."

"Gray Eagle . . ."

"Shh. There is more. Grandfather Buzzard flew back and told them of his amazing find. At last the earth was getting dry, so the animals descended. They couldn't see very well because there was no sun or moon to light their way, and so someone said, 'Let's get Sun from behind the rainbow!'

"The animals used all of their might and pulled Sun down.

"Mr. Fox said, 'Here's a road for you to

follow.' He showed Sun the way to go . . . from east to west because Mr. Fox was very wise.

"Now the animals had light, but it was much too hot. Sun was too close to the earth. The Crawfish's back stuck out of a stream, and Sun burned it red. His meat was spoiled forever, they thought.

"Together the animals pushed Sun up as high as a man, but the burning light was still too hot. So they pushed Sun farther, but it wasn't far enough. After four times, they managed to get Sun up to the height of four men. Everyone agreed it was the best they could do, so they left him there."

Joanie couldn't keep quiet. "What about humans? Wasn't it too hot for them?"

"Ah . . . before making humans, the Indians say that Someone Powerful created plants and animals and commanded them to stay awake and watch for seven days and seven nights. Our young men still do this today when they fast and prepare for a ceremony, but legend says that most of the plants and animals couldn't do this. Some fell asleep after one day, some after two days.

"Only the cedar, pine, holly, and laurel were still awake on the eighth morning, and Someone Powerful said to them, 'Because you were vigilant and stayed awake as you had been told, you will not lose your hair in the winter.' So these plants stay green all year.

"Once Someone Powerful created plants and animals, He made man and his sister. The man poked her with a fish and told her to give birth. After seven days she had a baby. And after seven more days she had another and every seven days the family grew to be many. The humans increased so rapidly that Someone Powerful began to wonder if soon there would not be enough room on this earth for everyone, so He changed plans. From that moment on, a woman could have only one child every year. And that's how it was."

Settling into his arms, Joanie considered the legend. "It's a lovely story."

"It is said there is another world beneath us."

"And how would one reach this other world?"

"You can only get there by going down a spring or a water hole, but you need underwater people to guide you."

"And what is this world like?"

"Exactly like ours, except that it's winter down there when it's summer up here."

He placed a hand on her shoulder as a glint filled his eyes. "Would you like to visit this world?" He pushed gently, as if to dunk her.

Squealing, she held tightly to him. "No!"

"Ah. Another day perhaps." He sobered and drew her back into his embrace. "I have told your story, Joanie Jornigan." He gently tilted her face to meet his. "And now I claim my reward." Slowly he lowered his mouth to touch hers. He tasted salty and sweet, like summer air and water. His touch sent waves of warmth rippling up Joanie's back.

The white man had his belief about this exhilarated glow that now coiled around her in a soft blanket of bliss. It was called love.

Thirty-Four

Beth paced beside her pallet. Joanie was off again with Gray Eagle, and the camp was quiet. Secretly, Pierce's plan to force Uncle Walt's hand scared the wits out of her, but she'd do anything to get this "war" over. She paused, noting her own reflection in the wavy-glassed mirror tacked to the lodge wall. Bending closer, she traced small lines around her eyes. She'd never been one to primp or even consider her looks, but lately she had a nagging desire for a pot of rouge or a touch of rose water to dab on her skin behind her ears.

At least a good scrubbing with scented soap and clean towels.

Irrational, Beth, her image whispered. *You've been filled with nothing but fanciful thoughts since the captain rescued you. No matter how kind he is, he would never want a work-worn girl like you. All you can offer him is trouble.*

Standing on tiptoes now, she smoothed tired lines with her fingertips. Would he notice her in her clean dress and the new yellow hair ribbon? The latter was a gift from Sister Mary Margaret for all her help in the garden. Preach had mentioned Pierce might have a girl waiting for him at home — how serious were they? Was this someone expecting to marry him, live on his land, and have his babies?

Is that what I want? The thing Beth once found insufferable didn't seem so bad at the moment, not when Pierce was the man she envisioned. He was gentle yet strong. Caring yet solid. Handsome but not pretty. He was rugged. He was tough as nails and soft as warm spring air when he wanted to be.

If a woman was looking for a husband, the captain would certainly exceed most expectations. After wearing trousers for several days, her dress was giving her funny feelings. She felt more feminine in it than she did in boy's clothing. She wasn't sure she was comfortable with that.

Beth stared at her image in the glass. Had Ma once looked at Pa the way she looked at Pierce? Sniffing the air, she half turned when she caught the brief scent of smoke. Eyes scanning the area she decided the smell must have drifted from a neighboring fire. Turning back to the mirror, she evaluated her features, examining her profile. Nothing unusual, yet nothing outstanding, either.

Switching positions, she lifted her nose and studied the opposite side of her face. It was a good thing she wasn't in the market for a husband.

Striding through the camp, Pierce spotted Beth staring in the mirror just inside the open door to her lodge. His footfalls paused, and he grinned when he caught her assessing her looks. He didn't figure her as the fussy kind, but then didn't every woman want to look her best? Leaning against a tree, he crossed his arms and watched her as she turned one way and then the other. She was mighty fetching in that yellow dress, with her golden hair hanging to her waist. It was loose again today. He tried to imagine her in a satin ball gown and slippers, waltzing beneath a crystal chandelier.

He shifted stances.

Most men would find her feisty nature aggravating. He found it likeable.

Shaking the thought clear, Pierce realized he'd been without a woman's company for too long. Beth came with a lot of complications — namely Uncle Walt and Bear. If Pierce was around either man any length of time he'd have to shoot him, and there would go his dream of a peaceful life. Shifting, his gaze caught a tiny wisp of smoke lightly drifting from the hem of her dress.

Immediately his arms dropped to his sides and his boots started to move.

Humming under her breath, Beth stepped away from the mirror, the words of the song she'd heard Joanie singing so often escaping her. "In the sweet by and by —"

Ooofff! The air left her lungs as someone pounced on her, knocking her to the ground. With a yelp, Beth grabbed hold of the beast's hair and yanked. "Let me go!" she shrieked.

"Hold still!"

"Pierce? Get . . . off . . . me . . . you . . . big . . . oaf!" What on earth had come over him? Some evil spirit?

"Your dress is on fire!"

"My — *what?*"

"Your dress is on *fire!*"

Stilling, Beth tried to catch her breath. The stench of scorched cotton filled her nose. "Oh no!" She gazed down at the smoke rising from her feet, and then her gaze switched to the fire pit burning low.

No wonder she'd felt so hot.

Pierce shook free of her grasp and took the rug he'd grabbed from a line and finished beating out the flames.

Glancing at her blackened clothes, she held back a scream. Her one dress, ruined.

Her eyes turned to Pierce, who was making sure the flames were extinguished. What was it with her and fire? The man must think she was a lunatic!

Grabbing her hand, he hauled her to her feet and made for the entrance. As they burst out of the smoky lodge, she realized the whole camp had gathered around them.

The children had dropped sticks in the dirt and run to watch the ruckus of the captain and Beth rolling on the ground. Preach stood to the side with his arms crossed over his thick chest and a grin planted on his dark face.

"Are you both all right?" he asked cheerfully.

Now that Beth was safe, Pierce went back inside to make sure no smoldering embers were outside the fire pit. He called over his shoulder, "Preach, check her to see if she's burnt."

Beth waved Preach's attention aside. Other than her pride, she wasn't hurt. Curious eyes peered at her. Clearly, the captain wasn't the only one who thought she had a fire fetish.

Gray Eagle and Joanie were walking into camp. When Joanie spotted the spectacle, she ran to help. Bending beside Beth's still-smoking skirt, she cradled her sister's heaving chest. "Goodness' sake. What's happened?"

The cough was gone this morning. After every one of Gray Eagle and Joanie's walks, Beth noticed, Joanie was visibly better. And wet.

Where did they go on these mysterious strolls? What occurred when they were there that would cause her life-long ailment to simply evaporate? Even more puzzling, why did Joanie refuse to tell her where they went?

"I'm not hurt." Beth pushed away Joanie's soothing hands. Smoothing her hair, she said quietly, "I'll get your dinner."

Pierce came back to stand beside her, grinning, and then he motioned for the crowd to disperse.

She could feel his laughing eyes on her back when she walked inside. She'd been so preoccupied with her appearance that she'd stepped too close to the fire and caught the hem of her dress aflame. Heat filled her cheeks. The man would think she was completely daft. Totally daft.

Turning, she tossed over her shoulder, "I wasn't minding what I was doing."

"I figured as much." His grin widened. A bit of black ash fell from her hem.

She would do better to keep quiet and allow the humiliating moment to pass. Yes, that was the only sensible course.

"Want me to hide the matches?" Pierce called.

"That won't be necessary." *Want me to hide the matches,* she mouthed, mimicking.

She should have known he'd show his man side.

Thirty-Five

"Sister Mary Margaret?"

The nun paused in her work, glancing up. Beside her a pile of weeds lay upended. "Yes, Beth?" From her kneeling position on the ground she gave her young friend a quick smile.

When Beth lifted her face, she realized the nun was studying her. She cleared her throat.

"What did you want to know, my dear?"

Beth sat down alongside her. Though the nun's hands were covered in dirt, a wedding band was still visible on her left hand.

"Have you ever been in love?"

The sister gave her a puzzled look. "With Christ . . . but I suspect that's not what you mean."

"No, I mean the earthly kind."

The sister smiled to herself and pulled up another weed as she weighed her answer. "Once, when I was young, there was this boy in our church." Mary Margaret sat back on her heels, lost in thought. "His name was Fred. He brought me a peppermint stick every Sunday morning. We planned to marry someday."

"Really?" Beth glanced over. "What happened?"

"He fell from his barn loft. He was helping his father put up hay for winter." The sister's usually cheery voice grew tender. "His mother found him when she came in from milking. The good Lord took him quickly." With a sigh the sister went back to work. "I decided then that God would be the love of my life. I joined the convent when I was sixteen and took my final vows two years later."

Beth tried to imagine the stout, rotund woman with laughing eyes as a wife and a mother. She would have been a good one, so caring and kind.

"Why do you ask?"

Beth started, returning to the present. She paused before answering. "I never thought I would marry or have children."

"Have you changed your mind?"

"No." Her eyes rested on Pierce and Preach, who were working on a large tree across the meadow from the garden. The woodpile grew larger every day. "But I think

I am starting to change my mind about men in general."

"Explain," the nun said, jerking a tenacious weed from the ground and adding it to her pile.

Smiling, Beth wondered what Mary Margaret had done for excitement before the Jornigan sisters came around. "Pierce, Gray Eagle, and Preach have shown me that not all men are bad. Some are quite . . . admirable."

Laughing, Mary Margaret straightened and shaded her eyes against the hot sun. "I should say so. Those three are the most pleasant men I've ever met." Then she whispered, "I think Gray Eagle is sweet on Joanie. And if I'm not mistaken, Preach seems to have taken a fierce liking to Trella and Esther."

Beth thought of all the good things that had happened since they had fled the shanty ten days ago. She'd met Mary Margaret. She'd come to appreciate the Cherokee and their kind ways. And truth be told, she was falling for the captain, though she dare not let anyone — even Joanie — know her thoughts. God had opened her eyes to many things during this brief time. To His love. To Pierce. To men in general. Right now she felt as though she could stay here forever in this peaceful world, but deep down she knew her past still waited for her. Walt and Bear. The inevitable showdown was bound to come soon, and then all of this would be over. She thought of her former plan to locate her land and start a new life. While that thought had once excited her, she now dreaded this blissful time coming to end.

"Oh my goodness." Sister Mary Margaret's hands paused. "I've been meaning to tell you something for days. My memory — it flitters away like a hummingbird. We found your Bible."

"You did!" Beth's heart leaped with joy. Joanie would be thrilled. And she would have the deed to her land again. What wonderful news. "Where? We thought we'd lost it somewhere on the trail."

"Not at all. Sister Helen found it when she was cleaning. It's been safe in the library where you left it that morning. I'll bring it tomorrow."

"Thank you." Beth's grin widened. "This has been the most perfect day."

"Yes," Mary Margaret said, laughing. "God gives us joy in small measure." She grinned. "If He didn't, we wouldn't be able to take it all in."

THIRTY-SIX

Bright stars twinkled overhead when Beth was caught up with the flow of Indians who moved to the council lodge Saturday just after sundown. All day an air of expectancy had hung over the camp. Beth wasn't sure what was happening, but apparently the Cherokee were preparing for a celebration. The camp had been alive with preparations in anticipation of the event.

Pierce wandered into the large room, and his eyes located the open spot beside Beth. Settling on the blanket next to her, he answered her unspoken question. "I believe we're about to witness a wedding."

Embarrassed, Beth glanced down at her beat-up dress.

Chuckling, the captain said quietly, "We are fortunate to be allowed to attend this event. The bride is the chief's granddaughter. She and the groom have traveled far in order for the chief to perform the ceremony." His gaze skimmed her and rested on her face. "You look very pretty, blistered dress and all."

"You're too kind."

Her eyes traced Joanie and Gray Eagle seated in the front row. They looked for all the world like a couple. The picture nagged at Beth. Soon she and Joanie would be moving on and Gray Eagle would be gone. Didn't Joanie understand that this brief interlude was only that? Brief. She halted her thoughts as the wedding couple approached the council fire. Beth's breath caught with the bride's beauty. Her eyes rested on the simple white embroidered deerskin dress and white doeskin moccasins. She carried a matching bag. The groom wore a rose-colored shirt, black pants, and moccasins.

Beth recalled the afternoon's hectic activities. Women had torn pieces of fabric into squares and rectangles. She now indentified those pieces as part of the wedding attire — the couple was also wrapped in blankets.

Leaning toward Pierce, she whispered, "Why blankets?" Outside, the air was suffocating.

"The blankets represent their old ways: weakness, sorrow, failures, and spiritual depression."

Beth's eyes focused on the two older couples who accompanied the bride and groom to the fire. She assumed they must be the parents.

She recognized the "holy man" when he stepped to the fire and blessed the union in a deep baritone. The ceremony was elaborate, and Beth didn't understand a word the chief said, but the affection that shone through the bride's and groom's eyes was evident.

Beth's eyes moved again to her sister, and she noted that Joanie was clasping Gray Eagle's hand. She frowned. What were they thinking? Displaying their affection so freely would only cause trouble.

Shifting back to the wedding couple, she saw that they were now exchanging woven baskets. The groom's contained meat and skins.

Pierce spoke close to her ear. "His gift signifies his promise to feed and clothe her."

The bride accepted the basket and then offered hers. Bread and corn.

"Her offering represents her promise to nurture and support him."

The simple beauty unfolding before her left Beth breathless. Nodding, she silently reached for Pierce's hand. The gesture was unlike anything she'd ever done. His strong fingers closed tightly around hers as the couple shed their blankets and relatives approached wrapping them in white ones.

Pierce said softly, "The white blanket signifies their new way of happiness, fulfillment, and peace."

Beth turned her head to look at him, and the captain's eyes locked with hers mere inches away. In that intimate moment, Beth felt her waning doubts melt like spring snow.

Doubts regarding men and God. She had seen her sister's faith lived out day in and day out. Even when she failed, Joanie believed God loved and accepted her. She had been crushed under Walt's abuse as well as the curse of a weak body, but she had never lost hope. And now look at her. Not only had God answered her prayers, He had given her the deepest desires of her heart. Years of Joanie's teachings and Bible readings suddenly made sense to Beth.

You are there, God. You really are.

Dancers appeared in brightly colored dress, pulling her attention away from her thoughts and back to the ceremony. They stomped and whooped and chanted. Soon a prayer was issued unlike any prayer Beth had ever heard before. Not on bended knees or privately in a closet. And there were no beautiful beads. Only the holy man saying a prayer of blessing to end the ceremony.

Leaving the tent a little while later, Beth discovered she was again holding Pierce's hand. On the walk back to their pallets, they shared a companionable silence.

Finally she said, "The ceremony was beautiful."

She had only ever seen one other wedding. It was for one of the pickers, but the couple had looked more trapped than anything else. The couple tonight seemed meant to be together.

"It was. They appeared to be deeply in love." He squeezed her hand as he glanced at her. "Sorry about tackling you to the ground this morning —"

"Actually, I should thank you — I need to thank you. You couldn't let me go up in flames." They met each other's eyes in the moonlight, and Beth's heartbeat sped up. A silver glow outlined his strong profile. He looked so handsome.

"No. I couldn't do that."

Two hours ago Beth would have considered the term "deeply in love" laughable. But tonight, after witnessing the beginning of a new family, the words made sense. They were enviable — and scary. The recognition that God was indeed there had shaken her. Tonight, when she prayed, she would tell the Lord that He could now truly claim her as one of His own, but if Beth were truthful, she knew she'd always been His child. True, a wayward one who needed an extra guiding hand, supplied by Joanie and Mary Margaret, but a child nonetheless.

Captain Montgomery didn't speak often of spiritual matters, but Beth saw the way he treated people, how he observed God's commandments. He had to know God to share the story he'd told the day of the picnic. *Push the rock, Beth. You don't have to move it.*

Stars winked overhead. A soft, honeysuckle-scented wind blew. Joanie had spoken once of the Garden of Eden. Surely it must look and feel something like this. God was easily discernible once she looked for Him.

Approaching the lodge she shared with Joanie, Beth's pulse quickened. They stopped walking and Pierce moved closer, his gaze on her lips. He was going to kiss her again. The knowledge was as real as the sound of laughter and the joy permeating the camp. She'd only been kissed by another boy once, and that was a stolen peck behind a row of tomatoes when she was fourteen. The attempt had been more childish silliness than romantic, and she never liked the boy anyway, but a man's kiss . . . one from this man . . . Her mouth went dry. He leaned forward and she closed her eyes when the sound of hoofbeats filled her ears.

They moved apart and turned toward the approaching rider. "Who would be visiting at this late hour?" Beth sensed that the visitor was friend. A call from a scout would have gone out if it were otherwise.

The horse and rider came into view, escorted by a young Indian. Beth's heart lodged in her throat when she recognized Reverend Mother. There was no good reason for her to come hurrying into camp at this late hour. Something was wrong! Dropping Pierce's hand, she raced to the horse. "Reverend Mother? Is someone ill?"

The nun met Beth's and then Pierce's eyes. "I hesitate to disturb you, Captain, but can you come back to the abbey with me?" She looked at Beth again. "You too, child."

"What is it?"

Reverend Mother averted her eyes. "I can't say here, but I would deeply appreciate your coming."

Glancing at Beth, Pierce said, "I'll get my horse." He turned and strode off.

Beth drew closer to the nun. "What's wrong? Is someone ill?" The sight of blood didn't bother her, and she'd wrapped many

341

a nasty-looking injury. She wanted to help if she could.

Despite the offer Reverend Mother's stern expression remained firmly in place. The sobriety in her expression chilled Beth. She stared at her, suddenly wondering if the emergency were somehow connected to her. But how could that be?

A few moments later Pierce galloped up astride his horse. "We'll follow you."

Nodding, Reverend Mother turned her mare and the animal moved off.

Pierce offered Beth a hand. He swung her up behind him. Then the sounds of his horse's hooves filled the air as they hurried after Reverend Mother.

Moonlight filtered through the sugar maples as the horses made for the abbey. Visions of the kindhearted nuns lying sick or incapacitated filled Beth's thoughts. Had they come down with consumption? Once Uncle Walt's slaves had suffered with something like that, and so many — young and old — died. The horses quickly covered the short distance, and soon they rode into the silent yard. Not a breeze stirred.

Pierce dismounted and turned to help Beth down. Then he stepped over to the aged nun, who was already in the process of tying up her animal. "Allow me, Reverend

Mother."

"Nonsense." Her tone bristled as she glanced nervously at the abbey. "I've been taking care of horses since before you were a babe in swaddling clothes."

Pierce just left her to it, and moments later they strode to the abbey. Reverend Mother was uncommonly silent during the short walk, which further alarmed Beth. Just how sick was everyone? Could she risk carrying the disease to Joanie?

Entering through the kitchen, the three paused at the sight that met them. The sisters sat at the table, wearing white night-dresses. Their hair was mussed, and they all looked half blind. None were wearing their spectacles. Beth searched for Mary Margaret, and her heart thumped in her chest. The bubbly nun looked as scared as a spring jackrabbit, and no wonder.

Standing behind the row of sisters, Uncle Walt and Bear grinned wickedly as they pointed their shotguns at the frightened women.

Beth's heart sank. This was Walt's trap. She whirled to face Reverend Mother, and the nun spoke, "God forgive me. I had no choice."

Beth turned back to assess her uncle and cousin. They were covered in ugly red welts.

"What happened to you?" Pierce asked in a detached, calm voice.

Walt's face screwed into a snarl. "I'll git you for this, Montgomery."

Stepping forward, Pierce said sternly, "Then point those guns at me."

"Don't do it, Pa." Bear's voice was tinged with a whine. "He's a sneaky one." Lifting the stock of the rifle, he scratched a welt on the tip of his nose.

"Gentleman," Pierce said, "this fight's between the three of us. Let the sisters go back to bed so we can settle our differences like men."

Walt's gun lifted now, centering on Pierce's chest. "Let's don't, Montgomery. I'm on to your tricks."

Beth's vision swirled. She couldn't let Uncle Walt and Bear hurt Pierce or these women. They served the Lord and never hurt anybody. She stepped forward too. "It's me you want. Let the sisters go and I'll come with you, Uncle Walt."

"Beth," Pierce warned in a low voice.

"No." She lifted a hand to stop him from saying anything else. "It's the only way, Pierce. I can't involve innocent women in my troubles." She had prepared for this moment. She had agreed to her role when Pierce shared his plan with her. She was the

344

bait, and Walt had just taken it. Her heart thumped like a war drum. Swallowing, she faced her uncle and cousin. "Let the sisters return unharmed to their rooms, and I'll go with you."

Bear glanced at his father. "I don't know, Pa." He rubbed angry red welts. "It could be a trick."

"It's not a trick," Beth assured him. "I promise I'll go with you without a fuss."

A sound like a growl came from Pierce's throat. "No, you won't —"

"Yes, I will. I have to, Pierce. This is my fight."

"It was your fight until I took on the problem myself and let the bees express my anger."

"Yeah." Bear sniffed. "Me and Pa are gonna get you for that, mister." He glanced at his father. "Ain't that right, Pa? Gonna git him real good."

Fear nearly blocked Beth's airway. She tried to find comfort in Piece's words running over and over through her frightened state. *"He'll set his own trap. We'll just spring it."* She hoped he knew what he was doing.

Her calm voice shattered the tense silence. "I'll go with you, Uncle Walt, and I'll take you to the deed."

Walt's head tilted.

Beth smiled. *Come on. Take the bait.*

His thick brow lifted. "You'll take me to the deed?"

"On one condition."

His burly brow furrowed. "I don't bargain. You belong to me, missy. Now git your sister, and we'll be leaving these fine folk alone."

"That's the condition."

"What?" He leaned and spat on the floor. Mary Margaret's eyes widened in disapproval.

"Joanie stays here. Those are my terms."

"Not a chance."

"Come on, Pa." Bear was growing more nervous by the minute. "Let's git the women and hightail it outta here." Bear's beady eyes skimmed the nuns' indignant expressions. "Religion gives me hives."

Walt's black eyes turned to the captain. "We need a couple of fresh horses."

"Well, as much as I hate to admit it, I guess you and your son have us over a barrel. Leave the nuns unharmed, and I'll not stop you taking your nieces," Pierce said, crossing his arms over his chest. "But I need to warn you. Those Jornigan women are a handful."

Walt gave a nod.

"And if you like, I'll ride with you."

346

Walt let out a scoffing laugh as his eyes narrowed. "What do you take me for, Montgomery? A fool? You ain't ridin' with us. You're stayin' put. Got that?"

"Got it."

"Bear here will make sure you stay put." Walt's eyes indicated the shotgun. "Afore we ride out."

"Yasser, Daddy."

Beth glanced to Pierce and then to Walt. "I won't go with you unless Joanie stays where she is."

An angry red flush dotted her uncle's cheeks. "You don't have a say, girl!" he shouted. "I said *both* of you were a'comin'." He lifted the shotgun.

In a firm yet calm voice, Pierce said, "Your niece said she wasn't going with you unless her sister is allowed to remain in camp. She's offering to take you to the deed. What more do you want, Jornigan? The truth is, Joanie's a sickly woman who hasn't got long left on this earth —"

Reverend Mother cleared her throat, halting Pierce's words.

The heavily bearded man scratched, appearing to weigh his options.

"It could be a trick, Pa," Bear warned. "You know this here is a wily bunch."

"No trick," Pierce said. "What interest

would we have in these women? We're just bystanders, caught up in a situation we had no control over nor did we ask for." He turned to face Reverend Mother. "I'm sure the same goes for these women."

Nodding, Mary Margaret piped up and said, "Why would we want trouble?"

Walt's eyes slid from one nun to the next. "That right, Sisters?"

If Beth didn't know better, she'd swear Pierce was stating his true feelings on the matter. Did he care about her? Doubt flared and then it receded when the captain's earlier words flashed through her mind. *Do what they say. Play along. Let them set the trap.*

Walt's gaze focused on Beth. "You sayin' you will take me to the deed if I let Joanie stay here?"

"That's what I'm saying."

"If you lead me astray, Bear will be here to take care of Joanie and these women." He turned back to his son. "Don't ride off until I get back, boy. You hear?"

"I hear, Pa."

Walt's eyes turned to flint. "And you'll not move a muscle."

"But Pa —"

"I said you'll not move a muscle!"

"Yasser," Bear conceded, though none too

348

heartily.

Walt's wild eyes pivoted back to Beth. "That deed is gonna be mine now after all. Yore pa thought he was pulling some big joke on me, hidin' it an' all — well, the joke's on him."

"You know Pa. He was a laugh a minute."

Frowning, Walt motioned to Pierce with the gun barrel. "Get her an animal and let's get started."

Outside, with Walt holding a gun on them, Pierce lifted Beth into the saddle and their eyes met. She read something in their compassionate depths she'd never seen in another person in her whole life. True concern. Love — perhaps?

The idea was so foreign to her that she wasn't sure if that's what she saw. The only certainty in her mind was that she trusted this man with all her heart and soul. Squeezing her hand, he said quietly, for her ears alone, "Take your uncle to the deed like a good niece and then come back to me."

"Take good care of Joanie," she whispered.

"I won't have to. Gray Eagle will."

Gray Eagle would. She took comfort in his calm assurance.

Lifting her head high, she turned her mare

and followed her uncle through the moonlight.

THIRTY-SEVEN

It was still dark when Walt's plantation came into sight. Beth took the lead then and walked her horse past the house and toward the ravine, stopping well away from the edge. Reining up, he spat on the ground and then pinned her with a hard look. "What is this? A joke?"

"No joke. This is where Pa hid the deed."

Was Pierce far behind? Or was he still under Bear's watchful eye? Beth didn't see how Pierce could know that everything would turn out well, but she was determined to play her part as though she knew the ending.

Dismounting and tying off the reins on a nearby tree limb, she turned to face her uncle. "The deed is buried in the fifth cave on the right."

Walt's jaw dropped when his eyes followed hers to the caves. For the first time in her life, Beth witnessed the man's total astonishment. "This ain't funny, Beth."

"No, sir," she agreed. "But like I said, Pa had a sense of humor." Correction: He was downright brilliant.

"Why . . . why . . . the low-down, conniving . . ." He paused and then spat on the ground again, his eyes assessing the deep gorge by the light of the moon. "How did Emmett get to the other side without killing his fool self?"

Beth didn't say anything.

Walt focused his attention again squarely on the ravine. "Girl, if you're lying to me, we're going back, and I will horsewhip Joanie and make you watch." His angry words broke through her silence.

"I'm not misleading you. The deed is in the fifth cave on the right. Pa said it was in plain sight."

Walt snatched off his hat and threw it on the ground. "Of all the . . ."

Beth turned away at the string of oaths pouring from her uncle's mouth. If Mary Margaret were present she would probably pray for him, but Beth felt nothing but revulsion.

They stood, silence settling around them. Now what? She glanced toward the woods, straining to detect any sign that Pierce was nearby. Instinct told her he wouldn't follow that closely. It would take a while to over-come Bear, escape, ride to the planta-tion . . .

What if he doesn't come? What if he mounts up and rides in the opposite direction?

She wouldn't blame him, yet somehow she knew he'd be there for her. Maybe Preach would come with him, but Gray Eagle would never desert Joanie. Her heart longed for the same devotion. How she'd changed. In the brief time that she'd known Captain Montgomery, he'd stolen her heart like a seasoned pickpocket.

Wasn't that just like a man?

"Well?" She asked as the silence stretched between them. "You're not going to cross that ravine, are you?"

Walt focused on the gaping chasm, and she knew he was weighing the matter. "Your pa made the jump?"

"He said he did, but he was lucky. If the rope had slipped or frayed, he would have been at the bottom of the ravine."

"But he made it."

She didn't intend to lie. "He did. He said he did." Her eyes discreetly searched the brush lining the gulch. *Pierce, where are you?* The sounds of night birds were her only answer.

Time stretched. Walt sat on the ground,

deep in thought. Beth saw all sorts of emotions play across his frazzled features. Fear. Logic. Greed. Anger.

Greed won out. "Come daylight, I'm going to make the jump."

"Uncle Walt, I . . . I wouldn't." She detested the man like raw liver, but she couldn't watch him leap to his death without arguing on behalf of sanity.

"Shuddup. That deed will set me up for life."

"Not if you don't *have* a life, which you might not if you attempt that jump."

"I can do anything Emmett did."

"True, but Pa might have had the Lord's blessing."

"Emmett's dead. Hardly seems like one of them there 'blessings' to me."

The party of three rode through the darkness. Bear had proved no match for the Cherokee warriors who had followed behind the nun, Pierce, and Beth. Bear was now secured to a pole in the sweat lodge, whining and crying for his pa. Pierce hoped time spent in the sweltering tent would sweat the meanness out of the headstrong cousin.

Gray Eagle, who was more than willing to support his friend and help rescue Joanie's sister, knew of a back road to the cotton

plantation, so the three men arrived unde-
tected. They now squatted in the thick
undergrowth watching the scene play out
before them. Beth stood back while Walt
knelt, fashioning a thick rope.

"Obviously, he's planning to make the
jump," Pierce whispered.

"He won't make it," Preach predicted.

"Beth's pa did."

"He was lucky," Gray Eagle said.

Sweat rolled from Walt Jornigan's temples
as he stood at the precipice in the morning
light. Wandering over to a rock, Beth sat
down, weariness evident in every line of her
posture. She glanced over when she heard a
faint hissing. Eyes widening, she spotted
Pierce. He was bent, peeking through a
bush, finger to his lips. She almost called
out but caught her response. *He's here! He
came!*

Then he let go of the branch and faded
silently into obscurity.

Walt rummaged in his saddlebag and took
out a lead pencil and a scrap of paper. Sitting down on the ground, he began to write.

Beth couldn't control her curiosity. "What
are you doing?"

"I'm cipherin'." He focused on the task.
"Ever heard of that, girlie? Smart folks don't

355

just leap over ravines. They cipher their moves on paper so's they don't make a mistake. That's what your pa did. He ciphered his move. I'd bet my life on it."

"I don't think Pa knew how to cipher."

"Oh, he was wily. Yes, ma'am. Real wily, and I'd bet cash money he learned how to cipher from your fancy book-learned ma." Walt bit the tip of his tongue and drew. "Now, lemme see. My rope is about sixty-eight feet long. That'll have to be enough for me to make a seventy-foot jump." He glanced up, scratching his chin. "I wish I could measure exactly how far across that is."

Beth didn't know how to cipher, so she couldn't dispute his figures. All she knew was that there was no deed on earth that would make her leap that canyon.

His tongue wedged between his teeth, Walt scribbled. "You're gonna be glad you decided to cooperate with your ol' Uncle Walt. You know that, girl?"

Beth didn't respond, but that didn't stop Walt from going on. "Yes, ma'am. Once I get my hands on that deed, we'll be sitting pretty. Might even share some of my riches with you and Bear once you get hitched."

"I've told you before that I won't marry my cousin. I've heard that terrible things can happen when a person does that."

"Oh, yes you will. You'll do what your uncle tells you. You hear that?"

Beth turned away from the man and the pencil stub feverishly bobbed. "You think I'm a fool," he said.

Beth remained silent.

"Fess up. You think I'm an idiot."

Drawing a deep breath, she said, "Yes, sir."

Pausing, he lifted an angry brow. "Are you sassing me?"

"No, sir. You asked a question and I answered you."

"You'd better watch your tongue!" Moments passed and he paused. "Go over the details again," he demanded.

"What details?"

"How did Emmett jump this here span without falling into it?"

Heaving another deep sigh, she said, "Pa said he tied a rope to that hickory."

"Yeah. Go on."

"He told me he climbed the tree, tested the rope, and then swung over." She lifted her eyes. "He said it was close. He almost didn't clear the canyon."

"But he did." Walt focused on the chasm and then switched back to his notes. "That's the point. He did, and so can I."

"I wouldn't try it."

He stood, stuck the pencil behind his ear, and began to scale the tree, a rope hanging over his arm. "That's the difference betwixt you and me. You're scared of your shadow, and I'm not afeard of nothing."

"Except honey," she muttered.

His face turned red and his eyes bulged. "When I come down from here," he hissed, "you're gonna feel the sting of my whip on your sassy back."

Beth met his gaze steadily, not a whit of fear in her being. "Make your silly jump."

"That's exactly what I'm gonna do. I'm here to stay, darlin'. I'm gonna be your new papa-in-law." He steadily climbed upward. "Ain't that a happy thought?"

Beth ignored the taunt as she watched him scale the tree to its top and then tie a thick knot. Testing the hemp with his weight, he swung out and then back under the tree a couple of times. The rope and branch held his weight.

Her eyes skimmed the brush, taking comfort in knowing Pierce was here. Did he plan to intervene or simply let Uncle Walt do what he would? The rope looked sturdy, and Pa had successfully swung over and then back. Maybe Pierce was waiting until Walt made the jump, retrieved the deed, and returned. And then what?

Walt paused at the edge of the canyon and retied the rope, slightly adjusting its length. He tested the rope one more time, and then giving a one-finger salute to his temple, he grinned. "I'll be back with the deed. Don't you run away — you hear me? I'll find you, Beth. Wherever you go, you'll never have a moment's peace. But if you're a good girl and stay until I get back, your ol' uncle might decide to give you and Bear a fair chunk of the plantation."

"Wonderful," Beth murmured. She had no reason to run with Pierce waiting nearby.

Giving a confident nod, he grasped the rope. "Adios!"

Springing to her feet, she watched her uncle leap. But even before he was halfway across the ravine, the tree branch groaned, and Beth watched in horror as it gave way, lowering Walt's body by several feet as he swiftly approached the other side. She realized in an instant that he wasn't going to make it. He hit the opposite wall full force, and the shock caused him to let go of the rope. She could hear him cursing at the top of his lungs as he disappeared.

She went to the edge of the chasm and peered over, staring at the tiny, motionless form of her uncle far below. "Oh my goodness!" He'd actually done it. He'd actually killed himself. Beth stared in shock. "Oh my goodness!"

Pierce, Gray Eagle, and Preach appeared. Pierce took her arm and gently led her away from the horrific sight. She gasped, trying to comprehend what she'd just witnessed. Gray Eagle peered over the rim.

"I . . . he . . ." Beth's voice caught in her throat as she turned into Pierce's waiting arms.

Glancing over his shoulder, Pierce consoled her. "It's okay, sweetheart. It's over. Common sense should have told him that it was foolish to try such a jump. The tree branch giving way wasn't your fault."

Tears slid down her cheeks, though she didn't know why for the life of her she was crying. He'd been nothing but a cruel taskmaster to her and her family. Perhaps it was relief that she was finally free of the burden of being hunted by him, that she could actually begin to think about living her life as she chose. As Joanie chose.

"What about the deed?" she finally whispered against his chest.

"Is it important to you?"

"No. I don't care if remains there for eternity. I have my land — and if the deed stays in the cave, then no one can sell the plantation. It will belong to the slaves."

He sighed. "No, Bear will probably still run roughshod over the plantation, but that can't be your concern now. Joanie is your concern." He rubbed a hand soothingly over her shoulder, his chin on top of her head. "Let's go home. Preach and Gray Eagle will never mention a word about any of this to anyone."

"But . . . wait." She drew back to look at him. "The sisters could use the money from the sale of the plantation." Beth thought about how frugally they lived. That deed could provide much: ample food, new material for clothing, spring seed for their gardens. The slaves would be set free. No longer would they have to spend hours picking rows of cotton or separating the lint of a cotton plant for its seed.

Pierce shook his head. "And which sister would make the jump? Sister Mary Margaret?"

Beth perked up. "She would!"

He laughed. "She won't, and I guarantee that the deed wouldn't hold any temptation for them." He watched her smile even as she swiped at her tears, and he pulled her close again. "What do you say about heading on home?" he whispered with his lips against her hair.

"Home? Where is that?"

Lifting her face to his, he smiled into her eyes and then kissed the end of her nose.

"Pierce?"

"Yes, Beth?"

"I know this seems odd . . . but Walt was kin. May I say a short prayer over him?"

He nodded. "I think that would be real nice."

The party stepped to the rim of the canyon and the men removed their hats. Beth took a calm breath, aware that this would be her first public prayer. She bowed her head and concentrated hard on the words that wanted to come, so wanted to come. "God . . . I know You don't hear from me much, but I'm going to get better about talking to You more regularly. Thank You for bringing me and Joanie this far." She glanced over at Pierce, aware of him standing beside her, hat in hand, head bowed. "I . . . didn't love Uncle Walt . . . not the way the Bible says, and I ask forgiveness for that. I hope he finds . . . something in death he couldn't find here on this earth. Amen."

"Amen," the men chorused.

"That was very nice, Beth. I'm proud of you," Pierce said as he draped his arm around her waist and they walked back to the waiting horses.

Nice, but he hadn't answered her question. He had acted as though he knew something about the matter she didn't know.

So, where exactly, did the captain think her home was?

THIRTY-EIGHT

Uncle Walt was dead. Bear was tied up and sweating in a Cherokee lodge. The pursuit was over. Joanie was breathing easy, and Trella and baby Esther were thriving.

There was no longer anything blocking their way from leaving, Beth concluded the next morning.

Pierce could go home now too. The idea of not seeing him every morning, hearing his low whistle, watching his jaunty stride . . . She bit her lip and pushed back breakfast that suddenly tasted sour.

Joanie broke the silence between them. "I don't want to leave, Beth."

Beth pitched the last of her coffee. "Our plan from the beginning was to go to the next community and find help for you. We have no reason to stay."

"But I'm better — so much better here."

"I know." Pausing, Beth studied her sister. Her cheeks bloomed with color and her eyes were bright. Her cough was infrequent these days. What had brought about this miraculous change?

"Joanie," Beth ventured. "Has Gray Eagle been giving you some sort of new herbal treatment in addition to the lobelia?"

Joanie's gaze dropped. "No . . ."

"But Gray Eagle *is* responsible — am I right? Tell me at least that."

"I can't, Beth. I promised."

With a soft sigh, Beth leaned closer. "I hate it when you keep things from me."

"Nothing's happened. Let's just say that Gray Eagle found a way to help, but neither of us can say how."

"You can tell me, Joanie!" Beth was practically shouting now.

"I truly can't. I made a solemn vow." She reached for her sister's hand. "Can't you just be happy that I've found relief? If I leave here, I'll get sick again."

"That doesn't make sense. What is *here* that you can't take with you?"

Shaking her head, Joanie insisted, "I have to stay."

"Well, we can't. This is the Cherokee summer home. When autumn arrives, they'll be moving to winter grounds."

"I know, and I've thought of nothing else for days. I felt sure that the hour would come when we would be free of Walt and Bear and have to move on, but if I do I'll surely die."

"Joanie! You're talking in circles. You're much better!"

"It's true, Beth. Now I'm better, but if I don't have . . . my treatments . . . then my lungs will close and someday that will be it for me."

Burying her face in her hands, Beth took a deep breath. None of what she said made sense. "Does Pierce know about these treatments?"

"No one knows. And no one must know, or they will be taken away from me."

"Then . . . perhaps we can ask special permission to live here. Maybe at the abbey with the nuns. They could use our help once the Indians leave for their winter home." Beth's eyes roamed the camp. The people here had been wonderful. If Joanie's condition could be treated, then Beth was willing to stay. She'd never been happier or more at peace. She loved Sister Mary Margaret and the sisters, and if she and Joanie left, she would miss them with a fierce longing.

"I pray that we can stay, but I fear we won't be allowed," Joanie admitted. "The sisters have been good to us, but we are intruders."

"They don't think of us as intruders. Mary Margaret said so."

Joanie turned soulful eyes on her. "It won't be the same. Gray Eagle is leaving, and so are Pierce and Preach."

"When?"

"In the morning."

"Who said?"

"No one *has* to say, Beth. Their business is finished, and we've known all along that they want to go home."

"Does Trella know Preach is leaving in the morning?"

"I'm not sure. I fear she's fallen in love with him."

Beth met her sister's eyes. "And you have fallen in love with Gray Eagle."

"Yes. Very much so." She flashed a sudden grin. "And you, dear sister, have decided that not *all* men are evil."

"Guilty," Beth confessed. How easily she had made the leap.

"Are you in love with Pierce?"

"I . . . yes, I suppose I am, but he's never to know. Nothing can ever come of this madness."

"You two haven't discussed your feelings?"

"I haven't acknowledged mine, and I haven't the slightest idea how he feels about me. Honestly, I don't know how he could even like me. I've given him nothing but

367

trouble since the moment we met."

Joanie's expression turned pensive. "By fleeing Uncle Walt and Bear, I fear we've landed ourselves into a deep marsh."

Beth reached for her sister's hand. "It isn't a marsh that traps us, but rather quicksand."

Nodding, Joanie said, "We both need God's guidance this morning." She reached for her Bible and opened it to the book of John, her favorite gospel. A note fluttered to the ground. Retrieving the paper, she skimmed it and then looked up. "It's from Ma."

"Ma? Why would she leave us a message?"

Joanie looked down at the note in her hand again and read the words aloud.

My dear girls,
I have done little in your lives to protect you from Walt. I beg that you will forgive me. Your pa loves you deeply, but he refuses to relinquish the deed to his brother. I fear that both Walt and Emmett have lost their way in this senseless dispute. Perhaps you will see the hour that it ends on a satisfactory note. This is my prayer. My hands are tied. I love your pa and I trust in his wisdom.
I will love you forever.

Ma

"The noted was dated the night before she died," Joanie whispered.

Lifting tear-filled eyes, Beth sighed. "Oh, Ma."

THIRTY-NINE

That evening Pierce stood in the abbey's kitchen doorway and watched the sun sink in the west. The invitation for Preach, Gray Eagle, and Pierce to have supper with the order took him by surprise. Except for their inclusion of the Jornigan sisters, the nuns usually kept to themselves.

The order had taken to Beth and Joanie like hummingbirds to sweet jasmine.

So have you, a voice in his head reminded him.

Reverend Mother arrived, looking worn. The men removed their hats and waited as Sister Mary Margaret helped the matriarch to her seat.

Dinner consisted of new potatoes, carrots, corn on the cob, roast beef, and blackberry cobbler swimming in heavy cream. Pierce feared he'd made of pig of himself until he saw the food Preach and Gray Eagle put away.

Over coffee, Reverend Mother got down to the purpose of her summons. "Gentleman, I imagine you found my invitation rather puzzling."

"Ma'am . . . I mean, Sister," Pierce said, "we're much obliged for a fine meal and well aware of your kindness and generosity. No explanation is needed."

Smiling, the sister nodded. Pierce noticed the tired lines around her eyes. How old was she? He thought most likely her late eighties.

"I'm ninety-one," she answered his silent curiosity. "Longevity runs in my family." She paused, thoughtful. "My mother lived to be one-hundred-and-seven."

Gray Eagle and Preach made sounds of amazement.

"I fear I might exceed her." She laughed at the men. "It's not that I don't have a keen appreciation for life, gentlemen. I merely long for my eternal home." Sighing, she lifted her coffee cup. "Some days more than others."

Sister Mary Margaret giggled. "Me too, Reverend Mother."

"Now, then." The nun set the cup back on its saucer. "My reason for summoning you here. I gather that you will be leaving soon?"

Pierce briefly looked at the others and

then assumed the spokesman role. "Yes, ma'am. Tomorrow morning."

"Ah. I'm sure you are anxious to see your families."

Nodding, the men's eyes focused on the nun.

"Would you stay if — as they say — the price was right?"

Pierce's brow lifted. "Ma'am?"

Settling back in her chair, the sister waved away Sister Prue's efforts to drape a light wrap around her frail shoulders. "We have so much land here. I've lost count of the acreage. My memory isn't what it used to be, but we have vast amounts. It was donated to the order by a benefactor in the late seventeen hundreds. We promised — or the sisters before us promised — to faithfully use the land for God's purpose."

"I'm sure you've kept that vow."

"We have, sir." She focused on Sister Mary Margaret. "Now, I intend to ask a favor of you that all of us —" her blue-veined hand swept the seated sisters — "have diligently prayed about for some days now. The request will seem outlandish, but I believe it is the Lord's hand — and His only — in what I'm about to request."

Pierce smiled. "And that would be?"

She focused on the three soldiers. "The

order would like to give you twenty-five acres, providing you will live here and organize a small community."

Pierce's jaw dropped.

"By you, I mean all three of you men, and naturally the women you will eventually marry." Her brow lifted. "I assume you boys do plan to settle down and raise families?"

The men, for once, were speechless.

"Ma'am?" Pierce said a few moments later.

"I am offering the three of you twenty-five prime, North Carolina acres if you will remain here and shepherd a small community."

Swallowing, Pierce asked, "What community?"

"The one that's about to be formed."

"Why would we do that?"

"Gentleman, I have watched you. You have good hearts. Hearts God can use to further His kingdom. You are exactly the kind of men we've been asking God to send over the years. You are godly people, much like Christ's twelve disciples, filled with respect and compassion. You're persuasive, good with the Indians . . ." She paused as her eyes took on a glint. "God often singles out the unsuspecting to do His work."

"Ma'am," Preach said. "I'm not like one

373

of the disciples. Peter, Matthew, John . . . those men were saints."

"Those men were simple fishermen, sir. The thing that made the twelve worthy was their willingness to follow."

Shaking his head, Preach said, "I'm sorry, ma'am, but I'm on my way home to take over my father's flock."

"Hmm . . . yes, but I would suppose that perhaps Peter and John set out one day merely to catch fish when Jesus called them to follow Him."

"Sister," Gray Eagle ventured, "I, too, have family responsibilities. I must see about my brother and his wife. I don't know if they have survived the war."

Pierce glanced at him. "You have a brother?"

Gray Eagle said, "Two sisters, one brother."

"I'm not asking you to stay right now," the elderly nun said. "Of course you should do your duty, sir, but then return to us." She turned to also give Preach a reassuring but tired smile.

"Now, wait a minute," Pierce objected. "I haven't felt this calling. Surely God can talk to me directly. And I am anything but a disciple like the twelve."

Granted, he tried to live by the Good

Book, but he wasn't worthy of being singled out for something like this. Yet even as he spoke the words of his objection, the truth of her words struck a chord. He felt ties to this peaceful haven, ties he'd never felt anywhere else. But there was still the matter of his land, the site of his own home, where he planned to sip sweet tea and live in harmony. "What would we do for a living in this new community? I don't know how to do anything but grow cotton."

"In the last week and a half, I have seen you do many other things, Captain. You are a gifted leader. As for your future, you'll do what God asks. He'll amply provide."

Pierce shook his head. "Maybe I was shot and killed on the battlefield." He glanced up. "That's it. I didn't make it to heaven, so I'm here instead." His eyes scanned the other men. "You didn't make it either."

"Gentleman." Reverend Mother chuckled as her eyes searched each man's features. "I know what I ask is overwhelming and, of course, ultimately the choice is yours. God will lead you where He wants you to go, and if that place is here, in Sanctuary, then you will have nowhere to run, for when He calls a man He won't let up until His purpose is served." Even though a nun, her smile was a bit impish. "But then you know that, don't you?"

Pierce knew that only too well. When he'd been called to fight for the North, against everything his family held dear, the decision had eaten him alive but he'd gone.

He sighed and said, "Sanctuary?"

"The town will be a haven for the broken-hearted and downtrodden."

"Why would God want us to start such a community?" Preach asked. "And how will people know where to come if they're hurting and broken?"

Reverend Mother pinned him with a stern look. "He knew where to find you, didn't He?"

"Yes, ma'am, but —"

"No buts. He will send whom He pleases. You need only fill the position He's offering." Her eyes shifted from one thoughtful face to the next. "Gentlemen, the Lord knows your credentials far better than I do. Pray about this, and do so with an open heart."

"I have to see to my land, Sister," Pierce insisted.

"Exactly where is this land you speak about?"

Pierce reached in his pocket and took out the documents he carried with him. Pushing back cups and saucers, he spread the plat map on the table. Chairs scraped the wood floor when the sisters rose to peer over his shoulder. "It's . . . here." He pinpointed the spot.

"Hmm." Reverend Mother studied the piece of paper. "You're certain?"

"Yes, ma'am. I purchased it from a Savannah newspaper advertisement."

"Oh, dear." Reverend Mother focused on a much younger nun. "Mary Margaret."

The nun backed away from the table. "I can explain, Reverend Mother. We . . . we needed money to buy seed. It seemed a logical solution. This is a tiny speck of land compared to what we own. I thought . . . selling a small piece of property . . . why, we'd never miss it. And we still grow a garden there."

"You *sold* the land? But —"

Color crept up Mary Margaret's face. "I know, Reverend Mother. I've had many a restless night thinking about it." She swallowed. "Actually, I believe I . . . I may have sold it twice. I've never had a good head for business."

Gasps broke out. Pierce overheard a hushed whisper. "This will put the Reverend Mother in bed for a month," Sister Prue predicted.

"Sister Mary Margaret." Reverend Mother

drew a deep breath. "You cannot sell land that does not belong to you, however worthy you deem the cause."

"Wait a minute." Pierce pushed away from the table and stood up. "Are you saying I don't own this land after all?"

"I'm afraid not." Reverend Mother smiled ruefully, and then her expression softened. "I am deeply sorry, Captain, but you and some other unsuspecting soul have been sold our bean and turnip patch, which, of course, cannot be purchased." Her eyes turned to Sister Margaret. "The order will reimburse any monies owed to you and the other buyer, and I can only repeat how sorry we are for this most unfortunate incident."

Pushing away from the table, she stifled a weary yawn. "Still, I can't help thinking that it looks as though God has already been at work in all this." Her smile was back again, kind and compassionate. "Pray about the situation gentleman. Heed what the good Lord says to you."

A bright moon rose higher as the group rode back to camp. Gray Eagle broke the strained silence halfway there. "It's a crazy idea."

Preach's relieved tone agreed. "Craziest notion I've ever heard. I've never been

378

personally called by the good Lord to do anything except get saved on a Sunday morning when I was nine years old."

"Well, maybe He found another thing you need to do," Pierce noted.

"Now don't go saying that! I got to get on home, Pierce. I haven't seen my family in years."

"Nor have I," Gray Eagle said. He glanced at Pierce. "Are you taking this seriously?"

"Are you?"

Gray Eagle shook his head. "I don't like to be put on the spot, and I'm about as far from a disciple as a man can get. Start a town? The three of us?"

"Count me out," Preach said. "If you want to stay, Pierce, you stay, but I'm going home." He lifted his chin. "I haven't heard any calling other to spell my pa."

Pierce glanced at Gray Eagle. "And you?"

Gray Eagle pursed his lips in thought. "At first my reaction was to say no, but now . . . maybe. I don't want to leave Joanie. And if she goes she won't have access to the pools. They're the only thing that helps her breathe."

Pierce set his jaw, and then agreed. "And I don't want to leave Beth, though she's a wildcat. How will the women view this cockeyed notion?" Beth — to his knowledge

— was still getting used to the idea of talking to God. "Those three women don't have a real plan. They think they do, but what sort of plan is it to take them and the baby to a community and just leave them there?"

"Don't forget Beth has land too. The community is just a stopover until Joanie is well and they can settle on their property."

"Is that right?" Preach said. "Well, I've been studying about it all day, and I can't say that I want to leave Trella or Esther." He groaned softly. "Oh, man. If . . . *if* we stay and put our trust in Reverend Mother's 'vision,' then what?"

"She didn't say she had a vision, and Reverend Mother doesn't have anything to do with the decision. We have to put our full trust in the Almighty."

"So," Gray Eagle said thoughtfully, "we're supposed to drop our lives, settle down here, and build a town."

"A town called Sanctuary," Pierce supplied.

"And then wait for troubled souls to come our way," Preach finished.

"There'll be a stampede," Pierce said, frowning. "Do you think God answers all prayers?"

"I've had a few go unnoticed," Gray Eagle admitted.

"That don't mean He didn't answer," Preach said. "Just that God knew better than to give you the answer you were looking for."

The men fell silent, each wrapped in his own thoughts. One thing Pierce knew for certain; there'd be a lot of praying going on tonight, and he had a hunch the answers wouldn't be to their liking.

Or understanding.

Glancing up, he muttered, "Never even thought about starting a town." *Me? Pierce Montgomery advising anyone on how to live their life?* The idea was laughable. He'd disappointed Pa. He fought for the North, wasn't married yet, and his sole ambition was to drink sweet tea.

Then it hit him. Beth's land — the deed she kept in Joanie's Bible. His heart sank. Was it possible she had purchased the same piece of property from a good-hearted nun who had no right to sell it?

Shaking his head, he said quietly, "Maybe the sister has an inside track on what God wants us to do." Then he smiled, somehow at peace with that idea.

FORTY

Fog shrouded the massive rock overhang when Gray Eagle led the way up the steep incline. Pierce hadn't known this section of the camp existed. He and Preach and the Indian scout had walked for more than a mile before they found the secluded place where the chief went for morning prayer.

When Gray Eagle paused, Pierce saw the object of their search. The chief stood tall and proud, his eyes fixed on the far horizon, his black hair streaked with silver ruffling in the light breeze. He turned, his gaze centering on the intruders. Stepping aside, Pierce let Gray Eagle assume the spokesman's role.

"Forgive us, Chief. I know this is private time for you —"

Focusing on the scout, he said, "Speak."

Stepping closer, Gray Eagle said quietly, "I have come to ask yet another great favor."

The chief's dark brow quirked. "You ask many favors, son of Walks-with-Sun."

"Always for the good of others."

The chief nodded. "Continue."

"Reverend Mother summoned us last night to supper."

"I know of the matter."

"The sisters consulted you about their desire?"

"When one asks for special privileges, it is wise to consult with the affected party."

"You speak the truth in grace and knowledge."

"Go on."

"You know that the nuns have asked that we start a new community, one adjoining Cherokee land?"

"I do."

"The order wants me, Pierce, and Preach to form an . . . unusual town."

A hint of a smile touched the Indian's features. "At least you ask."

"I want to consider your feelings on the matter."

The chief's eyes skimmed Pierce and Preach before coming back to the Indian scout. "You have decided to accept the task?"

Gray Eagle shook his head. "Before making a decision, I seek your permission."

Turning back to face the lifting dawn, the Cherokee chief fell silent. The day gradually brightened. It appeared to Pierce that he was staring at his past, acres and acres of former Cherokee land now divided among immigrants. Time had caught up with the man, his once-tall frame shrunken, his eyes not as vibrant, his senses dulled. Many heartbreaking changes had taken place in his lifetime, yet his heritage was still a symbol of the proud nation that refused to walk the Trail of Tears. Pierce wondered how the events of his life had not left him a broken man.

An inordinately long stretch of time passed before he spoke again. "I love this land. It is not the place of my birth, but I have enjoyed its bounty for many years." His gaze skimmed the gently rolling hills and deep ravines as tears rolled down his cheeks. "The wife of my heart is buried nearby. She was twenty summers when the Great Spirit claimed her."

Pierce shuffled, uncomfortable with the sight of the great man's grief.

"The sisters have been good to my people," the chief continued. "The land they offer is not Cherokee land."

"No, but it is the pools that the sisters also ask for."

"Ah . . . the pools."

"If we start this community that the

Reverend Mother visualizes," Gray Eagle went on, "we will need use of them. They have brought great help to the one called Joanie. She is able to breathe here. If what the sisters ask comes from the Great White Father, then He will use the comforting waters for the good of many."

Pierce watched varying emotions play across the chief's features. Pain. Sorrow. Hope. Despair. They were asking him to share yet another part of his heritage with the white man. After long thought, he turned to face Gray Eagle.

"Our tribe, like the sisters, withers like a plant without water. Soon now we will be forced to make our summer camp where the buffalo isn't as abundant, depleting our ability to feed our children. Already the white man has killed so many."

"The sisters are not asking that you give up your land," Gray Eagle said. "Only that you allow limited access to the hot pools."

"Limited?" The Indian chuckled. "You cannot make such a promise. For many years strangers have come from far away in search of the pools. We have turned all away but the good women in black and your Joanie."

"We will do the same." Gray Eagle's eyes met the patriarch's. "Only the ones in most need of the waters will be allowed to use them. I make you this promise."

"You will be the judge of such important matters?"

"Not I or Pierce or Preach. The Great Spirit will send the neediest."

"If I refuse your request, what will keep you from using the pools?"

"Nothing but my word." Gray Eagle's somber gaze met his. "I give you my pledge I will honor your land as my own."

"So you have decided to accept the task."

Shifting to face Pierce and Preach, who had remained silent during the exchange, Gray Eagle said quietly, "Yes. And these men, my friends, offer their word also."

"I can trust this word?"

"You can trust."

The chief turned back to stare at the now-risen sun, which was casting brilliant beams across the rich fertile land below. The sound of the gurgling pools met them. Pockets of steam rose from their waters. "If my people are able to make the long journey come spring, we will be welcomed and left alone?"

"Yes. You have my word."

His dark gaze shifted from man to man. Finally he said, "The pools belong to the Great White Father. They are not mine to give. You have my blessing to use them during the long winter months."

"We would need the summers too."

"This I will consider when I see this new town you will create. If the land or pools are misused . . ."

Pierce spoke up. "They won't be, sir."

The chief's sharp gaze pinned him. "I offer this grace to the Cherokee, not to the white man."

"Yes, sir."

Turning, the men walked away and the chief lifted both hands in a pleading stance toward the rising sun.

Morning prayer had begun.

FORTY-ONE

Joanie clung to Gray Eagle's arm the next morning. This would be the last time she'd feel the strength of his touch and revel in the warmth of his eyes. All things ended. Joanie had known this since she was a young child, but the reality of losing Gray Eagle was intolerable. "You will be leaving soon?"

"Yes." He focused on the thorny path that led to the hot pools. A smile played around his lips. "For a while."

"For a while?" Her heart skipped. What did that smile mean? "For a while indicates that you plan to return."

"It does."

Footsteps pausing, she turned to face him. "Gray Eagle, stop teasing me. Are you leaving forever or are you coming back?"

"Would my answer make a difference to you?"

"Yes." Her tone dropped to a whisper. Propriety didn't concern her. If all it took to bring him back was a yes, then she would shout it from the rooftops!

"I will come back." His grin widened. "You haven't spoken with Beth yet this morning?"

"No. Pierce came by earlier and asked her to join him on a walk."

They approached the pools, and after taking off her socks and boots, Joanie stepped barefooted into the swirling water. Gray Eagle followed.

"Why did you ask me if I'd spoken with my sister?"

"If she had come back from her conversation with Pierce, and you'd spoken to her, you'd know that there's a plan in the making."

She dipped her hand into the warm water and let it filter through her fingers. "What plan?"

"Don't you want to sit first?"

She murmured, "Apparently I should. You sound so mysterious." Settling into the water, she met his gaze. "Now, tell me the secret."

"No secret."

"Surprise?"

Moving beside her, he said softly, "I doubt that what I have to say will come as a total surprise."

"Which would be?"

"How would you feel about living here?"

"Here? At the camp?"

"Close by."

Her breath left her. Stay here, at this tiny piece of heaven? Was it possible? "I would love it, but there's no way . . ."

"There's always a way."

"How?"

"Last night, the sisters invited us for supper —"

"And?"

"They offered us a parcel of land adjoining the convent."

"Why?"

"Reverend Mother asked us to form a small community."

"Here?"

"Here." His grin resurfaced. "The town will be called Sanctuary. It will be a place of refuge where the downtrodden can come to find peace and healing."

"Reverend Mother has the authority to give you this land?"

"It would appear so." His eyes locked with hers. "What do you say, Joanie Jornigan? Should we stay?"

"We?" She mouthed the word as she drowned in the love she saw in the depths of his eyes. "But, Gray Eagle, you said you had to leave."

Nodding, he said, "For a while — a short while. I will go home to see my family, see that they have survived and are well, and then I will return."

The enormity of what he was suggesting, or at least hinting at, began to sink in. "We will stay here forever?"

"Not forever." His smile was warm and tender. "We have an eternal home, and it's not here."

"What are you suggesting?" Was he proposing?

Scooting closer, he reached for her hand. "Will you wait for me? I mean, when I return, will you —"

Grasping his hand, Joanie's heart felt as though it would come through her chest. "Yes."

"Yes?"

"Yes. I will marry you when you return."

Smiling, he drew her face closer and whispered, "I will only be gone for a short while. You will stay here, soak in the springs, and get better."

"What about Beth and Pierce? I so long to tell Beth about the hot springs. She wonders about my improvement, and I feel dishonest not telling her how the waters have helped me."

"I know it is hard to keep silent about this wonderful thing, but you must for just a little while longer. Until the new town is formed. Then you will be able to share the news with your sister. It is my belief that the Father will use these pools to help many."

"Is Pierce staying too? Beth would be heartbroken if he didn't."

"Pierce's feelings are apparent in his eyes; he will stay. There are responsibilities we must fulfill, but I sense that both he and Preach will answer the call."

The news was shocking and exciting. Joanie was trying to take it all in at once. "The Indians . . . how will they feel having a new community so nearby?"

"Reverend Mother has discussed her dream at great length with the chief. He is resigned."

Gray Eagle briefly explained the nun's strange request as Joanie shook her head. "She must feel strongly about this idea of Sanctuary."

"She does. The Cherokee prefers his space, but this is a summer camp. In the fall, the Indians will move south where the temperatures are warmer and the buffalo are many. At first the community that the sister envisions will be small: Pierce and his wife, Preach and his wife, and me and my wife."

Wife. The word sounded so wonderful to her ears. "What about Trella and Beth?"

Giving her a patient look, he said, "I somehow think they will be accounted for. Reverend Mother wants the community to be small. A refuge for weary travelers."

Shaking her head, Joanie said, "What travelers?"

"The ones God sends our way."

"That's sounds crazy."

"Do you feel it was crazy that God led us here, to this place?"

"No. I prayed for a miracle and God answered."

To her way of thinking, God sent her here, to these springs, to these sisters, and to the Cherokee, and it seemed He had another grand plan — one of those special things He did that appeared to have no basis in logic. "I would love to make this land my home."

His eyes lit with joy.

Leaning up, she kissed him. His lips were warm, strong. Amazing.

"Forever, if God wishes," she whispered.

"I'll only be gone a few short weeks."

"They will feel like a hundred, but I will

wait," she said before fully surrendering to his kiss.

FORTY-TWO

"Miss Trella?" Preach parted the thick hide that was the doorway and stepped inside the tent.

Trella glanced up and smiled when she saw her visitor. "Preach. Good morning."

"Good morning." Squatting beside her, his eyes took in the sleeping baby. "How's our little Esther this morning?"

"Good. Very good. We switched to cow's milk at the last feeding, and she's handling it well."

Preach made a few cooing sounds before his eyes grew serious. "I came to tell you I'll be leaving tomorrow."

"I figured as much. I'll . . . miss you."

"I'm going to miss you too. And the baby."

Blinking back tears, the young black woman averted her eyes.

"Trella? What are you going to do when you leave here?"

She didn't look at him but gazed instead

at the sleeping infant. "I've been giving the matter much thought and prayer. I can't afford to raise Esther. It breaks my heart, but I've decided to leave her in a foundling home —"

"No!" Preach's deep baritone shook the tent.

She glanced up, tears streaming from the corners of her eyes. "Preach. I've never heard you speak so forcefully."

"You've never said something so . . ." He bit back words.

"Wrong?" she supplied. Her eyes returned to the infant. "I've prayed and prayed about the matter, but the only answer that comes to my head is this: If I can't care for Esther properly, then I should give her to someone who will."

"I won't let you give your baby away, Trella."

"Preach, I . . . I don't have a choice."

"Yes, ma'am. You do." He got to his feet, hat in hand. "Now, I got something to ask you, and I don't want you saying a word until I finish. You hear?"

"I hear."

"Well now, seems God has a funny way of taking care of business, but here's what's happened." He explained the nun's offer to provide land if the men would oversee the formation of a new community. "Don't rightly know why anyone would make such a suggestion, but appears to me that the good Lord must want this place called Sanctuary." His eyes met hers. "It sure will be a godsend for us."

"Yes, sir. And your point?"

"Ma'am . . ." Preach kept his eyes straight ahead. Bending to his knees, hat in hand, he went on. "Miss Trella, would you do me the honor of marrying me?"

Trella's jaw dropped. "Preach!"

He met her stunned gaze. "Yes, ma'am?"

"You . . . can't mean it. I'm . . . soiled. I'm nothing —"

"You're wrong about that. You're a good woman, Trella Jones. You're sensible, and loving, God-fearing, and the best mother on earth, and that's what I want in a woman I'm going to spend the rest of my life with. You're everything I want in a wife."

Still on his knees, he reached for her hand. "You understand what I'm saying? There's not a bad bone in you. You've been forced to do bad things, but that part of your life is over. Nobody is ever going to force you to do anything you don't like again. I'm asking you to be my wife. To help me start a church in this new town. It wasn't my idea when I rode off almost three weeks ago for home to marry and become a father all at once, but then it wasn't your idea to fall in with the likes of Walt Jornigan."

Tears coursed down Trella's cheeks. "No, it wasn't."

"Hush now." His big, clumsy fingers wiped at her tears of joy. "We're not ever gonna speak of the past again. You hear? If you'll do me the honor of marrying me, and allowing me the privilege of being Esther's papa and your husband, you'll make me the happiest man on earth."

"Oh, Preach. You deserve so much better than me."

His hold tightened. "If you'll accept my proposal, you'll be giving me all I'll ever want or need." He gently shook her clasped hands. "I love you, woman. I fell in love with both you and Esther. I don't see how I could go without either one of you in my life."

Laughing through her tears, Trella admitted, "You do sound serious."

He sobered. "Serious as drought. Marry me, Trella."

Slowly rising, she met his adoring gaze. "I would be honored to marry you, Preach."

He took her in his arms and kissed her soundly. Then he gently pulled away, meeting her gaze. "It's my honor, Trella.

All mine."

"Give you land?" Beth frowned. "Why would Reverend Mother want to do that?"

Pierce explained, and then added, "It does sound a little far-fetched."

As they walked beside the stream, he reached for her hand to help her over a fallen log. Beth had sensed Pierce had something other than exercise on his mind when he'd shown up so early. Now she knew.

"Actually, you're not going to like this part."

"Like what?" She stopped, facing him. "What's going on?"

He focused on her, his expression sheepish. "It seems, Miss Beth, that we may be co-owners of a turnip patch."

"What?"

"The land you bought?"

"Yes." Her heart thumped. Her and Joanie's future.

"I think you and I might have purchased the same plot from the same newspaper source."

"That's impossible."

He cocked a brow. "You think anything is impossible? After what we've been through?"

"You're not making a lick of sense."

"The *Savannah Daily News and Herald,* six months ago, three dollars and a nickel an acre?"

Beth nodded hesitantly, her heart sinking.

"Sister Mary Margaret sold both of us land that wasn't hers to sell."

Beth reeled. "Mary Margaret? She sold us —" Her hand moved involuntarily to cover her mouth. "We own the bean and turnip patch? Oh dear me!"

"Oh dear us. Truthfully, we don't own anything. Reverend Mother — or God — wants us to take that parcel of land and make it a town."

"This can't be happening."

"That's what I thought, but it is."

"Reverend Mother offered us land anyway?"

"Twenty-five acres. For all of us to use. Me, Gray Eagle, Preach . . . and our mates."

She wouldn't look at him now. "Then it wasn't offered to Joanie and me. It was offered to you."

"I knew you'd say that."

"It's the truth."

"I reminded Reverend Mother of the fact that none of us are married, and of a more serious problem. You hate men."

Smothering a chuckle, Beth kept her eyes

fixed on the stream. "Well, maybe not *all* men."

"Oh? You've had a change of attitude?"

Heat rose to her cheeks as she looked up at him. "You take such delight in teasing me."

"I surely do." Sighing, he winked. "If I couldn't tease you, Beth, my life wouldn't be worth a fig."

"Well, Pierce, anything to make your life worthwhile."

She sighed inwardly. She didn't own land. She'd bought turnips. She and Joanie and Trella would have to hope to make a new life elsewhere. No sweet tea for her.

They walked on in silence. He hadn't dropped her hand once they cleared the log, but she had to admit that she didn't mind.

"My brother can run the plantation back home."

She glanced sideways. "What did you tell Reverend Mother?"

"Nothing, yet." He turned to meet her eyes. "If you and Joanie won't stay, then I'll have to do some more praying about the matter."

Her heart thrummed. What was he suggesting? After a moment of hesitancy, she said, "I think . . . we could be convinced to stay."

That was as far as she would allow herself to commit. But then she said, "You *have* to do as Reverend Mother asks, Pierce. It's not such a bad idea — to provide a haven for hurting souls." She, Joanie, and Trella could have used such a place. But then, God had already provided it. Here, in this lovely valley that surely must look a whole lot like heaven.

Squeezing her hand, he winked at her again. "Then it's settled. We stay. You, me, Joanie, Gray Eagle, Preach, and Trella."

"I don't think it's proper for six unmarried men and women to form a community."

"I've been giving that matter considerable thought," he agreed, pausing to meet her gaze. "It wouldn't be proper."

"There's always Bear to consider," she reminded. "He's still around."

"I eat bear for breakfast."

He was teasing, but Beth knew this man had no fear of her kin. Since his father's death her cousin had changed. He seemed broken now. Contrite almost. He had gone home, promising to never come near them again, but maybe his old nature would spring back to life one day.

Her hand tightened in his. "Will this new community have sweet tea?"

"I'm not staying if it doesn't."

"You're seriously considering this notion?"

"I am. There'll be sugar. You can count on it."

They walked on. "The sisters have offered rooms on the third floor of the abbey to you, Joanie, Trella, and Esther. When we return from checking in with our families, we'll begin work on housing."

"Preach's father will be disappointed that he can't pastor his flock."

"Preach figures God has someone else in mind for his father's church. Sanctuary will need Preach's spiritual guidance."

"Sanctuary?"

He flashed a grin. "Reverend Mother has her heart set on the name."

"Sanctuary." Beth's hand tightened in his larger one. "Sounds like a lovely place." One she'd gladly spend the rest of her life building.

Pausing, he faced her and took her other hand. "We've come a long way in a short time, you and I," he said. His gaze locked with hers. "I have to leave for a little while, but I'll be back. Will you be here?"

A smile touched her eyes. "I may have run away in the past, but my intent all along was to find my property and settle there. I guess the Lord has fulfilled His part in the matter." She squeezed his hands. "Go home, Pierce, and check on your family. I'll be waiting for you when you come back."

He took her in his arms and leaned down to kiss her. "I will return. You know that."

"Hmm . . . do I?"

His second kiss persuaded her that she knew that perfectly well.

"Pierce, when you come back, would you mind taking me to the plantation to get my mother's things? Joanie and I hid them in the root cellar before we left."

He chuckled softly. "Beth, I'd be willing to take you to the moon if I could manage it."

Her lips touching his, she whispered, "How long will you be gone?"

"I'll make it as fast as possible." He kissed her again. Then, lifting his head, he whispered, "By the way, Miss Jornigan, I've fallen in love with you."

"Honest?" Her fingers threaded golden locks of sun-kissed hair.

"Have I ever misled you?" His mouth lowered to take hers in yet another kiss that was nothing less than a sealed bargain.

The future stretched before her. Exactly what kind of future wasn't yet clear, but something told Beth she'd be drinking a lot of sweet tea in her old age.

DISCUSSION QUESTIONS

1. At the beginning of the story, we see three different men: Pierce, a white man; Gray Eagle, an Indian; and Preach, a black man. Do you think it is their faith in God that unites them even more than the fact that the war is over? Does the war being over make close friendships for them possible now?

2. After their parents are gone, Beth and Joanie decide to strike out on their own, taking a very vulnerable friend along with them. What do you think of their decision to do that? Was it brave or foolish or both?

3. Sadly, the women on Walt's plantation were not treated well. Fortunately, God led the soldiers to the ladies just in time. How does a good man change Beth's view of men in general? Did Gray Eagle and Preach have the same effect on Joanie and Trella?

4. The kindness of the Cherokees made a

huge difference in these women's lives. Even in light of the fire, they showed Beth mercy. What about the nuns? How did they make a difference for Beth and Joanie?

5. How does greed play into Walt's decisions to chase his nieces without mercy? What consequences do he and his son suffer because of their bad decisions?

6. When Walt and Bear show up drunk at the Indian camp, did you think Pierce's actions were justified? Did he go too far or not far enough in trying to teach those Jornigan men a lesson? Do you think Pierce, Gray Eagle, and Preach should have handled the situation with Walt and Bear differently? Dealt with it more decisively sooner? What would you have done?

7. Beth begins a personal search for understanding about prayer. What did you think of the different ways to talk to God discussed in the story? Were all acceptable to you? If not, why not?

8. These three couples were blessed to find true love and hope for their futures during the course of their adventures. What do you think of the idea of waiting on God for the things you long for?

9. Reverend Mother asks her new friends to form a community that is all about sanctu-

ary for troubled souls. Is there a way you can be a refuge for anyone in your world today?

10. 1 Corinthians 2:9 tells us "Eye hath not seen, nor ear heard, neither have entered into the heart of man, the things which God hath prepared for them that love him" (KJV). Which character in this book saw these words most poignantly fulfilled in his or her life?

ABOUT THE AUTHOR

Lori Copeland is the author of more than 90 titles, both historical and contemporary fiction. With more than 3 million copies of her books in print, she has developed a loyal following among her rapidly growing fans in the inspirational market. She has been honored with the *Romantic Times* Reviewer's Choice Award, The Holt Medallion, and Walden Books' Best Seller award. In 2000, Lori was inducted into the Missouri Writers Hall of Fame.

Lori lives in the beautiful Ozarks with her husband, Lance, their three children, and five grandchildren.